Fear tightened Melanie's throat

Gently, she eased from under Chris's arm. The sheets rustled as she slipped off the bed. Bricks were cool under her feet, but a deeper chill caused the gooseflesh prickling her skin. She groped at the foot of the bed for her robe.

She padded to the door and with one finger eased aside the drapes. Her backyard, illuminated by a sliver of moon and starlight, was tiny, flat and bare. She searched the shadows against the fence. Hoping she wouldn't awaken Chris, she tested the locks.

Heart pounding, she crept into the living room. Standing in the middle of the room, she held her breath and listened. Her scalp prickled, and hammers tapped her nerves. He was out there, watching, waiting. She felt him....

ABOUT THE AUTHOR

Sheryl Lynn lives with her family in Colorado Springs. Unlike her hapless characters, her past is secret-free, and she likes it that way. Sheryl says reading and writing romantic suspense is a marvelous release, a way of living dangerously without getting hurt. She even likes it when writing a story like *Deadly Devotion,* which kept her awake many nights wondering what exactly were all those strange scratchy noises and thumpety-thumps.

Books by Sheryl Lynn

HARLEQUIN INTRIGUE
190—DOUBLE VISION

Deadly Devotion

Sheryl Lynn

Harlequin Books

TORONTO • NEW YORK • LONDON
AMSTERDAM • PARIS • SYDNEY • HAMBURG
STOCKHOLM • ATHENS • TOKYO • MILAN
MADRID • WARSAW • BUDAPEST • AUCKLAND

To Tom, for investigating all the odd noises in the middle of the night

Harlequin Intrigue edition published April 1993

ISBN 0-373-22223-8

DEADLY DEVOTION

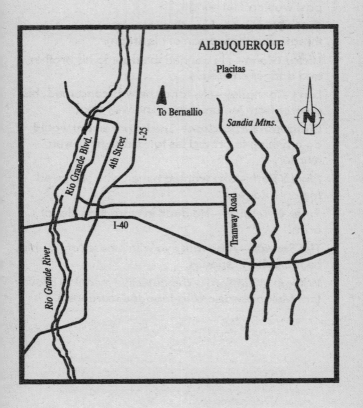

ALBUQUERQUE

Placitas

To Bernallio

Sandia Mtns.

Rio Grande Blvd.

4th Street

I-25

I-40

Tramway Road

Rio Grande River

CAST OF CHARACTERS

Melanie Rogers—She wanted a new life, but the past wouldn't let her go.

Chris Glenn—His haunting secrets were threatening the woman of his dreams.

Victor Glenn—He opened the door to his brother, and danger entered.

Larry Connalley—As far as he was concerned, his divorce from Melanie was in no way final.

Charleton Richardson—The knight errant would do anything to protect his fair maiden...even murder.

Phyllis Rath—She wanted a man who still loved Melanie Rogers.

Peter Osterman—He dealt in more than illegal arms.

Tim Service—A private eye with a nose for trouble, he found it—in spades.

William Whiteford—The detective meant to prove that Melanie was a cold-blooded murderess.

Chapter One

While the garage door lifted, Melanie Rogers craned her neck to see into the BMW's rearview mirror. The red-yellow-and-blue balsa-wood parrots swinging from her earlobes made her smile.

Remembering Larry's astonishment when she'd walked into the judge's chambers made the smile widen. What had he expected? Widow's weeds? For her to mourn the end of their marriage? Certainly he hadn't expected bright red walking shorts, a tropical print blouse and three-inch parrots nearly brushing her shoulders.

She flicked an earring with a finger, relishing the memory of Larry's battle to hold nasty words in check. His public persona was one of cool self-control—the unshakable, ice-for-blood attorney. Only Melanie knew the private Larry Connalley, the autocrat obsessed with power and control.

He'd never have the opportunity to abuse her again. The cage door was open—she was free!

She pulled the BMW into the garage. As she gathered her purse and the folder of legal papers, she recalled reading an article about depression following a divorce. So wrong. Six years of marriage to Larry had been hell; he'd made the year of separation horrible. Now the divorce was official and irreversible, and she felt elated.

She hugged the folder to her breast. Then, recalling Phyllis Rath's snide smile as she'd waited outside the chambers for Larry, Melanie laughed. Phyllis thought herself so discreet, pretending her affair with Larry hadn't begun until after the separation. She had sat there in her white silk suit, her black hair pulled back in a demure bun, smiling that bitchy smile while her eyes said, "I won. The better woman always does."

Melanie wondered what would have happened if she had given in to temptation and said, "Larry claims you squeal in bed. Is that true?"

Stricken by sudden guilt, Melanie looked down at the folder. Should she warn Phyllis about Larry's darker nature? Did Phyllis know? Guilt faded, replaced by the philosophical notion that Phyllis Rath was Larry's female counterpart—icy, ambitious, and willing to do anything to get her way. Phyllis could hold her own against Larry. Besides, anything Melanie said against Larry now would sound like sour grapes. Phyllis wouldn't listen anyway.

She got out of the car and, drawn by the delicious scent of freedom, walked into the street. The Albuquerque sky had never looked so blindingly, beautifully turquoise before. She tasted the breeze gusting off the high desert plains; the air had never smelled so sweet. To the east, the Sandia Mountains towered over the city, purple and serene. Clouds, like fat sheep grazing in the sky, cast azure shadows across the foothills.

The first time she'd seen Albuquerque, it had nearly overwhelmed her. As a young bride—out of Ohio for the first time—she had been awed by the vast open spaces, the sweeping rockiness of the Sandias and the primeval volcanic fields west of the Rio Grande.

She'd grown to love the New Mexico city. The mild weather; the contrasts of the pine forests of the mountains to the lush cottonwoods of the river valley to the manzanita of the desert plains; the soothing colors of the Southwest— gold, gray-green, purple, sienna, rose and turquoise; the melding of ancient Pueblo cultures, Spanish influence and modern urbanization. She couldn't imagine a nicer place to live.

Especially now, free of Larry.

A flash of scarlet caught Melanie's eye.

"Carmen?" she breathed and set her purse and folder on the trunk of her car. She hurried across the compound street to a parked Cadillac, then crouched with one hand on the asphalt to look under the car. "Carmen?" She clucked her tongue at the scarlet macaw.

Tail dragging in the dust, the big parrot looked back at her. Carmen tongued a piece of gravel, then chuckled and dropped it.

Melanie looked at the house opposite hers. Camellos Court was a collection of patio homes connected by free-flowing adobe walls and surrounding a wide circle street. The macaw belonged to her neighbor, Victor Glenn. Victor traveled extensively, and since Melanie worked in a pet store, he gladly pressed her into service as a pet sitter. Melanie knew the macaw well—or at least she'd thought she did. Carmen had never left Victor's courtyard before.

Melanie played her fingers on the pavement, stirring up bits of gravel and blown grass. She clucked and coaxed until Carmen waddled out from under the car.

"Bad bird," she chided gently as she extended her arm.

"Bad bird," Carmen said. With mischievous humor in her white-rimmed eyes, she nibbled Melanie's hand.

Melanie *tsk*ed a warning and tensed her muscles as the macaw climbed onto her forearm. Carrying a macaw without a glove or stick was rough work. Carmen's claws were like an eagle's talons.

"You're a pain, my friend," Melanie said as she slowly straightened. Her arm quivered with the effort of holding the bird steady. "Victor isn't going to be happy with you."

Bobbing her head and swinging her blue-yellow-and-scarlet tail for balance, the macaw said, "Bad bird."

Talking nonsense and fending Carmen's bill away from her dangling earrings, Melanie carried her to Victor's gate. She touched the latch, and the gate swung open. Victor must not have latched the gate, allowing Carmen the opportunity to simply walk out.

Great, Melanie thought. Winston is probably out, too. She looked back over the compound in search of the black Labrador retriever. Seeing the front door stood open, she called, "Victor?"

Silence.

"Well, since you won't stay on your perch, inside you go."

"Bad bird," Carmen replied as she strained toward the bleached branches of the outdoor perch.

Wincing at the flexing of the macaw's claws, Melanie went to the door. "Victor! Got a runaway for you!" Carmen's claws were too rough for politeness. She knocked, then entered. "Hey, Victor!"

The clattering and scuffling of big paws preceded Winston. All Labradors were endowed with an endearing goofiness, but Winston was an especially charming example. He was big for a Lab, weighing nearly eighty pounds, and his shiny black body was tough and muscular. His rudderlike tail wagged furiously, and he barked a muffled greeting around the Frisbee in his mouth.

Carmen clacked her mandibles at the dog and tried to hang upside down. Melanie gritted her teeth as claws pierced her forearm like needles. "Victor!"

"There's that damned bird!" said a harsh voice.

Carmen knocked Melanie's ear with the knob of her wing. Melanie shook her head against the stinging, and Carmen clamped her claws and screeched. The screech turned into a whistle that cut through Melanie's eardrums and made her teeth ache.

Unable to care who was in Victor's house, Melanie hurried to the perch in the far corner of the living room. Carmen flapped her wings and screamed like an actress about to get chopped to bits in a horror movie, and Melanie had to forcibly remove the macaw from her arm. The bird climbed to the top of the perch, hissing and holding her wings wide in a threatening display.

Rubbing her scratched arm, Melanie stared at the man hobbling into the living room. The sight of him made her forget her stinging arm, and fear knotted her belly. He was about five foot ten and heavily built, yet compact, with a broad chest and narrow hips. A lime-green tank top revealed a muscular neck and chiseled arms.

His heated gaze was directed at Carmen, not Melanie. As she relaxed, she noticed that he was bronzed the glorious golden shade that suntan lotion companies loved to promise. Then she saw his eyes. Wide and angry, they were the bluest eyes Melanie had ever seen. Paul Newman had nothing on this guy.

Locking gazes with him was like scuffing a carpet in nylon-clad feet, then touching a light switch. The tingle went under her skin—until reality struck. Victor was gay. Hence, any man in his house had not the slightest interest in the opposite sex.

Despite the cane he used to limp cautiously across the floor, what a waste of a terrific body, she thought.

"Carmen was taking a stroll through the parking lot," she said, backing a step toward the door. "Where's Victor?"

The man cast the bristling macaw a baleful look, then grinned, somewhat sheepishly, at Melanie. Her heart tightened as mixed signals made her head spin. His grin was crooked and friendly. So was the down, then up, flick of his gaze over her legs, then back to her face. Instead of making her feel like meat, that friendly once-over made her feel pretty.

"I've been looking all over for that stupid bird. I put her out, and then she was gone. I thought she had come back in the house." He leaned on the cane, his right foot lifted slightly off the floor. "Vic said she wouldn't leave her perch."

"Usually she doesn't. Where is Victor?" Beads of blood gathered on her arm. The scratches burned.

"Vacation. Europe." He rolled those gorgeous blue eyes, then glared at Carmen. "That bird hates my guts." Then the scowl disappeared, and his smile turned sunny, focused on her. "Thanks for bringing her back."

Melanie smiled. "No problem. Carmen gets a little antsy when Victor's away. I doubt she hates you."

He grunted and extended the cane. As she studied the deep bite marks on the dark wood, clear signs of the macaw's powerful bill, Melanie curled her lips inward.

He said, "She attacks this every chance she gets. It's personal, all right." He cut his eyes at the macaw. "Don't know why Vic can't keep a parakeet like a normal person." Then he noticed her arm and stiffened. "Jesus, you're bleeding. I'm sorry, come clean that up. I'm really sorry." Beckoning to her to follow, he hobbled into the kitchen.

More to continue listening to his pleasantly rough-edged voice than to doctor the scratches, Melanie followed.

He ran water in the sink. Under the skylight, his sun-tanned face was weather-beaten, deeply lined around the eyes and in his brow. His eyes were brilliant, startling—bluer than the Albuquerque sky. Melanie judged him to be in his thirties, but his smile was boyish.

His short sandy hair was haphazardly cut, and he had a crooked nose and a heavy brow. His eyebrows had an aggressive cant. Not particularly handsome, yet the combination of boyish smile and devastating blue eyes struck every feminine chord. She could stand here and moon at him all day.

"I'm Chris, by the way," he said. "If I lose that stupid bird, Vic'll kill me. He has a first-aid kit somewhere."

Melanie held her left arm under the running water. She caught his glance at her ring-free hand. "Don't bother. They're just scratches. I've had worse," she said. He seemed interested…in her? She winced as the water stung the welts encircling her forearm. "I'm Melanie Rogers."

He nodded. "The bird lady. Vic said to call you if I had problems with the critters." His smile revealed very white teeth.

His smile threatened to melt her knee joints. "Bird lady?"

Chris lifted a shoulder. "He never said you were so pretty. Guess Vic doesn't notice things like that." He clamped his lips, looking startled, then shifted his attention to her arm. He mumbled something about Victor she didn't catch.

Mixed signals turned into absolute confusion. She watched him rip paper towels off a roll, then pat her arm dry. Instinct said this man was definitely interested; but common sense said any man in Victor's house was interested in attractive men, not pretty women. Had she been away from normal society so long she couldn't tell anymore?

Carrying his Frisbee, Winston came into the kitchen and looked from man to woman, his gaze hopeful. Chris thumped the Lab's broad head. "Winston and I get along fine. I just don't know what I'm gonna do about that idiot bird."

"Maybe she sees the cane as a threat." She wondered what had happened to his leg. He looked too healthy for a chronic problem, and those muscles didn't come from lying around the house. Car accident? Skiing accident? "You haven't been using the cane to prod her, have you?"

A guilty duck of his head and a sheepish smile said he had.

Charmed, Melanie shook her head. "She's very gentle and calm-natured. It might be best to leave her alone. Keep her food and water bowls filled, but ignore her. She'll make up to you if she gets lonesome enough." Remembering her open garage and the purse sitting on her car, she made a move toward the door. "I'd better be going."

"I'm glad you found her. I was looking all over the place." He reached across the counter and touched a Crockpot—Melanie grew aware of a spicy aroma. "I've got a big pot of green chili stew here. The least I can do is feed you. You know, say thanks."

Gorgeous blue eyes, filled with sweet invitation, made her want to sigh. "I'd like to, but I...sort of have a date. Thanks for the thought."

"A date." He made a face. "Figures."

"Oh, no, it's nothing like that." She wondered why she bothered explaining, why she felt the urge to let Chris know she was unattached. Marveling at the easiness she felt, she said, "It's a man who's been asking me out for a long time. I ran out of excuses."

"I see." He played his hands over the crook of the cane and cocked his head. Despite his rough features and his powerful body, sweetness shone through and left her fluttery. "Maybe some other night?" he asked.

"I'd like that." She headed for the door. Chris started to follow, and feeling sorry for him because of his leg, she held up a hand. "I know my way out."

"Okay." He leaned his weight against the counter.

She gave him a little wave, then walked out the kitchen door.

"Melanie?"

She stepped back into the kitchen.

"Vic gave me your phone number." He shrugged, as if to prove the casual innocence of his words. "In case I had problems with the bird. I misplaced it. Could I get it from you?" She gave him the number, and he wrote it on a piece of paper. Hopping on one foot to the refrigerator, he made a show of sticking it under a magnet. "I won't misplace it again."

He was definitely flirting...and she wished there was some way she could break her date. "Call if you need anything," she said, hoping he'd take her literally.

Outside, she blinked in the sunshine. Laughing at herself, she thought, great—finally she had gotten rid of Larry, then met a knockout man, only to discover he's Victor Glenn's boyfriend. Wasn't that the story of her life?

CHRIS WAITED until he heard the front door shut before letting loose a whistle. Winston pricked his ears and he patted the dog. Meeting Melanie Rogers had turned an otherwise boring, rotten day into something special. He smelled traces of her perfume and envisioned the glossy brunette curls bouncing around her shoulders and the gentle humor in her big brown eyes. The sweet fit of Bermuda shorts on rounded hips added a nice touch to the picture.

Vic had told him about the charming lady who lived across the compound. "An absolute maven of aviculture." Chris had assumed he meant a little old blue-haired lady who liked canaries. Never in a million years would he have guessed it meant a lovely lady with a baby-bow mouth and a touching fragility that made him feel too big for his skin.

He grinned at Winston. The Lab sat on his Frisbee. "Almost makes Carmen worth it, huh, Winston, old boy?" The Lab's tail thudded against a kitchen cabinet. "Isn't she pretty? You like her, too? Good taste, Winston, very good. Let's hope her date isn't too hot. Okay, Winston?"

The phone rang.

Chris lurched onto his bad leg. Fire shot like bullets through his thigh and hip. Gritting his teeth, he grabbed the counter for support and, with sweat beading on his upper lip, glared at the telephone. His heart pounded.

On the third ring, the answering machine activated. Victor's voice said, "You know the routine. Don't forget to leave your number." Then the beep.

Chris held his breath until the moment when a youthful voice said he'd found a supply of handcrafted pottery Victor had to see for himself. Chris exhaled deeply through his mouth. He told himself, assured himself, that no one knew about him and Victor, but still he was twisted up inside.

Winston whined anxiously. Chris ruffled the Lab's ears. "Nerves, old boy. Funny how getting blown up will do that to you."

Gripping the cane tightly, he tested his bad leg. The pain subsided to a taut thrumming. Bearable. He hobbled to the back door and looked out over the swimming pool. Beyond the high wooden fence, the Sandia Mountains ruled the horizon.

Victor claimed the skiing was excellent on the eastern slopes. Chris wondered if his leg would ever heal well enough to let him ski again. He tried to picture himself hip-deep in powder, charging downhill with more enthusiasm than sense. Instead, he saw Billy Scopes's confused face, heard Peter Osterman's cultured voice, felt the explosive heat, smelled hair burning, tasted blood . . .

Fresh sweat broke on his forehead.

He pulled the sliding-glass door shut and locked it.

He went to the living room, placing the cane carefully—the brick flooring had a nasty habit of catching the rubber tip. Carmen hissed at him and he made a face at her. Pain-in-the-butt bird. He liked animals, but the scarlet macaw could have made Saint Francis take up hunting.

Telling himself he was being ridiculous, he checked the lock on the door leading to the front courtyard. Ridiculous. Osterman had a network that put the CIA and the FBI to shame, but he couldn't trace what he couldn't find. Not even Chris's mother knew about him and Vic.

Chris shifted his grip on the cane and wiped his sweaty palm on his shirt. No reason for fear. Albuquerque was safe.

He unlocked the door and slid it open to let the breeze enter through the screen. Distant traffic noise came over the adobe wall surrounding the courtyard, mingling with the faint murmur of the next-door neighbors. Someone had started a charcoal grill; the smell made him lonely. High overhead, flocks of birds flew toward Bosque del Apache, and he watched them, feeling as if he were locked in a cage.

He wandered aimlessly through the luxurious house, which boasted brick floors, plastered walls with the soft lines only true adobe possessed, a kiva fireplace and viga ceilings. Each of the spacious bedrooms had a sliding-glass door leading to a small courtyard. Skylights made the rooms bright and airy.

As the fear dissipated, he grinned, recalling his initial uneasiness at the thought that Victor's house would be crammed with frills and ruffles. But Victor didn't make ninety grand a year decorating offices because he had prissy taste. The house was furnished with spare-lined furniture and decorated with southwestern art in muted colors. What would Victor say about Chris's apartment? Were motorcycle posters and used pistol-range targets considered tasteful decor?

He sat heavily on the guest bed, absently massaging his throbbing leg and staring at the sliding-glass door. There were no windows in the house, only doors and skylights. The expanses of glass made him feel exposed.

He opened the drawer of the bedside cabinet and pulled out the Desert Eagle .44 Magnum he had stashed there and checked the load. It held nine rounds in the clip and a tenth in the chamber. Its sixty-four ounces of stainless steel eased him; the oily smell assured him he wasn't helpless. Extending his arm, he looked down the sights, envisioning Peter Osterman's face. One round from the Eagle could erase that supercilious smile.

Chris put the automatic pistol back in the drawer.

Had he only been here a week? It felt like a century. He couldn't drive a car or walk any distance. He'd watched every movie Vic owned, and enough television to make his eyeballs ache. A week? If Peter Osterman didn't get him, boredom, frustration and loneliness would.

Winston jumped on the bed and flopped down beside Chris. "Lie low," Chris said as he ruffled the Lab's dense fur. "Yeah, right. Winston, old boy, I'm starting to think getting blown up is better than this. I'm going nuts."

He lay back and studied the stripped log beams—vigas, Vic called them. His thoughts drifted to Melanie Rogers. Nice how she'd made it clear there was no significant other in her life. His fingertips tingled with imagining how her clear, pale skin might feel.

How did a pet-store clerk afford this neighborhood?

"Quit!" he growled. Winston flinched. Chris snorted and grabbed the dog's head and rocked him back and forth. "Not you."

Why did he have to be so suspicious all the time? Save your suspicions for Osterman, he told himself, and leave slim brunettes with knock-'em-dead legs for more pleasant thoughts.

TALKING NONSENSE in reply to the greetings of her African Gray parrots, Melanie opened a diet 7-Up. Her stomach growled, reminding her she had skipped lunch today. She thought about green chili stew and clear blue eyes, then made a wry face. Chris had only been thankful because she'd brought Carmen home. His invitation didn't mean anything.

Seated at the kitchen counter, she leafed through her mail. Advertising, junk, bill, junk... A movement caught the corner of her eye. She *tsk*ed as Abelard waddled across the floor.

"Get back to your perch, silly bird. You aren't climbing up my bare leg." Abelard veered to the right, pretending interest in something under the dining-room table. She sorted through the bills, then noticed a pink envelope addressed to Melanie Rogers. She had only recently gone back to using her maiden name.

A soft press against her ankle made her look down. Abelard cocked his head and peered up at her with one gleaming eye. She plucked a grape from a fruit bowl and gave it to him. He waddled to the middle of the floor, where he could tease his mate, Heloise, with his prize.

Melanie smiled at his clownish antics. For the past five years, Heloise and Abelard had been her only friends, her substitute children. She and Larry had entertained often and socialized at charity functions and parties in the homes of Albuquerque's finest families, but she had had no friends. She hadn't dared talk to other men, and speaking to women beyond impersonal chitchat had been a risk—she'd never trusted herself to keep the bitterness out of her voice.

She had to relearn how to make friends, how to trust again. Her thoughts drifted to Chris. It was odd how comfortable she'd felt with him. Strange men usually made her nervous.

Heloise climbed down the perch. She scuffled in the sawdust and seed litter in the catch pan, complaining to Abelard in squawks and squeaky whistles. Heloise didn't like leaving the perch, even after nearly a year in this house.

Melanie remembered the day the judge had awarded her this North Valley house. The place was a shack compared to the adobe mansion where Larry lived, but Larry had been furious. After the hearing, he'd told her, "Don't you ever forget who gave you that house. You didn't do anything to earn it." He'd spoken in the hallway outside the courtroom, surrounded by other lawyers and spectators. He'd wanted everyone to know what an ungrateful, chiseling little gold digger he'd had the misfortune to marry.

"Earn it?" Melanie had replied. "Is that what I was supposed to be doing while we were married? Do pardon me for misunderstanding." Those words had garnered stifled laughter; Larry had almost lost his infamous cool in public.

She still couldn't believe she had dared smart off to him. Couldn't believe she'd gotten away with it. Couldn't believe how good it felt. Still felt . . .

She opened the pink envelope. The stationery was pink, too.

"Dear Cookie . . ."

Melanie nearly dropped the paper. Cookie? Memories bloomed. The reddish hair, the pitiful excuse for a mustache, the shy grin and shy eyes. Only one person had ever called her Cookie. Doug Harland.

A bittersweet smile curled her lips. She and Doug had been high school sweethearts. After graduation, she'd gone to college and he'd joined the navy. For nearly two years they'd maintained a love affair through the mail. Then Doug had come home on leave after they hadn't seen each other for over a year, and they had no longer had anything in common. They'd parted friends, but lost track of each other. She wondered what kind of man he'd become.

Dear Cookie, My dear, dear, dearest love. For years I sought you and now I've found you again and this time I will never let you go. Our hearts are one, our souls entwined. The stars decree our union, my darling Cookie. It is fate. From the first moment I stared into your beautiful, shining, soft and knowing eyes I knew it was true...

Melanie wrinkled her nose and turned the envelope over, seeking a return address. The typewritten letter didn't sound like Doug at all. If anything, it sounded like her own adolescent mush. She groaned, wondering if some of that purple-prosed nonsense she had written all those years ago was still floating around.

She skimmed the letter, looking for a punch line or a "Gotcha!" Cookie? Doug must have found out about her divorce from her parents. Did he think this was the way to stir up old fires?

"C'mon, Doug, it's been years." She stuffed the letter back in the envelope. Throwing a glance at the clock, she sighed.

She had promised Roddy Nordstrom a date, and he was due at seven o'clock. She turned a wistful gaze east. Green chili and bright blue eyes tempted her far more than Roddy.

She mentally kicked herself. Roddy hadn't even asked her out, but had gone through Annie to set up the date. The poor man was so shy he could barely speak. For weeks he had lurked around the pet store before making it known, in his oddball way, that he was interested.

A pity date. She felt mean for having agreed to it. Roddy was a good-looking man, she supposed, but his shyness and mumbling and inability to look her in the eye turned her off. She didn't find him attractive, but lots of women would—Annie, for example. Annie thought he was the best-looking thing on two legs.

Melanie especially felt bad because of the real reason she'd agreed to go out—because Larry couldn't tell her not to.

She stared at the folder of legal papers. When she walked out on Larry, she had vowed he would no longer control her life. Now she was going out on a date with a man she didn't care for, only to prove that Larry no longer owned her.

Disgusted with herself, she swung off the bar stool. She was determined that after this date there would be no more doing anything because of Larry. He was the past, and he was going to stay that way.

Chapter Two

Unsure whether she felt angry or relieved, Melanie glared at the kitchen clock. It was eight-thirty, and still no sign of Roddy. Her belly grumbled with hunger and three diet 7-Ups had left her woozy. She made a cheese sandwich.

As she ate, she thought about Chris and his offer of stew and fine company. She laughed at herself. *Hi, my date stood me up, can I settle for you? And by the way, what exactly are your sexual preferences?*

Chewing slowly, she tried to picture Chris and Victor as a couple. Impossible. Victor Glenn was an elegant man, tall and thin and always impeccably dressed. He even pressed creases in his casual denims. As far as Melanie knew, Victor never dated—men or women. Where did Chris fit, then? Victor's walk on the wild side?

"Forget it," she muttered.

Chris didn't matter, and Roddy Nordstrom was a jerk for standing her up. She counseled herself to stick with birds. Birds she understood; men were impossible.

The next day dawned clear and sunny. With the entire weekend to herself, Melanie turned her energy to the house. While a Drifters album played on the stereo, she swept the floors, amazed by the amount of sand she gathered in the dustpan. The house was two years old, but the bricks were still settling into the sand base. She washed the sliding-glass doors until they sparkled.

Singing along with "Under the Boardwalk," she opened her closet and stared at her clothing. Jewel-colored silks, tropical print cottons and richly hued linens hung side by side. She gathered up the few suits and dresses left over from her marriage and laid them on the bed. They were all white, cream or beige; they were all exceedingly expensive. Larry had a weird thing about color. He hated it.

His mansion in the foothills was a wasteland of neutral colors and glass. White walls, white carpeting, white furniture. As if even the suggestion of color offended him, he had insisted that Melanie wear only neutrals, too.

She fingered the hem of a beaded cocktail dress. Of ecru silk and hand-sewn white beads, it cost nearly three thousand dollars. A smile tugged her mouth as she caught a glimpse of her fuchsia-and-green tropical print blouse in the mirror. White and beige would never touch her skin again.

She went to the garage to find a garment bag.

Through the narrow strip of window, she saw Chris in the street. Leaning on his cane, he threw the Frisbee for Winston. The Lab was a high-flying fool. No matter how high or how hard Chris threw the red disk, Winston had a spectacular leap to counter it.

Her admiration drifted to the man. His white T-shirt molded to his chest and back, and as he tossed the Frisbee his muscles moved with fascinating fluidity. He was a bulky man, yet graceful, as if he knew exactly how much space he occupied. His faded Levi's were not so tight that they looked uncomfortable, but they were tight enough to fuel a few fantasies.

As Winston leaped high and twisted to snag the Frisbee, Chris threw back his head and laughed. The man was undeniably a looker. Melanie frowned. At the very best, he was bisexual. Definitely too weird for her.

She bagged the suits and dresses. Some lucky shopper at Goodwill Industries would find herself a tasty bargain.

By afternoon she'd done all the busywork she needed or wanted to do. Euphoria over her newly won freedom lingered. She felt like doing something fun, something... spontaneous.

She exchanged her blue jeans and blouse for a scarlet sundress and studied herself critically in the mirror. She still appeared a tad on the skinny side, but there were no more bags under her eyes, and her hair was shiny. She flicked a curl with a finger, glad her perm had finally relaxed. Her white skin was an anomaly in sunny New Mexico—she hoped the magazines were right in saying untanned skin was back in fashion. Still, she looked good and, better, she felt good.

With no particular destination in mind, she got in her car and drove. She headed south, then turned into Old Town. Admiring the plaza, she inched her car along the narrow street. Tourists strolled along the grassy square and broad sidewalks. Indian craftsmen displayed silver and turquoise jewelry, wood crafts and woven blankets. The spicy scent of roasting chilies drifted through the car window, making her hungry.

Melanie studied the old church dominating the plaza. Odd, but in all these years living in Albuquerque she'd never taken a tour through the historic church. She eyed the crowds and decided some other day. Someday she'd do all the touristy stuff—ride the tram to Sandia Crest, take the Molley Trolley on a historic tour, maybe even learn how to golf or hang glide.

She followed a one-way street back out to Rio Grande and continued south to Central, the old Highway 66.

Traffic was thick and slow, but she smiled, studying the scenery with a fresh eye. Each time she saw an empty storefront she wondered if now was the time to begin seriously planning her own pet store. She wanted to open a bird shop, specializing in the hard-bills—parrots, macaws and cockatoos.

She cruised past the University of New Mexico and wondered if she should finish her degree before starting her business. Maybe a major in biology and a minor in business? Or vice versa?

She turned north onto Carlisle. College students rode bicycles, played games or washed cars. She caught herself envying their youth and laughed at herself. Twenty-eight was a long way from old. Larry had only made her feel old.

As she stopped for a traffic light, she noticed a Chevrolet dealership on the southwest corner of the intersection. Rows of colorful, sparkling cars, trucks and vans transfixed her. Absently she caressed the beige leather seat of her BMW. It was buttery soft, rich...bland. When the light changed, she crossed the intersection and turned into the car lot.

She parked in front of the showroom. As she wandered the rows of cars, admiring the glossy colors, a salesman approached. The name tag on his blazer read Jim.

"Thinking about a second car, ma'am?" he asked.

She ran her fingertips over the glassy finish of a maroon Beretta GTZ. The dealer sticker called the color medium garnet. She liked the sound of it. "This is pretty," she said as she peered in at the plush velour interior. It was called garnet, too.

"Not as pretty as that BMW you drove up in, but almost," Jim said. He expounded on the Beretta's good mileage, durability, reliability and warranty.

Fixated on the maroon finish, Melanie half listened. She saw herself behind the wheel, surrounded by all that lovely garnet. The BMW was a fine car and reliable, but it was white, and its interior was natural leather.

"I'll take it," she said.

Jim stopped in midsentence and blinked at her.

Melanie ran both hands over the Beretta's sun-warmed hood. "I like it. I'll take it. Can I trade in the BMW?"

Jim cleared his throat as he brought out a calculator. He talked about having to clear things with the manager and having the mechanics check out the BMW.

Melanie belatedly registered what she had said and her eyes widened. Larry's face superimposed itself over Jim's, full of censure, sneering. She backed up a step, then caught a glimpse of herself in the Beretta's window, with her shoulders rounded and her head ducked submissively, and hated it. Once upon a time her mother had complained, "You got so much temper, you should've been a redhead." Friends had teased her with the nickname "Spitfire."

Was her spirit broken beyond repair?

She forced her shoulders back and her head up. "How about an even trade? It's paid for. We switch titles and call it even."

Jim looked at the white BMW. "Uh, ma'am, that's a very expensive car."

Biting back the urge to agree timidly, Melanie said, "I know how much it cost. My husband liked to remind me every chance he got." She patted the Beretta. "Look, I want this car. I don't want the BMW. If you don't want the trade, I'll shop around until I find somebody who does. So yes or no?"

Jim had to talk to the manager. He drew the attention of other salespeople, and they eyed Melanie from the show-room. She didn't care. She didn't care that the mechanics who checked out the BMW—it was in perfect condition— looked at her as if she were crazy. Maybe she was crazy. There was no way to explain it to Jim, or even to herself.

She drove away in the medium-garnet Beretta. As she shifted the gears, surrounded by the plush garnet interior, she felt happy. Her wandering led her to Winrock Mall. The parking lot was jammed with cars, and the mall was full of Saturday shoppers. Inside, she strolled aimlessly, window-shopping. She stopped at a clothing store that advertised shorts on sale.

Starting to enter, she noticed the reflection of a man behind her. Uneasily she tightened her grip on her purse and glanced over her shoulder. Staring, he sat down on a bench and idly plucked at the drooping leaves of an overgrown schefflera. He grinned at her. Melanie hurried inside the store.

When she found the shorts, her nose wrinkled. Khaki, olive and desert gray were the big colors this spring—too dull for her taste. She left the store, then faltered. The man was still there, still staring. Hurrying away, telling herself that ill-mannered men stared all the time and it wasn't one of Larry's goons, she put him from her mind.

She entered Elise's Boutique and sorted through huge brandy snifters filled with hair accessories. A barrette with a bow made of bright red-and-white polka-dot grosgrain caught her eye, and she held it against her sundress. Nice match.

"May I help you?" the salesclerk asked.

"I'm just looking, thanks." Then she noticed the perfume display. "Maybe you can." She pointed. "I've been wearing Shalimar, but I think it's too heavy for me. I'd like something lighter, more flowery."

The young woman moved behind the counter and waved her hand over the tester bottles. "Here's a new one. It's called Last Night. Isn't that sexy?" She spritzed a tiny amount in the air. Melanie sniffed, smiling at the hint of jasmine. She held out her wrist. "That's pretty. May I?"

"Well, if it isn't Mrs. Connalley. Or should I say Ms.?"

The voice grated on Melanie's nerves like sandpaper. Forcing a smile, Melanie turned to face Phyllis Rath. "It's just plain Melanie, Phyllis."

Phyllis Rath slunk through the store. A jolt of discomfort shook Melanie. Phyllis looked the way Melanie used to look—the way Larry wanted a woman to look. She wore a tailored beige dress, tastefully accessorized with gold jewelry, and her hair pulled back in a French twist. Though, Melanie grudgingly admitted, the hairstyle accentuated Phyllis's exquisite bone structure and long neck.

Melanie fumbled in her purse for a credit card. "I'll take the perfume and the hair bow," she told the clerk.

"Talked to Larry lately?" Phyllis asked as she picked up a bottle of perfume and sniffed.

"Since yesterday? No." She wondered if Larry had suddenly gone cold on Phyllis. Perhaps she was finding out what many other "other women" learned the hard way. They made terrific mistresses, but not wives. Poor Phyllis, she thought, but she couldn't quite feel sorry for her.

"Spending your alimony well, I see," Phyllis said coolly. "Must be nice to gain so much for such a small effort."

The day wasn't so fun anymore. Melanie accepted her bag and card and started to turn. Then, on impulse, she scanned the perfume display and picked up a bottle. "Here," she said, plunking it down in front of Phyllis. "Larry loves Obsession."

She headed for the exit. Working her tongue against the sour taste Phyllis left in her mouth, she reached for the door. A hand beat her to it. A big hand with thick black hair on the knuckles. She jumped and gasped.

It was him, the staring man. He was huge, well over six feet tall, and slabs of muscle strained his T-shirt. Smiling, he pushed the door open.

"Thank you," she murmured, and hurried out. To her dismay, he followed.

"Hey," he said, "you dropped something."

Drawing her purse and bag over her bosom, she shook her head. "No...no, I didn't."

He thrust out a hand. "This is yours," he said mildly. He opened his fingers, revealing a tiny envelope like the ones flowers shops used.

She knew what it contained. A note from Larry. A command for her to come home, to return to him. Her calves flexed, and her feet itched to run. Instead, she walked, as normally as she could, down the concrete steps and toward the parking lot.

"You better take it," he called.

She kept walking.

She found her car, jumped in and flicked the automatic door locks. Listening to her pounding heart, she murmured, "Stop it. Larry doesn't pay those creeps enough to hurt you."

Clenching the steering wheel to steady her shaking hands, she closed her eyes and leaned against the headrest. When her breathing slowed and her heart stopped pounding, she opened her eyes.

She looked around the parking lot. "Send all the creeps you want, you coward," she whispered as she started the car. "I'm not crawling back to you, and I'm not running. This time I'm winning, Larry. Me!"

She drove home.

When she pulled into her driveway, her hand automatically went to the visor for the garage-door opener. It wasn't there. She groaned, knowing she'd forgotten it at the car dealership, and parked in the street. As she opened her gate, her eyes widened at the sight of a huge bouquet of creamy white roses, wrapped in cellophane and bound with streamers of curly ribbon, sitting before her front door. Bemused, she crouched and opened the card.

Inside was a typed haiku:

Single rosebud, all
    Tear bedewed and baby breathed,
    An apology.

"Right, Larry. You jerk." She crushed the card, cast the roses a disgusted look and tried to feel more angry than scared. The restraining order specifically stated that Larry wasn't allowed within a hundred feet of her or her house.

It wouldn't do any good to call the police, though. Larry would deny leaving the flowers, just as he denied his threats and harassment. Everyone always believed him. She dumped the roses in the garbage can beside the garage, then pushed the button to raise the door.

After she parked the Beretta, she was about to close the garage when she saw Chris and Winston. Chris waved at her and started to hobble across the street. Feeling sorry for him she crossed to him.

"I'm warning you," she said, "Winston is tireless."

"I'm finding that out." He gave her an admiring once-over, making her feel fluttery and feminine.

Again confusion swept over her. She was dying to ask, but how? *Excuse me, sir, are you gay?* Right.

He held out a hand, and Winston gave him the Frisbee. The dog watched the man's every move. His body quivered with anticipation, his thick tail rigid. Chris flicked his wrist, sending the Frisbee sailing in a smooth, high arc. Winston bolted into a dead run.

"I've never seen him miss," Melanie said. How did one ask a man about his preferences? And how would she know whether he was telling the truth?

"He's quite a dog. How was your date?"

She laughed as Winston leaped six feet in the air to snag the Frisbee. "He stood me up."

Chris made a disgusted noise.

"Too bad you're not a girlfriend. I could be catty and give you all my nasty opinions on the subject." She watched him from the corner of her eye.

He snorted a laugh. "The last thing any man wants to know is what a woman really thinks. We need some delusions to cling to."

Winston brought the Frisbee to Melanie. The more the merrier, his laughing eyes seemed to say. Not minding the saliva-slick surface—at least not too much—she took it. She tried to give it a good toss, but it wobbled slowly. Winston shot her a tolerant look, then trotted after it.

Meanwhile, she mulled over Chris's words.

"Want a beer?" he asked.

"That would be nice." She added quickly, "Stay with Winston. I know Victor's house pretty well."

As she went through the living room, she paused to talk to Carmen. The macaw was contentedly chewing on a rawhide toy. Melanie fetched two beers from the refrigerator.

She couldn't resist a quick peek to see if Chris had left anything telling lying around. Nothing except dirty dishes in the sink and something that smelled heavenly bubbling in a pot on the stove.

Quit, she chided herself. Having gotten rid of one obnoxious man, she didn't need to be scouting out Victor's boyfriend. Maybe she was suffering from some weird symptom of postdivorce depression. Instead of feeling bad, she sought a bad relationship.

Outside, Melanie gave Chris a beer. The sun was going down, and the air had acquired a nippy chill. Winston didn't mind the dusky light; with unerring aim, he caught each Frisbee throw. Hugging one elbow, Melanie sipped beer. It tasted funny, but then, she hadn't had a beer in almost seven years.

"So, how do you know Victor? You must be pretty... close for him to let you stay in his house." She hoped that sounded innocent to him; it sure sounded loaded to her.

He handed her his beer, then gave the Frisbee a hard throw that sent it speeding straight across the compound. Winston was a black blur in pursuit. "Vic's sort of..." His voice trailed off, and he raked his fingers through his hair, leaving it sticking up in spikes. Then he whipped his head around. "Hey, you don't think...me and Vic, that I'm..."

Thankful for the poor light hiding her flaming cheeks, Melanie blurted, "I never said..."

He planted a fist on his hip. "Vic's my brother."

She nearly dropped the two beers. "Excuse me?" No way, she thought. Victor Glenn was nearly fifty, tall and thin, with dark hair and eyes. He looked like the actor Jonathan Frid, who had played Barnabas on the old *Dark Shadows* soap opera. Chris looked like a construction worker or a boxer or a lumberjack.

"Christopher Glenn. You think I'm—?"

Unsure whether delight or embarrassment was stronger, she said, "I didn't realize Victor had a brother."

"Yeah, well, the family still hasn't figured out which one of us is the black sheep yet." Then he let out a throaty and good-humored laugh. He rubbed his arm briskly. "Damn, but it gets cold here at night."

"It's the altitude." Melanie wished she could see his face more clearly. "You aren't from around here?"

He whistled for Winston, then said, "Want to come inside and finish your beer?"

"Let me close up my garage."

Inside Victor's house, Melanie baby-talked to Carmen but kept a covert eye on Chris. He sorted through compact discs and made a wan apology for Victor's taste in music, hinting that he preferred rock and roll. Melanie couldn't believe she had ever entertained any doubts about his interests. But Victor's brother? She failed to find the slightest resemblance.

She sniffed the mellow aroma coming from the kitchen. Her stomach growled. Leather squeaked as Chris eased himself onto the couch.

"Pet shops must pay pretty well," Chris said. "That's a nice Beemer you drive."

"The BMW? I sold it today." An urge arose to tell him about Larry, and she put a clamp on it. Instead, she said simply, "The house and car were part of my divorce settlement."

She sat on the couch, opposite him, and rested her bare arm on the cool leather armrest as she sipped her beer. His frown bothered her. Did he think her some rich divorcée raking in alimony and living the useless life? "I'm working in the pet store to gain experience. I'm going to open my own shop someday."

He nodded. "Been divorced long?"

She flashed to a situation comedy she'd seen. A character went on her first postdivorce date, then spent the entire evening boring the man to tears with every sordid detail. It was funny. Now, Melanie found herself wanting to blab everything about her own miserable marriage, but it wasn't funny.

"Long enough." She couldn't resist asking, "What about you? Married?"

His smile was sunshine, filling his blue eyes with light. "Never. Women take one look at my apartment and decide I'm too far gone to housebreak."

Melanie relaxed. No hard feelings or suspicions here, only some friendly checking each other out. He didn't care that she was divorced; he wanted to know if she was available. That was undecided, but worth exploring.

"So, you and Victor are brothers. I never knew he had any family at all."

Chris focused on his beer can. He ran a finger around the rim and traced the dewy sweat. It took Melanie several seconds to guess that he was...embarrassed?

She opened her mouth to change the subject, but he said, "He's fifteen years older than me. He left home when he was seventeen, so I never got to know him." Then his expression grew wistful. "He called me a couple of years ago, out of the blue. Despite everything Dad had said about him, he turned out to be okay." His gaze drifted, then settled on the rounded contours of the kiva fireplace. "Vic's okay." His shoulders hitched with a discomfited little laugh.

Melanie began to doubt that Chris could say anything wrong. Lord, but he was charming. "I like Victor. He's a great neighbor." She winked. "And he gets me discounts on furniture and fabric." That earned her a sunny smile. "What do you for a living?"

For an instant, those blue eyes were startled. Then, quickly, they turned guarded. He drained his beer, then crushed the can in his hand. He shook his head. "Nothing right now."

He obviously didn't want to talk about it. A pang of sympathy twisted her heart. Was he completely disabled and unable to work?

She groped for a neutral subject. As she told him about a business class she'd taken, Chris relaxed. The way he listened unnerved her. No one had ever paid that much attention to what she said, and the absence of the "hurry up so I can talk about me" face she'd come to associate with men loosened her tongue.

Chris sniffed, scowled, then sat bolt upright. "My clam chowder!" He shot her a quick grin. "I forgot my dinner." He grabbed his cane and struggled off the couch. "You eaten?" he asked.

She followed him into the kitchen. He grabbed the pot lid with his bare hand, yelped, then used a pot holder. An atrocious burned stink rolled out in a steaming cloud. Grimacing, he lifted the pot off the stove and set it in the sink. He explained that he'd meant to exercise Winston, then eat, but... Melanie stifled laughter as he stirred the thick glop, scraping through the crust on the sides and bottom of the pot.

"Looks like Winston eats well tonight." He flicked the vent fan to High. "How about a ham sandwich?"

Bothered by the way he was hopping around on his left leg, she said, "Only if you'll sit down and let me fix it."

He hesitated, and she opened her mouth to apologize, but then he hopped around the kitchen counter and sat on a bar stool. She gave him another beer.

His fingers brushed hers, and his impish smile indicated that the touch was deliberate. Melanie caught herself holding his gaze a few seconds too long. It wasn't their brilliant color that made his eyes so beautiful, it was their open expressiveness. They said, I like you and I like looking at you and I want you to like me, too.

Divorced one day, thinking about getting serious the next? It didn't feel as absurd as it should have.

Melanie made thick ham-and-Swiss-cheese sandwiches with lettuce, tomato and dill pickle. She found potato chips in a cupboard.

They ate at the counter, talking about trivialities. Melanie dominated the conversation and knew she talked too much. Her easiness amazed her. Big and tough-looking as he was, Chris offered no threat. A fleeting memory of the creep at the mall shook her. She shoved it from mind.

The phone rang and Melanie leaned back so that Chris could reach it. His fingers dug into the soft bread of his sandwich, and lettuce crunched. His smile disappeared, and his eyes became flat orbs of blue ice. Melanie slowly set down the potato chip she'd been about to eat.

Chris's glare at the phone transformed him. Gone was the rough-and-tumble boyishness. He was cold and hard-featured, his mouth a thin white line. His eyebrows formed a fierce V. His shoulders bunched, and cords stood out on his neck. Sweat beaded his upper lip.

On the third ring the answering machine activated. A woman said she had tickets for the symphony, and if Victor wanted one he'd better act fast.

Chris exhaled deeply. He wiped his face with a furtive gesture and relaxed. He took a big bite of his sandwich, swallowed, then resumed their conversation as if nothing had happened.

Strident alarms *ping*ed at the back of Melanie's brain. It suddenly struck her as very odd that Victor had left town on an extended vacation without telling her—if only to mention that someone would be staying in his house. She'd seen him a little over a week ago, and he hadn't said a word about Europe or a brother.

Bands of fear tightened her rib cage. Chris didn't look like Victor's brother. Why wouldn't he answer the phone? Why did he look at it as if it might bite? Why did he evade her when she asked where he came from or what he did? Had he misplaced her telephone number, or had he ever had it? Why didn't Victor's friends know he was out of town?

She pushed her plate away. "Uh, how long will Victor be gone?"

"About two weeks."

Something hard lurked behind his eyes, something secretive that made her neck prickle and her stomach knot. She realized then that his arms were nearly as big as her thighs, and the house was very quiet, and no one knew she was here.

She swung her head. "Gosh, look at the time!" She almost stumbled getting off the stool. She didn't want to know his secrets. She wanted to run.

She babbled about expecting a phone call, telling Chris not to bother seeing her out. It was all she could do to keep from running out of the house. She forced herself to walk.

CHRIS GAVE the remains of Melanie's sandwich to Winston. He drained his beer and considered getting drunk. Instinct said—and his instincts were always good—he had scared her. Her big brown eyes had telegraphed that she thought him strange, possibly dangerously strange.

He wanted to go after her and explain himself, but he couldn't. Truth was dangerous where a man like Osterman was concerned. If Melanie knew the truth, suppose she slipped and mentioned something to a friend, and that friend told another, and suppose somewhere in Osterman's vast network of ears and eyes someone was paying attention?

He doubted Osterman would hurt her. Osterman was funny that way. He never used women in his organization. No murders of women had ever been traced back to him. Some sort of twisted chivalry, a quirk of Old World courtliness.

No matter how lonely and frustrated he was, no matter how great his need to talk honestly to another human being, Chris couldn't take the chance. He couldn't even tell Vic the whole truth. Fortunately, Vic was an expert at discretion.

He looked down at Winston. "Figger it, old boy. Meet a pretty lady who makes the domestic life look sweet, and she thinks I buried Vic in the garden."

He studied her phone number which was posted prominently on the refrigerator. He wanted to call her, assure her that Vic really had taken a vacation.

He wanted to assure her . . . of what?

He gave Winston the rest of his sandwich. The dog gobbled it down in one chomp, licked his chops and begged for more.

Chris wanted to assure her that freaking out over telephone calls was a temporary affliction caused by the aching fear that Peter Osterman might blow him up again. He groaned and slumped against the counter. His bad leg drummed a nasty reminder up his hip. For the first time in his life, he felt helpless and useless—victimized.

Melanie Rogers made him feel normal again.

It was more than that, though. Just as Melanie was more than a lovely collection of interesting parts. She was special. Her direct gaze, soft laughter, gentle air and oddly tender vulnerability made *him* feel special, made him feel strong and whole again.

He chuckled; it sounded dry and bitter. Melanie Rogers was a lady, a woman to dream about. Not the kind who'd be interested in a scarred-up cripple with a price on his head.

Chapter Three

As she unlocked her front door, Melanie felt stupid. She and Victor were neighbors, not best friends. If he went on vacation, he was under no obligation to tell her.

Larry again. Coloring her perceptions, making her paranoid and suspicious. Damn Larry! How was she ever going to purge him from her thoughts?

Yet Chris had stared at the telephone as if it...scared him.

Or had he? In the past year she changed her phone number several times because of Larry's harassment. She still hesitated before answering. Had she projected her own fears on to Chris? Chris probably thought she was an idiot now. She pushed open the door. A fluttering at her feet made her jump. She turned on the light, then picked up a pink envelope with Melanie Rogers typed across the front.

With a little cry, she slammed the door and locked it. As she gaped at the envelope, her flesh crawled and her scalp prickled with the sensation of thousands of tiny marching feet. She worked her tongue in her dry mouth, steeled herself, and opened the envelope.

My dearest, dearest Cookie,
I carry your banner, me, only me. Purity is your shield.
You are quest's end. You belong to me!!!

A rise of fury overcame the fear. Melanie crushed the pink stationery in her fist. Larry. Either he had come across some old letters or he had thought up the pet name Cookie on his own. Or maybe that sleazy private investigator who worked for him had found out about Doug and the letters.

She stomped into the kitchen and threw the note away. "Leave me alone, Larry!" she muttered. Arms crossed tightly over her breast, she leaned against the counter and told herself over and over she wasn't scared of him anymore.

Once she had been so eager to please him, so willing to be the perfect wife. Yet if she bought him gifts he would return them. She would arrange the table for a dinner party, and then, when the guests arrived, Larry would call her into the dining room and in his "lecture" voice, force her to rearrange the settings.

He left receipts for expensive perfumes, lingerie and furs on his dresser—gifts she never saw. When she demanded the truth, he smiled. He'd call her on the telephone dozens of times each day, and if she didn't answer quickly enough, he shredded her with a razor tongue. Yet if she called him at work his secretary always said he was in a meeting.

Still, he knew when he had hurt her too badly, pushed her too far. At those times he filled the house with flowers, plied her with jewelry, and for a week or two would be the perfect lover, the perfect husband.

Those times were worse. Larry's declarations of undying love and devotion, and his insistence he couldn't live without her, made her wonder what she was doing wrong. It made her believe that if only she were a better wife Larry would change, that he would love her and treat her with kindness and respect.

When she'd finally had enough of his cruelty, infidelity and constant belittlement of everything she did or said, when she demanded he treat her as a human being and a wife, he resorted to violence.

A counselor at the Woman's Center had warned her that Larry might not see the divorce as final. Melanie had ignored her at the time, but now she was beginning to see it as wishful thinking. Fear tingled through her, and she scrubbed down the gooseflesh on her forearms. Knowing that Larry held the restraining order in contempt chilled her bones.

She snatched up the phone and started punching in Larry's phone number. She'd tell him to go straight to hell, to leave her alone....

She slowly hung up the phone. He wanted her fear and trembling voice. He wanted her anger.

If he forced a reaction, he won.

CHRIS CHECKED HIS WATCH; he'd been playing Frisbee with Winston for over an hour. The Lab caught the latest throw, but instead of racing back to Chris, he walked. Chris sympathized. His hip and thigh throbbed.

Winston dropped the Frisbee at Chris's feet, then flopped down on the asphalt, panting. Chris glanced at the open end of the compound. Did Melanie work evenings? He looked at his watch again. He'd give her five more minutes.

Twelve minutes later, the racy rumble of an engine slowed, and then the maroon Beretta pulled into the compound. Chris checked his back pocket for the postcard.

Melanie's garage door began creaking upward. Chris hobbled across the street. With a grunt and a put-upon sigh, Winston got to his feet and followed.

"Hi," Chris called as Melanie got out of her car.

She nodded a stiff greeting. She held a portfolio-style purse protectively against her breast. Her sapphire-colored dress reflected the cool lights in her dark hair and made her skin look like ivory. Chris forced himself not to look overlong, not to appear too eager.

He pulled out the postcard and offered it. "Vic wrote me," he said. Her big brown eyes, fawn-colored, almost golden, were wary. Caught in their spell, Chris felt clumsy and stupid. But no guts, no glory.

She studied the photograph of a round conservatory tower in Copenhagen, Denmark. Chris urged her to flip it over and read Vic's cheerful note and see the Danish postmark. She lowered the purse. Fine eyebrows knitted, she handed back the card. "Sounds as if he's having fun."

"He needed a vacation. He works like a maniac," he said. "Some guy he knew got sick, so Vic got the ticket at a cut rate. It was sort of a last-minute thing. Do me a favor. Don't tell anyone I'm staying in Vic's house."

The line between her eyebrows deepened, then eased. Chris wanted to stare into her eyes forever. A twitch of a smile curved her lips. She lowered her chin, and a fall of soft hair obscured the side of her face. Chris curled his fingers against the urge to push it behind her ear.

She invited him in for a drink.

Her house was built in the same style as Vic's, but smaller, with the long side running parallel to the street. The kitchen, dining area and living room were basically one room.

The colors first startled Chris, then made him smile. The furniture was upholstered in stripes of blue, green and pink, and pillows in wild patterns and hot colors dotted the chairs and couch. Throw rugs made islands of tropical brightness on the warm red-brick floor. Prints and framed posters, many of exotic birds, enlivened the walls. Even the dining-room table was bright, with place mats and cloth napkins in hot pink, electric blue and vibrant green laid around a huge centerpiece of multicolored silk flowers.

"Nice place," he said. He noticed the pair of gray parrots in the living room. The smaller one, swinging its red tail for balance and using its bill like a third hand, climbed down the perch. Chris kept a wary eye on it as he sat on a bar stool and accepted a diet 7-Up.

"Not too jarring?" she said. "I'm as bad as the birds. I can't resist anything colorful or shiny." She snuck Winston a piece of cheese before closing the refrigerator.

The dog gulped it down, then, panting, wandered to the parrot perch. The parrots fussed as Winston emptied their water bowl.

"Hey!" Chris said.

"It's all right. They're old friends." She pulled a stainless-steel bowl from a cabinet and filled it with water. She called Winston and set it on the floor for him.

Playing her fingers over her 7-Up can, she said, "You didn't have to show me that postcard." Color bloomed on her cheeks.

"Yeah, I did. I really am Vic's brother and he really is in Europe. So...I did." He used his thumb to erase the wet ring his soft-drink can made on the countertop. "To be honest, my life is a mess right now. I can't give you any details. Feels stupid being so mysterious." Looking away, he wondered why he felt like a clumsy kid. He'd been around, romanced his share of the ladies.

Maybe it was the way she curled her lips inward, or the way she dropped her eyelids, her eyelashes casting shadows on her clear-skinned cheeks. Or the tantalizing way her big blue earrings brushed her shoulders. Whatever it was about her, it made his heart feel too big for his chest.

"Okay," she said, in her low, pretty voice. "I can sympathize with a messed-up life." Her smile widened. Her mouth enchanted him. Her upper lip had a bow curve, like a child's, and even when it was closed there was a slight gap between her lips. "Have you eaten?" she asked.

"I was going to ask if you'd have dinner with me. Vic raved about a place called Conchita's. Do you know where it is?"

She nodded.

"Can I be a jerk and ask you to drive? My leg is a little stiff."

"Give me five minutes." Her eyes were sparkling.

Chris barely felt his leg as he took Winston home. He checked to make certain his trousers were clean and tamed his hair as best he could. He left the house, but as he locked the front door, he hesitated.

For years Chris had hunted Osterman, but now he was the prey. Going out in public exposed him the same way a stag exposed himself by feeding in a meadow. His palms sweated.

Drawing deep steadying breaths, he reminded himself that if Osterman knew where he was he'd be dead already. Taking a lady to dinner made no difference. He was safe...so far.

He met Melanie in her garage. As he lifted his leg into her car, he wished he could get rid of the cane. It was temporary—daily swims, gentle workouts on Vic's weight machine and exercising Winston were speeding the healing process—and it didn't embarrass him. Still, Melanie was too beautiful for a physically handicapped man.

She backed out of the garage and used a remote to close the door. She told him about forgetting the other remote unit at the car dealer, then going back to get it. Which explained her lateness in getting home this evening. Except the BMW had been sold, and no one remembered the unit. Chris sensed Melanie was holding something back as she hinted that the salesman who'd sold her the Chevy wasn't happy about seeing her again.

She drove to the end of Candelaria and stopped at the sign. Chris noticed that another car stopped three car lengths behind them. When she turned south on Rio Grande, the other car followed.

Quit being so damned paranoid, he told himself.

Melanie talked about a shipment of baby caimans—often mistaken for alligators—that her boss couldn't remember ordering. He used the side mirror to try to get a make on the car. Dusky light made it hard to tell anything other than it was a late-model Ford, cream, white or pale yellow. He cursed New Mexico for issuing only one license plate. When Rio Grande widened to four lanes, other cars passed them and they passed others, but the Ford hung behind.

Melanie turned into the parking lot at Conchita's. The Ford slowed and drifted into the left turn lane as if to follow, but cruised past. Chris's left shoulder felt naked without the Desert Eagle.

They walked toward the restaurant. Melanie laughed. "Okay, what gives? Ask a girl out then spend all your time looking in the mirror? Am I that boring or do you think you're that good-looking?"

He shot her a guilty look. "Sorry. First time out of the house in a while. I guess I was wool-gathering." He swept a finger across his chest. "Cross my heart, you have my undivided attention."

He opened the door for her, then followed the soft sway of her hips as she entered the restaurant. Her silky skirt swished hypnotically, and through the slit in the back he caught intriguing glimpses of the backs of her knees. She was tiny—she probably counted fractions if asked her height—but curvy, despite her petite contours.

Low murmurs and spicy, meaty cooking odors assailed him. He looked back, but there was no sign of the Ford. It had probably just been a fluke, nerves.

By the time they finished salads of marinated jicama and green peppers, Chris was convinced that Melanie was the most beautiful woman he'd ever met. Candlelight made her soft eyes glow. Her hands were slim and white, as animated as little birds when she talked. Against the background of the booth's high back and the thick plaster swirls of the wall, she was a jewel, sparkling and lively.

He wasn't the only one who thought so. Several men cast her admiring glances. Their waiter, a pimply boy in skintight black trousers, could not do enough for the *señorita*. Chris couldn't help thinking that the people there were probably asking themselves what an ugly pug like him was doing with a vision like her.

Enjoying himself immensely, thanks.

By the time she'd finished her enchiladas de chili verde and he'd eaten his bistec de Jalisco—steak in orange sauce—

Chris also knew she was the smartest, brightest, most interesting woman he'd ever met. Her laughter was easy and inviting, her humor gentle. They had things in common. Both like televised baseball, but not football; both liked rock and roll music; she found dinosaurs fascinating and so did he, and she promised to take him to the Museum of Natural History.

And by the time he'd finished his ice cream while she nibbled at a strawberry ice, he knew he was seriously in danger of falling in love. It was easy to imagine spending the rest of his life staring into her big brown eyes.

Chris mulled over the best way to tell her about himself, but he couldn't find one. Knowing better than most how one piece of information led to other information, he didn't know how to tell her a little without having to explain everything. Besides, it might turn her off, knowing he made his living carrying a gun.

He laughed at himself. Friends called him Chris Cool, and said he had veins filled with ice and a heart of steel. Wouldn't they get a good laugh out of seeing him reduced to chicken meat by a woman? Of course, they hadn't been smacked between the eyes by her powerful brand of femininity, either.

When they returned to her house, he opened his mouth to invite her to Vic's for a drink, but she invited him first. She opened the door, casting him little sideways glances that made his chest feel too tight.

"I ate too much," she said, rubbing her flat belly. "I talked too much, too. I don't know what's wrong with me tonight. I usually don't prattle away like this."

"Talk away. I like it." He dreamily followed the wispy trail of her perfume.

Melanie froze in midstep. To keep from knocking her with his cane, Chris stumbled and struck his shoulder against the doorjamb. He started to tease her, but his sixth sense made his scalp prickle. She stared into the living room.

His gaze flicking around the room, his tingling shoulder forgotten, he asked, "What is it?"

"My birds." She tossed her purse on the counter and strode into the living room, turning on lights as she went.

The tall perch was empty.

"Heloise? Abelard?" Melanie made helpless noises as she reeled in an aimless circle.

Chris automatically looked to the nearest door for signs of forced entry. Was there a market for hot parrots? He checked the sliding-glass door. Locked. So was the front door.

A miserable-sounding squawk came from the direction of the fireplace. Murmuring pitying words, Melanie hurried to the draped doors leading from the living room to the court-yard. She stood on tiptoe to reach the top of the drapes. It didn't take a bird expert to know the parrot with the fluffed feathers and the gaping bill was unhappy. Melanie coaxed it down. It climbed to her shoulder and hunched into her hair, making gravelly noises.

"Oh, Heloise, where's Abelard?" Melanie turned wide, frightened eyes to Chris. "Do you see him anywhere?"

Chris moved cautiously through the living room, peering into corners and under furniture. The parrot on Melanie's shoulder loosed a half squawk, half whistle. A muffled reply came from under the couch. On hands and knees, Melanie coaxed the parrot into the open.

She put the parrots on their perch, and both climbed to the top. They huddled together, billing each other and making anxious noises.

Chris focused on Melanie. Skittishly clumsy, she checked doors, tugging the handles. "Did someone break in?" he asked. "Is anything missing?"

"Uh, no... Why would you say that?" Her slender throat worked as she stared at the doorway leading to the back of the house. Her hands fluttered over her breast.

She was lying. "What spooked the birds?" Chris asked. He watched her closely.

Melanie shook her head, causing falls of curly hair to half obscure her face. "Noise or something. They're very sensitive." Her eyes slid away from his; and she blinked rapidly.

Lying again. Chris touched her arm, and she flinched, her flesh quivering. "Hey," he said, "if you're scared, say so. It's okay. A woman living alone can't be too careful. Want me to check the back?"

Her wide-eyed relief nearly broke his heart. He headed for the back rooms, with Melanie crowding his heels and nearly tripping him. Balancing his weight on his left leg, gripping the cane tightly, he reached through a dark doorway and found the light switch.

Track lighting illuminated a spacious bedroom. A brass bed and an eclectic mix of antique-looking furniture filled the room. Blue, green and pink chintz on the bed and windows gave it a hothouse look. The bedroom was crowded, but neat, and there were no signs that anyone had tossed the place.

He checked the sliding-glass door leading to the backyard. The locks, keyed dead bolts going through both halves of the door and the frame intrigued him. The doors couldn't be jimmied or popped from the frame. Melanie was obviously the nervous type.

Chris went on to the closet and bathroom. Hugging her elbows, Melanie followed, but gave no sign that anything was out of place. He looked into the bathroom off the hallway, then went to the other bedroom. It contained a desk and floor-to-ceiling bookshelves. The desk was littered with paperwork. The bookshelves held novels and a lot of books about birds interspersed with college textbooks on business and biology. The sliding-glass doors were secure.

"Everything look okay?" he asked.

She stared at the desk, her focus lingering on a stack of papers. He took a step closer and saw they were credit card and utility bills. Melanie managed a wan grin and nodded, but when she met his eyes her smile faded. She left the room and Chris limped after her.

"Living alone," she said in a high-pitched, rapid voice, "I get spooked too easily."

Again, Chris sensed she was lying.

MELANIE WALKED CHRIS to the gate. He took a step, then turned. Even in the darkness she felt his longing to kiss her. His wanting was a palpable thing, teasing her, making her feel desirable.

She had never met anyone like him before. He was a study in contrasts. Except for his eyes, he had a rough face, a well-used face, yet he was the most attractive man she'd ever seen. He had a macho demeanor, somewhat cocky, perhaps chauvinistic, but his earthy naturalness indicated that he didn't take himself too seriously. He was big and tough and he knew it, but he didn't make her feel weak.

She wanted to kiss him, wanted to test that wide mouth and see if it was as sensitive as it looked, to see if it tasted as sweet as his words. She wanted to know if his arms were as strong as they looked. But, on the other hand, she didn't want to. She didn't want a hasty affair on the rebound. Chris flattered her with his attention, but her sensibility rebelled at the idea of using him to prove she was still desirable as a woman.

"Night, Chris," she said.

"See you tomorrow?"

Her heart fluttered. "I'll be home around six."

"I'll be waiting." He lingered a few seconds, then went home.

She slowly closed the gate. The chilly night air raised gooseflesh on her arms. She hurried into the house and locked the door. Leaning her back against the carved wood door, she laughed at herself. She wanted to do more than kiss him.

What a sexy man. His blue eyes could be so startled when she said something funny, then immediately fill with warm humor, and his laugh arrowed straight to her heart. He made her feel safe. Everything about him, from the throaty rumble of his voice to the protective hand he had placed on her elbow as he guided her through the restaurant, said he would never hurt her.

Amazing—she wanted to trust.

She looked at her sleeping parrots. They perched so closely together, with their heads tucked under their wings, they looked like one lumpy bird. Maybe a sonic boom or a gust of wind had spooked them tonight. There was no way Larry could break into her house. Besides, if he had broken in, he'd have done a lot more than frighten the birds.

She yawned and, anticipating sweet dreams, went to bed.

Two days later, Melanie discovered her parrot earrings were missing. She turned her jewelry box upside down looking for them. She searched both bathrooms, looked through drawers and purses, but the gaudy balsa-wood parrots were gone.

Fear tightened her rib cage. Someone *had* been in the house the night she had gone to Conchita's with Chris. The minute she'd seen the empty perch, she'd known. Heloise and Abelard never left the perch at night unless something drastically upset them.

The parrots hated Larry.

Melanie clutched the edge of the dresser and forced herself to breathe slowly. What was Larry trying to prove? She used one finger to sift through her jewelry. The only good pieces she owned were a sapphire ring, a few gold chains and a pair of diamond studs. Those were untouched.

Why would Larry take a three-dollar pair of earrings? Her hand recoiled from the jewelry box; she envisioned Larry's taint, like a black, creeping mold fouling the rosewood box. When she lifted her gaze, the white-faced woman in the mirror was a stranger. A frightened stranger.

Not a stranger to Larry, though. This was the face he loved. What better target was there for his nasty-mindedness than the earrings she had used to taunt him? What better way to shake her up than to flaunt his ability to get at her?

How had he gotten into her house?

The same way he always found out her phone number, a sick voice nagged. He meant to drive her crazy, to make her crack, to wear her down until her only alternative was to return to him.

The temptation to run nearly overwhelmed her. But where? To whom? Larry wasn't trying to run her out of town. He wanted her back so that he could control her again. He would find her. If she ran, tried to hide, she'd live in terror, wondering when he was going to show his face.

Phantom pains deep in her muscles gripped her. She caught herself anxiously tracing the scar on her scalp. Her mouth was dry and choking, filled with rank fear. Larry's face loomed in her memory, his lips pulled back to a taut, maniacal smile, his eyes glittering with twisted pleasure.

Melanie marched to the kitchen and picked up the phone, punching in the number for the locksmith. As she listened to the ring, it struck her as both funny and horrible that she knew the locksmith's number by heart. She'd changed her locks twice in the past year. Once when she'd moved in, a second time when her nerves had gotten so bad that every night sound made her believe Larry was trying to open a door.

The locksmith answered, and she made an appointment to have her locks changed, all of them. Only after she'd hung up did she realize she wanted to tell him to send someone other than Tony Ornales. She groaned, hoping very much Tony didn't show up.

Why didn't they have female locksmiths?

She hurried home from work that evening, arriving only minutes ahead of the van from North Valley Locks and Security. Repressing a sour sigh at seeing Tony Ornales, she let him in the house.

"Somethin' wrong with the locks, Miz Rogers?" he asked around a huge wad of gum.

At least she hoped it was gum. She tried to ignore the not-so-subtle flexing of his right arm, which was covered with an ugly tattoo of an eagle and an anchor. Tattoos were bad enough, but his nearly encircled his upper arm, and the eagle grimaced as if the anchor chains were choking it. Melanie knew he was married, because of the gold band on his ring finger; she wondered how his wife could stand looking at that strangled eagle.

"They're sticking. Change them, please." She focused on her mail, wishing Tony would stop staring at her legs as if he wanted to pop them off her body and lick them.

Tony might be a cretinous lecher with greedy eyes, but he was efficient. In less than ninety minutes he was putting away his tools. He wrote out a bill, then dangled a set of keys in the air. Melanie reached for them, and his arm twitched, raising the keys higher.

"Know what you need, Miz Rogers?"

My gun, she thought.

"Nervous lady like you needs a roommate." His smile was slow and syrupy. "Maybe a man roommate."

She grabbed the keys, then turned briskly to the counter and wrote out a check. "Thank you, Tony. I'll keep that in mind. Are you certain these are the only keys that fit those locks? I don't want any extras floating around."

"Oh, yeah. Have to make 'em special at the shop. Custom, special security. Those locks are good. Have to break the whole door to get inside. But too expensive for most folks. Most just use a broomstick. Not you, though, you're first-class."

She ripped off the check and all but threw it at him. Ten seconds, she told herself. Ten seconds, and if he isn't gone I will get my gun.

"Thanks a lot, Miz Rogers." One eyelid drooped as if he were about to wink. Melanie's flesh crawled. "Call me anytime. Ya know, if ya got problems with the locks."

She saw him out the front door, then shot the dead bolt home. Leaning her forehead against the wood, she sighed, loathing herself. Once upon a time she could have handled

a creep like Tony, or at least given him the attention he de-
served, namely none.

"I hate you, Larry," she murmured. "I wish you were
dead."

Chapter Four

Annie Guererro shut the cash-register drawer. She called a cheery farewell to her customer, then scooted around the service counter and approached Melanie.

Melanie turned to a fresh inventory sheet. She counted cat toys, then wrote the number on the sheet. The work was necessary, but mindless. It gave her plenty of time to think about Chris. He'd sprung ersatz paella on her last night, made from frozen fish and imitation crab—surprisingly good. Tonight he promised green chili stew. Despite his blustering about his clumsiness in the kitchen, he was a great cook.

Then she remembered how badly he'd beaten her at gin. She owed him $1.49.

"Guess who I saw at lunch?" Annie said.

"Tom Cruise." Melanie counted another hookful of plastic toys. She wondered if Chris was up for a rematch. Probably. He was an easygoing man, boundlessly good-humored, eager to laugh, eager to please.

Annie flipped back her glossy black bangs. "Roddy. He asked about you."

Not very pleased with what had happened the last time Annie tried to fix her up, Melanie made a noncommittal noise. She liked Annie, but the girl thought anyone who remembered when Paul McCartney was a Beatle was ancient.

At nineteen, she was still more girl than woman, and acted a lot sillier than she actually was.

"You never did say what happened on your date, Mel."

"He didn't show. And he didn't bother to call. A dream date he is not."

"You're kidding!" Annie made a disgusted click with her teeth and tongue. "Well, I think he wants another chance. Know what he said? Said he's leaving town. Off to Arizona or Colorado to build a building. I think he's an architect. Want me to tell him—"

"Nothing. Don't tell him anything." Melanie grinned. "I don't want to encourage him. I'm seeing someone."

"I can have Roddy?" Dark eyes bright, Annie leaned close enough for Melanie to smell her bubble gum. "Who is he?"

"You don't know him." She winked. "The boy next door turned out to be okay."

"Is he good-looking?"

"The most gorgeous baby blues you've ever seen."

"And the body?"

Melanie touched her lips with her fingertips and made a kissing noise. This conversation was a trifle embarrassing, but she'd been dying to tell someone about Chris. Annie was the closest thing to a girlfriend she had.

"This is too good!" Annie snorted giggles into her hand, then lowered her voice. "You have all the luck. So what does he do? What kind of car does he drive? Where does he take you? Any—?" She wiggled her narrow hips in a ribald hootchy-kootchy.

Melanie gasped out her laughter. "Annie! Your mother would be shocked at your dirty mind."

The girl rolled her eyes. "C'mon, Mel, spill all the juicy details. What does he do?"

Wishing for a way to end this conversation, Melanie counted toys. She and Chris could talk for hours about a movie they watched on the VCR, but ask him anything personal and he clammed up. Subtlety didn't work, either. No matter how back-door or sideways she couched questions, he would change the subject. Intuition told her he was honest, a good man. He was fun to be with, fun to look at, fun to talk to—but his evasiveness drove her nuts.

The doorbell tinkled, and both young women looked to the front. Annie froze, her eyes widening into dark moons.

A woman, her blouse untucked and one stocking badly torn, was trying to control a Great Dane. About eight months old, the puppy was a hundred pounds of sinewy muscle. The woman held on to a leash with both hands and the dog made gagging noises, flinging gobs of saliva. The choke collar, which was cutting into his fawn-colored neck, choked him but did not control him. His huge paws skittered on the linoleum.

Melanie set her clipboard on a shelf. "Uh, ma'am . . ."

The Great Dane knocked into a wire book rack, which teetered, then crashed to the floor in a spindly clatter. The Dane barked and reared, towering over the woman. Puppies in display cages began to yip and howl. The woman screamed and dropped the leash. Bolting away from the spilled books, the Dane leaped down an aisle, slipping and sliding on the linoleum and knocking the shelves as he went. Bags of birdseed and hamster litter thudded to the floor. Budgerigars, canaries and cockatiels shrieked, beating their wings against cage bars. Some kittens in a cage caught the Dane's eye. His hackles lifted, and he launched himself at them.

Melanie raced down the aisle and intercepted the dog. He reared back on his haunches and bared his teeth as he feinted to get around her to the kittens. His teeth clacked twice in rapid succession.

"Down!" she bellowed. The Dane froze, ears forward. "Bad dog!" She mustered full disapproval. "Bad, *bad* dog! Naughty!"

The Dane humped his back and tucked his tail. He held his head stiff and to one side, slaver dripping off his jowls.

She caught the leash and he bared his teeth. An image of what those jaws could do to the bones in her hand intruded on her concentration, but she forced it away. "Bad dog!" In a dominant pose, she dressed him down with harsh words. She jerked the leash, snapping the choke chain around his neck. He started and tried to run, but she snapped the chain again. Wary respect entered his eyes. His tail twitched, then wagged.

A wagging tail, Melanie knew, was a sign not of friendliness, but of either submission or confusion. This dog was confused; Melanie felt him testing her. Power telegraphed up the leash.

Melanie fully believed the adage that said there were no bad dogs, only bad masters. She tried not to think about how his withers reached her hip or that he weighed nearly as much as she did.

Ready to snap the chain again, she showed him her hand. He sniffed it, then licked her fingers. "Good dog, that's a good boy." She tugged the leash. When he resisted, she snapped the choke collar. He followed. "Good dog."

The Great Dane's owner stood red-faced and wringing her hands. Melanie led the dog outside and the woman followed. "Oh, my goodness, I am so sorry. That's why I must get him to obedience training. He's simply out of control."

"Uh, ma'am, the class isn't held here. You only sign up for it here. The class is on Osuna, next to the bowling alley." Melanie handed over the Dane's leash. "No harm done." She patted the Dane's huge head. "This is a nice dog." He grinned at her, his fangs showing past his floppy jowls. Once fully grown, he'd be a real monster. Obedience training wasn't a nicety, it was a necessity.

"I'll pay for any damages."

"No problem. Something you might find useful, ma'am, is not to put steady pressure on the choke chain. If he acts up, give it a good sharp jerk. The noise and surprise will catch his attention. Be certain to praise him as soon as he behaves."

Melanie watched the woman go, then allowed herself the luxury of a shudder. She went back inside.

Annie looked at her with something akin to awe. "Wow! That dog's bigger than you! I can't believe you did that. I was frozen stiff."

Melanie began picking up books. "Dogs don't scare me, Annie. It's people who give me problems."

Speaking of which . . . She saw her boss standing in the doorway to the back room. Emmett King had operated this pet shop for twenty years and had a reputation for carrying well-bred animals. Melanie liked him very much. What she had learned from him about handling customers and running a business was invaluable. For the past few weeks, however, he'd been cool—since about the time he had stopped hinting that Melanie would make a good store manager.

She guessed he'd found out she meant to open her own store. He probably felt she hadn't been honest with him.

Annie sang Melanie's praises to Emmett, telling him about her quick reaction. Emmett nodded as he surveyed the damage. Looking worried, he asked Melanie if she'd been bitten. She assured him there was no harm done and he went back to inventorying in the back room.

Annie joined Melanie in straightening shelves and righting the book rack.

Melanie said softly, "He's pretty upset with me, isn't he?"

Annie waved a hand. "It isn't your fault that dippy lady brought—"

"Not the dog, Annie. Did you tell Emmett that I want to open a bird store?"

Annie hitched her shoulders and ducked her head. Very slowly she asked, "Was it a secret?"

"No . . . Oh, never mind." It was her own fault. Nine-tenths of all her problems came from ignoring problems and hoping they'd go away, and now she'd blown it again. She wanted to explain to Emmett that she had no intention of competing with his store, but she didn't know how.

"He won't stay mad long. I've been here since I was sixteen. He's an old softy." Annie giggled. "He keeps me even when I'm late. The only thing he really hates is when customers get mad. You never knew Jewel. She worked here, uh, two summers ago. She told a customer that table salt was okay for her saltwater tank. Made the woman's fish sick." Annie whistled. "Now that was something, seeing Emmett mad about that! He yelled at Jewel in front of everybody. Fired her, too." She patted Melanie's arm. "Don't worry about him. I don't think he's mad, just a little sad. He likes you."

"If you say so . . ."

"Trust me. He's an old softy. Now tell me more about this gorgeous man."

After work, anticipating dinner with Chris and a gin rummy rematch, Melanie got in her car. She turned the key in the ignition. Nothing. Not even a run-down whir or click. She tried several times before giving up, then smacked the heel of her hand against the steering wheel.

A brand-new car and it was dead? She got out and stared at the Beretta, hoping the reason for the problem would somehow materialize. No such luck. She knew as much about cars as she did about flying jet airplanes.

"Problem?"

Melanie jumped and clutched her chest. Pulse racing, she turned a glare on Roddy. "Jesus! You scared me. What are you doing here?"

He ducked his head, one shoulder raised as if he expected her to hit him, and crammed his hands into his pockets. Unbidden images of dog packs filled Melanie's mind. In the canine world, Roddy would be low dog in the pack.

"I'm sorry, you startled me," she explained. "My car is dead."

Roddy muttered something unintelligible as he edged around her to the car. Melanie frowned at his back. He had a full head of thick brown hair, and his jacket and slacks were expensive and perfectly tailored for his slender build. What made him so stumble-tongued? Maybe he'd been a fat kid, or more likely a very skinny, sickly kid, or had grown up with a medical problem or a stutter. Or perhaps he'd never been able to overcome childhood shyness.

"Keys," he said, reaching backward.

She handed over her keys. He slid behind the wheel and tried the ignition, then popped the hood release. As he fiddled inside the engine compartment, Melanie tapped her toes and hoped this didn't mean her car was a lemon. It was so much fun to drive. Then a car cruising past the end of the parking row caught her eye.

A white Ford Fairlane, exactly like Larry's. He usually drove his Porsche, but when he visited seedier clients, he drove the Ford—his slumming-around car. The Ford passed before she could see the driver. She shivered despite the late-afternoon sunshine.

Roddy stepped back from the car, mumbled something, then strode across the parking lot. Brows lifted, she watched him go. Sighing, she slid behind the wheel and sat with her feet outside the car, making circles on the pavement with her toes. Cars. Four wheels and reliability—was that too much to ask?

She debated calling Chris to tell him she'd be late. Would he answer? His distaste for telephones was almost a joke now. What exactly did he do for a living? Construction worker? Why would he hide that? Industrial spy?—ridiculous! Darn that Annie and her questions!

Roddy returned with a wrench. Keeping his face averted, he bent over the engine. "Try it."

She turned the key, and the engine leaped to life. She stared at the RPM gauge in amazement. "You're a miracle worker, Roddy. Thank you! What did you do?"

"Nothing," he mumbled. "Battery cable slipped." He closed the hood, pushing with both hands to make certain it latched, then took a sideways step toward her. "Sorry about the other night. Uh, I sort of got...emergency, meant to call..."

Embarrassed by his fumbling apology, she said brightly, "You made up for it today by coming to my rescue. You are definitely forgiven." She sat, wanting to leave, but wanting to be polite, too. He had fixed her car, after all. "Annie says you may be leaving town. A construction job?"

His prominent Adam's apple bobbed and his jaw worked from side to side as he stared distantly. "I don't have to go."

That wasn't the answer she'd expected, or wanted. "Have to go where the money is. I wish you the best of luck."

"Uh, Saturday night? Tickets for a concert. You'll like—"

"I'm sorry, no."

His eyes darted toward her like quick black birds, then away, and his knuckles whitened where he held the wrench.

"I'm very busy these days." She smiled to show there were no hard feelings, rolled down the window and shut the door. Leaning her head out, she added, "That's sweet of you to ask, but with work and everything, I don't have time. Why don't you ask Annie? She loves concerts. I know she'd like to go with you." She put the Beretta in reverse, gave him a jaunty wave, then backed out.

In the rearview mirror she saw him watching her drive away. He looked so forlorn that her heart filled with pity. She hoped, for Roddy's sake, that Annie wasn't busy Saturday night. At least he could talk to her. Or, Melanie thought with a wry laugh, Annie would be so busy chattering that she wouldn't notice Roddy's silence.

At home, she noticed the blinking light on her answering machine and played it back. Chris said, "Hey, gorgeous. Dinner is ready whenever you are. Come on over." The message made her smile.

She exchanged her slacks and blouse for a pair of shorts and a T-shirt with a silk-screened macaw on the front. Then she called the Chevy dealer and asked for the service manager.

"Hi," she said when he answered. "I bought a Beretta GTZ from you recently. It's giving me some problems. I have Friday afternoon off, can I bring it in then?"

"Can you describe the problem, ma'am?" She heard him rustling paper.

"My battery cable slipped off. Fortunately, a friend was able to fix it. But if this is a chronic problem—"

"Pardon me, ma'am?"

"The battery cable slipped off."

There was a long silence. A thudding noise in the background grew loud. Finally he said, "Ma'am, battery cables don't slip. They're bolted on."

Melanie's neck prickled. Roddy and the wrench—a Ford Fairlane cruising the parking lot. Her heart thudded dully while the service manager explained that battery cables were affixed with heavy bolts and clamps.

"I see," she said. "Then you're saying that this isn't going to happen again."

"If you want to bring it by, I can look. But unless someone tampered with your engine, I don't see how it could have come off."

"Uh-huh." She licked suddenly dry lips. "Well, thank you very much, then. I may swing by Friday to make sure." She hung up, then sat, clenching her hands to stop the trembling.

Larry. He couldn't get her back, so now he was getting even? Everything tightened inside her, and her shoulders ached with every breath. It wouldn't do any good to call the police unless someone had seen him tamper with her car. She knew Larry too well to expect there would be any witnesses.

A domestic abuse counselor had once told her, "Abusive men thrive on power and attention. The antithesis of love is not hate, but apathy. When a victim reacts emotionally or physically, the abuser assures himself she still cares.'' Those were easy words to say in the safety of a counselor's office. Nice, safe, clinical words, lifted from a sociology textbook. Still, Melanie knew the counselor was right. As long as she engaged in battle, whether one-on-one or through the legal system, as long as she cared, Larry owned her.

She went to Victor's house.

A knock earned only a muffled bark from Winston. When she opened the door, the dog skittered around the floor with the Frisbee in his mouth. ''Chris?'' she called.

''Bad bird,'' Carmen replied.

Calling again for Chris, Melanie followed her nose and Winston to the kitchen. Watery bubbles popped and hissed around the Crockpot's lid, releasing the spicy aroma of chilies and pork. A cloth-covered basket tempted her, and she peeked. Wedges of corn bread, dotted with jalapeños and pimento, made her mouth water.

The sliding-glass door was open, and she went to it. Chris swam facedown in the kidney-shaped pool. Kicking his legs with more energy than grace, he reached the side, dived under, turned, then pushed off the side. Melanie went to poolside and crouched. The white tile radiated warmth through the thin soles of her sandals.

When Chris came up for air, she called, ''Hi.''

He swiped water from his eyes and grinned. ''Is it that late already?'' He swam lazily to her side and rested his forearms on the edge of the pool. His eyes were bluer than the sky. Water sheeted off his sun-golden shoulders and his hair molded, otter-sleek, to his skull. ''Feels great. Got the pool heater on. Want a swim?''

Melanie shuddered at the very thought—water terrified her. ''Maybe later.'' She arose, aware of the way he followed her legs as she picked a towel off a deck chair. ''I'm starving, and smelling that chili is making me desperate.'' She started to hand him the towel, but his smile stopped her.

A bolt of envy pained her. Chris was so strong, so sure of himself. She couldn't imagine him being afraid of anything—or anyone daring to harass him or make his life miserable. A wave of weakness and helplessness made her sway.

Damn you, Larry! I am not weak and helpless!

"What's the matter?" He planted his hands on the poolside and hoisted himself out of the water, twisting lithely so that he sat on the edge.

"Huh?" She looked away. His knotted shoulders and the feline sinuousness of his broad back caught her off balance. She wanted to touch him . . . taste him.

"You've got a funny look on your face. Problem?"

Problem? One woman's problems, one man's delight. She had vowed before, and reaffirmed now, never to allow Larry to interfere with her life again. If she waited out his petty harassments, he'd tire and quit.

She settled a neutral expression on her face. Chris stood. His body was almost hairless except for a downy dusting below his collarbones that thickened in the center of his chest and ran down his ridged, steel-plated belly in a tantalizing dark gold line.

Then Melanie saw the scar.

Puckered and angry red, ridged by chlorine-whitened flesh, it ran a jagged course from his right knee across his thigh and disappeared under the leg of his swim trunks. As if someone had used a paring knife, carving out chunks, smaller scars dimpled his thigh, knee and shin. Melanie gasped, then bit her tongue.

Chris looked down. "Pretty bad, huh? Not exactly the body beautiful."

Her cheeks warmed. It looked so horribly painful. Imagining the injury made her heart ache. "I'm sorry, I . . ." She thrust the towel at him.

He hopped to a deck chair. While he toweled his hair and shoulders, he said, "It doesn't embarrass me." His smile was sunny. "Considering I almost lost the leg, the scar doesn't bother me a bit. Now you, on the other hand, what's bugging you?''

Compared to whatever had injured his leg, Larry's petty vandalism seemed ... petty. She smiled. "Nothing. Except I'm starving." She perched on the wide redwood arm of the chair and combed his wet hair with her fingers. "Did you have a car accident?" She winced inwardly, knowing she shouldn't have asked.

His expression turned thoughtful. "I need to tell you something."

His seriousness caused a tightening in her breast. Did she really want to know? Suppose he was disabled for life, forced to live off his brother's largess? Suppose it was worse—suppose he was a felon or a fugitive terrorist or a drug dealer.

He dried his legs, not looking at her. "Do you—? I mean, I know you think I'm sort of strange. I dance around your questions. I hate that. But what do you—?"

Oh, Lord, she thought, here it comes. We've reached the point in our relationship where honesty is imperative and now he's going to tell me he's a bank robber or running from the FBI. "Chris, what's going on? You can tell me." She tried to see his eyes; he avoided her gaze.

His chest rose with a heavy breath, and he straightened, resting his hands on the towel in his lap. "I can't tell you everything. I want to, but I can't. I'm in a lot of trouble, Melanie. I can't let anyone know I'm here."

Her appetite disappeared, and she felt too heavy to move. She wanted so much to be brave and noble and say nothing in his past mattered. But it did, and she knew it did.

"I'm on convalescent leave," he said. "Wounded in the line of duty. I'm a policeman, Melanie."

It took several seconds for the unexpected words to sink in. She gaped at him. Then she giggled. The giggles turned into a laugh, and she clapped both hands to her mouth. Chris's bewildered expression turned into a scowl. She gulped down the laughter and gasped, "Oh, Chris, I thought you were going to say you robbed banks!"

"Huh?"

Imagining the elegant Victor with a tough policeman for a brother caused fresh laughter. She laughed so hard her eyes teared. She swiped them away, then caught his face with both hands. Endearing bemusement twisted his brow; his jaw jutted pugnaciously.

"Why didn't you tell me? I have the most awful imagination. You can't . . . I'm embarrassed to admit what I was thinking." She pressed an impulsive kiss to his mouth.

His smooth lips tasted of sunshine and chlorine. Kissing him had been a spur-of-the-moment impulse, but once started, it demanded a finish. Her eyelids drifted shut, and she pressed her fingertips against his cheeks. He cupped her elbows, tugging slightly, and she canted her head, felt him rising to meet her. He brushed his tongue lightly, invitingly, against her lips. Startled by powerful yearnings, she pulled away.

Blinking rapidly, she fiddled her fingers on her lap, too aware of the sun-warmed redwood beneath her buttocks and Chris's size and bare chest and the golden streaks in his sandy hair. He released her elbows, slowly, his fingers trailing down her forearms.

"Why didn't you tell me?"

Grinning, he fingered his lower lip. "Guess I should have." He touched her knee, tracing a circle with a long, muscular finger. Shivers rippled under the skin. "I'm in a bad situation. I don't want to drag you into it." His hand, dark against her paleness, grew bold. The shivers widened and tingled up her thigh and danced in her groin. That kiss had been a teaser, a promise of delights to come. Sweet invitation warmed his eyes, and she knew his thoughts had nothing to do with police work.

She stood. Whatever was happening between her and Chris was too special to ruin with impulsive behavior. She'd been hurt so badly before; she couldn't jump into another relationship so quickly. She took a few steps, her back to him.

"Melanie?" He stood behind her, and she stiffened. He placed his hands on her shoulders; heat seared through the thin cotton of her shirt. "I feel stupid hiding things from you."

She rolled her head to the side. He stroked her cheek with his thumb. Everything felt all twisted inside her. "It isn't that," she said.

"Does it bother you that I'm a cop?" He touched her jaw softly, and she turned. "I didn't know how you'd feel about me carrying a gun, or how to say one thing without telling you everything."

Touched by his insecurity, she lifted her eyebrows. He worried about how she might feel? A staggering concept. She wanted to kiss him again, to reassure him. "It doesn't bother me. It's... it's us. You and me. I don't want to rush this. There's no hurry, is there? Can we—?" She looked away, ashamed of her own secrets and insecurity. *How much alike we are,* she thought in bemused wonder. "I don't want to blow it. You're too special, Chris."

His smile enchanted her, told her everything would be all right. He touched his finger to her chin and tipped her face, pressing a gentle kiss to her mouth. She sighed. Her knees trembled with the strain of holding back.

"No hurry, then," he said, and stepped away. He jutted his chin at the house. "Dish up dinner while I change."

Over dinner, she felt the change between them. She saw it in the way his eyes caressed her with new boldness. Each time he brushed her fingers, electricity jolted her, and his voice held a new tenderness. She barely tasted the stew.

When it was time to go home, he walked her across the street. He pushed her gate open, but before she entered, he wrapped one heavy arm around her shoulders.

"Sure you won't—" He checked himself. "See you tomorrow."

His arm tensed against her shoulders, the muscles tightening slightly. He could, if he wanted, overwhelm her, force her to submit, coerce her, seduce her...but he wouldn't. He never would. He was powerful, but he owned the power of self-restraint, and it telegraphed clearly, *You are special and I will never hurt you.* Knowing that sent thrills of desire coursing through her body.

She stood on tiptoe to kiss him good-night. He lifted stray locks of hair from her face, and the calluses on his palm rasped gently across her cheek. His scent of sunshine and masculinity turned her knees to jelly. "Night, Chris." She practically floated across the courtyard.

When she unlocked the door, she noticed a piece of paper stuck between the door and the jamb. With her mind filled with blue eyes and throaty laughter, she plucked it free, then went inside.

A piece of pink paper held the typed message: "Cookie, you can't live without me." Three slashes underscored live.

She crushed it in her fist. "Right, Larry. Truth is, I'm doing fine." Humming, she riffled through a junk drawer and found a padlock. She went outside and snapped it on the gate.

In fact, she thought, inhaling deeply, as if she could catch Chris's heady scent on the breeze, I'm doing wonderful.

Chapter Five

Whistling, Chris adjusted the table centerpiece. He had told the flower shop to deliver something colorful. They had obliged with a splashy bouquet of orange tiger lilies, red and yellow tulips, purple irises and bright pink daisies.

He eyed the dining room, satisfied, then hobbled into the kitchen to peek into the oven. Savory roasting juices made his mouth water. He'd never tried making pot roast before, but with time on his hands and Melanie to cook for, it was worth experimenting.

Winston lay on his chest in the middle of the floor, and Chris nearly tripped over him. He used his cane to nudge the dog. With a put-upon sigh, Winston moved.

"Don't give me that, you old faker. This dinner is special. Our two-week anniversary."

He filled a silver bucket with ice, then checked the label on the wine bottle—Chardonnay, in flowery script on a gold background. An elegant-sounding name for an elegant lady. He settled the bottle into the ice, then checked the dining room again. Following the diagrams in a cookbook, he had set the table with Victor's Limoges china, sterling flatware and Waterford crystal.

He laughed at himself, knowing he was acting like a schoolkid turning handsprings to catch a pretty girl's eye. He studied his reflection in the sliding-glass doors and slicked back hair with a hand; it had grown back enough that he needed a haircut. Half turning, he flexed his biceps, studying the definition. He exercised to diffuse energy rather than out of vanity—but it was a good body, it made up for the face.

He remembered his first undercover assignment, and nearly getting shot by an overeager uniform cop. "Christ Almighty, Glenn!" the policeman had said later. "Thought you were a street punk!"

Outside, the lowering sun turned the Sandias into a picture postcard of red, gold and bronze. He opened the door wider, amazed at how clean the air smelled. A lot nicer than Phoenix. He glanced at his watch, then went into the living room to light the fire. Balanced on one leg, he turned on the gas jets, then started the fire.

Carmen squawked. He imagined he saw a decidedly wicked gleam in her weird white eyes. Stupid bird. He'd tried doing exactly as Melanie told him, letting her warm up to him. Feeding her a cracker had earned him a nice reward. His thumb still throbbed under the bandage.

Winston pricked his ears. Whistling and chattering, Carmen craned toward the door. Hearing Melanie's soft knock, Winston snatched up his Frisbee and trotted to the door. Chris grabbed the coffee table and pushed himself upright, calling, "Come on in."

Melanie walked inside. Chris was so busy admiring her emerald jacquard blouse and her slim skirt, which revealed pretty knees and slender calves, that it took him a few seconds to register her expression. A strained smile and a trace of puffiness around her eyes made him wonder if she'd been crying.

She greeted him, Winston and Carmen with her usual cheeriness.

Chris gave her a friendly kiss. Her flowery perfume made his blood rush. Did she suspect what these "friendly" kisses did to him? He wanted to press her, but she flinched if he touched her unexpectedly; occasionally he caught a curiously fearful expression on her face. Once, during a gin rummy game, he'd slapped the table when she won, and she'd cringed, wide-eyed. He scared her—and he didn't know why.

Her words and eyes said she liked him; her body language said back off. The mixed signals befuddled him, but he wasn't about to run her off with a show of randy bad manners. And the kisses did give him pleasant dreams—he hadn't had a nightmare since meeting her. He doubted Melanie would appreciate the exact content of his sweet dreams. Definitely X-rated.

She lifted her head and inhaled. "It smells heavenly. Ever thought about going into the restaurant business?"

He caught the tense edge in her voice. Her eyes were red-rimmed and shiny. He touched a finger to her lips. "Shh... Cooking is my most closely guarded secret. Can't ruin my macho image."

She laughed. "You're such a jerk."

He hooked his arm with hers. "Want a before-dinner beer?" He guided her toward the couch.

"Sure."

"Sit, take a load off." He waved away her insistence on helping him. As he went around the couch, he couldn't resist brushing her dark, soft hair. He imagined her hair spread over satin pillows, gleaming, glossy, teasing his bare skin, imagined plunging his hands into it and letting its heavy luxuriousness fall away like water....

Muttering, "Down, boy," he fetched two glasses, tucked two beers under his arm and went back to the living room. He winked at her curiosity as he filled the glasses. Then he held up a finger for her to wait, and called Winston. Taking away the Frisbee, he gave the Lab the can. "Winston, old boy, deposit."

Winston trotted into the kitchen. A soft rattle said he'd dropped the can in the recycling bin. Chris repeated the trick with the second can.

Hand over her eyes, her legs curled kittenlike on the couch, Melanie laughed. "You taught him that?"

"A man can only watch so many soap operas." The edge was gone from her voice. She'd tell him what was bothering her when she was ready. He picked up his beer and leaned back. "So, glad it's Friday? Have a good day at work?"

Her expression tensed. Her eyes shimmered, and then tears spilled like water out of an overfilled glass. Startled, Chris reached out to her, but she twisted off the couch and ran into the kitchen. He snatched up his cane and followed.

"Hey, hey, what is it? What's the matter?" Her sobs made his chest feel weak and tight.

She scrubbed her face with a paper towel and shook her head violently. "It's so humiliating," she gasped, her voice raw and husky.

His hand wavered over her shoulder. He felt useless and stupid. Finally he pulled her against his chest and held her tight. Shoulders hitching, she sniffed and snuffled, dampening his shirt with her tears.

"What happened?" He rubbed his hand in slow circles over her back. It struck him, hard, how small she was. The top of her head barely reached his chin, and her slenderness curved against the hollows of his body. A rise of protectiveness worsened the heaviness in his chest. "Talk to me, honey. What's the matter?"

"Oh, Chris, Emmett fired me." She lifted an unhappy face, but her tears stopped. She dabbed at her eyes with the towel, smudging what remained of her mascara. "Larry did it!"

"What? Who's Larry?"

She pulled back, and he let her go. She ripped another paper towel off the roll and turned around to blow her nose. Huskily she said, "It isn't the job. I was going to quit eventually anyway, but he's driving me crazy! He's trying to ruin my life."

He fingered her shoulder. Her blouse was silky and slippery, and the flesh beneath it was firm. He wanted to hold her again. "What happened?"

She lifted both shoulders. "I knew Emmett was in a bad mood. Annie played hooky and didn't call. All day he was practically standing over my shoulder, watching everything I did." She blew her nose again.

Color bloomed like roses across her pale cheeks. "He called me into his office. He said a customer had complained, and he showed me a pedigree for a Yorkie. I could see it was faked, all whited out and typed over. I didn't do it. I didn't even sell the dog! But a customer swore I had and threatened to sue the store. He was obviously lying! I wanted to ask how much Larry paid him to fire me. I couldn't believe it."

"Who the hell is Larry?"

She squeezed the paper towel, and her knuckles whitened. Her eyes filled with haunting pain, and patches of crimson flared on the crest of her cheekbones. "My ex-husband. He's trying to ruin my life."

Chris guided her into the living room, had her sit and gave her the beer. Punctuated by shuddery sniffs and long, embarrassed pauses, her story came out. How she'd been a twenty-one-year-old college student when she met Larry Connalley while he was in Columbus for a law convention. After a whirlwind courtship, he'd married her and brought her to Albuquerque. She told him about the verbal abuse, Larry's infidelity, and the way he'd cut her off from friends and family.

She drained half her beer in a long gulp, then wiped her mouth with the back of her hand. "I went to a psychologist. I thought it was me. I thought everything was my fault. Then he came home from a trip. He said it was a business trip, but I knew that was a lie. He'd gone to Lake Tahoe with Phyllis. He left his receipts on the dresser.

"I told him I wasn't going to sit home feeling sorry for myself while he humiliated me with that woman."

Her voice had a quiet, eerie quality. Chris chewed the inside of his lip to keep from interrupting.

"I flipped. It was as if six years of anger boiled up to the surface. I grabbed up receipts in both hands and shredded them. I threw a bottle or something. And then he hit me." Pain rippled across her face. "He hit the side of my face and knocked me against a chifforobe. I felt my eye swelling, tasted blood, but I just stood there. No one had ever hit me before. I couldn't believe it.

"He was smiling. I'll never forget that smile. I tried to run, but he knocked me down the stairs. I passed out—a concussion, took ten stitches in my scalp."

Tears rolled down her cheeks. "I had him arrested. It didn't do any good. He came to the hospital, he brought flowers. I had a call button in my hand, but I was so scared I couldn't press it for help. All I could do was hope that he didn't kill me."

Jaw clenched, Chris stared at the fireplace. Domestic violence. Shrinks and do-gooders called it spouse abuse, as if somehow husbands suffered as much as wives. Chris called it plain old wife-beating, and it made him sick.

"Larry asked me if I had learned my lesson. I had. As soon as I got out of the hospital, I called the police. Two policemen went with me to the house, and I packed my luggage and collected my birds and walked out."

She hunched her shoulders in a defensive posture. "I had to leave him. I had to! I couldn't fool myself anymore that life would get better. He liked hitting me. That smile—like he'd found a new toy. If I stayed, he'd have hit me again... and again."

She wiped her eyes. "Larry fought the divorce. He had a judge order us to attend joint counseling. He made it sound like I was a neurotic idiot and he was the long-suffering saint. Everyone takes his side, always. He hired a private investigator to follow me around. I got a restraining order against him, so now he sends goons to carry his messages."

"Messages?" Chris asked.

"Stupid things. 'Come home,' and 'Larry loves you...all is forgiven.' Little cards and stuff. He leaves me notes and flowers." She drew a deep breath and dabbed her eyes with the shredded paper towel. "I hate him."

"Ever consider relocating?" Chris asked.

Her lips tightened, and her eyes sparked angrily. Chris mentally kicked himself for saying such an asinine thing. A man assaults his wife, then society kicks her while she's down—makes her go to counseling, change her name and hide out in safe houses. He's the criminal, but she's treated like one.

"I'm sorry, I meant . . ."

Melanie's bloodshot eyes held steel. "I refuse to run. For seven years he controlled me, jerked my strings. No more. If I run, it'll be a rabbit hunt. It's a game to him. He likes it." She nodded. "But he'll quit. He has a girlfriend. She wants to be what he wants her to be. If I refuse to play, he'll quit."

Her fingers twitched, then inched along the couch toward him. He folded his hand over hers and squeezed her slim fingers.

She said, "I didn't want to . . . drag a lot of old baggage between us. There is an us, isn't there, Chris?"

Thinking that some very bad things might happen if he ever met Larry, Chris nodded. "There is definitely an us." A curious tightness invaded his chest.

Her cheek muscles twitched, as if she were trying to smile but couldn't quite manage it. She entwined her fingers with his. "I didn't want to tell you."

"You can tell me anything."

She smiled; it was weak but real. Then, lifting her chin, she said, "I'm okay, I'm going to be okay. Getting fired isn't so bad. I've been procrastinating. Now I don't have any excuses to put things off." She raised her glass. "I'm going to open my own store. Here's to fresh starts."

Crystal rang softly as he touched his glass to hers. Watching her over the rim, he sipped his beer. Steely determination marked her soft and lovely face. Admiration for her swelled until he felt as if he would burst with it. He set down his glass, then took hers and set it down, too. He placed a hand on her shoulder. Watching her eyes, he slid the other hand around her waist. Her lips trembled in a tentative smile, and he gathered her into his arms.

He touched his lips to hers, then drew back, again struck by her smallness, by her china-doll face and her vulnerability. He wanted to make love to her, but, more, he wanted to protect her. Her lips parted, her eyelids lowered, and she lifted her face to him, seeking. He kissed her long and soft and slow, clinging to her mouth, never wanting to release her. The hesitant probe of her tongue made blood pound in his ears.

Winston's claws skittered. Chris opened one eye and glared a command for the dog to settle down, then traced the sleek contours of Melanie's narrow back and the sharp nip of her waist. With delicate fingertips, she teased the short, stiff hairs on his neck.

Carmen squawked. Winston whined and paced restlessly.

Damned critters, Chris thought. He longed to feel her skin, knowing it would be silkier than her blouse. Slowly, shivering with longing, he worked a hand along her delicate ribs and stroked the side of her breast. Her brassiere was lacy, underwired, and her breast was small and full. Cupping the sweet fullness, he kissed her deeper, wanting all of her, his nerves singing as she arched against him and clutched his back.

Winston loosed a lionlike roar and launched himself across the room. The Frisbee clattered hollowly on the bricks.

Chris and Melanie sprang apart. Winston leaped against the carved wood door, barking furiously. Carmen whistled and flapped her wings.

The door swung inward, and a man reached for the dog. Chris grabbed at his shoulder for the .44 magnum that wasn't there.

MELANIE STRAIGHTENED her blouse and shifted her thighs against the liquid ache of frustration. She hoped her cheeks weren't as red as they felt. "Hi, Victor," she said.

"Hush, Winston," Victor Glenn said, "I'm glad to see you, too. Well, little brother, I see you've met the neighbors." Lugging a large suitcase, he tried to get past Winston.

The Labrador whined and wagged his tail so hard he threatened to put holes in the wall. His big feet clattered on the floor. Victor finally dropped the suitcase and crouched.

Melanie chuckled into her hand as Winston gave Victor a face-washing. Chris struggled off the couch and, eschewing his cane, limped gingerly across the living room. "I wasn't expecting you until the seventeenth," he said, grabbing Winston's collar.

Straightening, Victor tugged his lapels. A silk handkerchief hung, just barely, from his breast pocket. He tucked it in absently, giving Chris a dry look. "It is the seventeenth." Then he smiled and opened his arms.

Chris ducked his head and shot Melanie a discomfited look, then stepped back and extended his right hand. Victor slowly dropped his arms, then, with a hint of a shrug, shook hands with Chris.

"You're looking great, Chris. Good skin tone, bright-eyed and bushy-tailed. I take it the climate agrees with you." He looked over Chris's shoulder and winked at Melanie.

Melanie stood.

"And you, Melanie, charming, as usual." Victor's dark blue eyes twinkled to match his impish smile. "I did think you had better taste, though. Chris is a Neanderthal." Winston was clamoring for his master's attention. "Please, Winston, get down. My goodness, hasn't anyone loved you? Have you been a naughty dog?"

The Lab bounded away and, in a scrabbling skid, snatched up his Frisbee.

Victor shook a finger. "Not now. Let me get my luggage inside." Chris made a move toward the door, but Victor waved him back. "I'll get it. If you want to be helpful, pour me a giant glass of water. I'm parched."

Chris hopped one-legged to the couch and retrieved his cane. Melanie wondered out loud if she should go home. Chris beckoned for her to follow him into the kitchen. "Sorry," he said. "Got my dates mixed."

"Are you sure I should stay? I'm certain you and Victor have lots to talk about." She stared at her feet, embarrassed about getting caught in a compromising position—and embarrassed that she had told Chris about Larry.

Chris caught her wrist. She started, stiffening, overwhelmed by a trapped sensation. Then she met the wicked gleam in his blue eyes, and tremors of smoky pleasure shook her insides.

He pressed a quick kiss to her mouth and whispered, "Stay. This dinner is for you, but if you don't mind sharing, I don't." He kissed her again, playfully. "Besides, we never have much to discuss. Vic doesn't talk about his life, and I don't talk about mine. Know what I mean?"

"I guess so." Chris's discomfort about Victor bemused her. Yet the fact that he tried to not be uncomfortable charmed her. She hugged his waist.

When the three of them sat down to dinner, Victor gave the table his vote of approval. Melanie felt very flattered by the bright flowers and elegant place settings. She met Chris's eyes across the table and saw his eagerness to please her.

Victor lifted a bottle of white wine from the icy bucket and looked from it to the roast beef and then to Chris. "This one is not quite aged well enough. How about a nice cabernet sauvignon instead?"

Chris's eyes narrowed in a good-humored glare. "Sure."

Victor exchanged the white wine for a red, then set about carving the roast. While they ate, he reduced both of them to helpless laughter with tales of his transatlantic flight.

Carmen waddled into the dining room. She gave Winston a haughty look, then ducked and bobbed like a begging baby bird at Victor's feet. Victor extended a fist.

Carmen climbed on, and he transferred her to the back of his chair. She billed his ear and nibbled his collar. Raising her head feathers, she closed her eyes as he scratched her breast.

"Bad bird," she said.

Taking small bites of her beef—it was perfectly medium rare, tender and juicy—Melanie studied the brothers. Chris was fair, yet Victor was almost Latin in appearance. While Chris was heavily built, with big, well-used hands, Victor was slim, with bony hands and manicured fingernails. But when they smiled she saw the resemblance. Both of them had the same boyishly crooked grin.

Victor dabbed his lips with a napkin. "Dinner is wonderful, Chris, but I'm still on European time. Jet lag—I couldn't sleep a wink on that wretched airplane. Next time I'm booking passage in the cargo hold. More legroom."

He stood and held out a fist for Carmen. "Come, darling, back to your perch."

"Bad bird."

"You certainly are." He bade Chris and Melanie a cheery good-night, and then, with Winston at his heels, left them.

With an oddly wistful look on his face, Chris watched him go. Then he refilled their wineglasses and smiled at Melanie. "Dinner okay?" he asked.

"Perfect."

"Sorry I messed up the dates. I wanted tonight to be special."

She placed a hand over his and lightly traced the thick knobs of his wrist. "It is special. And I like Victor. He's nice." She lowered her eyelids, then slowly raised them. "You aren't apologizing for him, are you?"

He played with a biscuit, shredding it into little balls. "I guess I am. Does that make me a Neanderthal jerk?"

"Sort of," she said honestly.

He pulled a face. "It's funny. I was my father's son through and through. Baseball, camping, getting in fights.

Played football in high school. I even became a cop because of him.

"I never told anyone I had a brother. I was always afraid they'd find out what he is." Again the wistful softness appeared in his eyes, and his smile was sad. "All that tough-guy stuff, and I couldn't even admit that I missed him."

He lifted her hand and kissed her knuckles, one by one, then rubbed the back of her hand against his cheek. "Vic and I talk on the phone, and write, and we get together whenever he's in town on business. I can't bring myself to tell anyone he's my brother. Can't introduce him to my friends.

"But when I ran into trouble, he never asked questions, never hesitated. Right off, he opened his door to me. I guess that says real plain who's the better man around here."

"There's hope for you," she said.

"Think so?"

"I know so." Melanie leaned slightly across the table, and he leaned slightly toward her. She knew all her instincts were right the moment he smiled. Leaning the rest of the way, she pressed a soft kiss to his mouth.

Then she felt suddenly rather foolish and shy for wanting to haul him over to her place and hop into bed. Even thinking such bold thoughts shook her. She sat back and fiddled with her napkin.

"What about you?" he asked. "You never mention family."

She lifted a shoulder and played with her wineglass. Tracing the cut pattern, she examined the highlights formed by the crystal and the dark red wine in the dim light of the dining room. "We're not very close. People in my family do not divorce, no matter what. My parents blame me for divorcing Larry."

Chris grunted. "The old, let's-jump-on-the-victim-because-it's-easy syndrome. Yeah, I've heard that one."

She shot him a hard look. "I'm not a victim, Chris. Don't think that, please. After I walked out on Larry, I swore I would never be a victim again, ever." She shook her head and thought how odd it was that this conversation felt so natural. For once she felt neither shame nor defeat, merely a simple need to assert herself. "Victims cannot help themselves. I can."

"Lady, you're really something." He kissed her hand again, his breath warm against her skin.

Wishing for eternity to hold this moment as she stared into pools of pure, clear blue, she murmured, "You are, too."

They ended the evening early. Melanie wanted to invite Chris to her house, but she knew where that would lead. She wanted to make love to him, spend the night in the comfort of his strong arms and share breakfast with him in the morning.

But Chris wasn't some fast-food hamburger to grab on the run. He was a fine seven-course meal to anticipate, lovingly prepare, linger over and savor, and always remember. She could not see the future, but intuition said he was part of it.

Right now, they didn't know each other well enough. She had once made the mistake of blindly following her heart and her hormones. She couldn't bear to make the same mistake twice.

At Victor's gate, Chris kissed her long and lovingly, filling her with fresh wonder that a man so big could be so gentle. She went home, walking backward part of the way, watching him watching her. She pulled her mail out of the box and locked the gate.

Inside the house, she kicked off her shoes and worked her toes against the rough brick floor. As she looked at her sleeping birds, a pang of regret cut through her. She wanted to call Emmett and convince him that she'd never do anything to hurt him or his customers. Maybe it was for the best, though. She had been procrastinating, heeding self-doubts. As long as opening her own store remained a dream, she couldn't fail. For once, Larry had done her a favor. It was fly or fall now.

She opened an envelope from the bank.

A bad check? She stared at the returned check and the officious Insufficient Funds stamped in red over the face. She read the terse notice saying the bad-check charge was twenty-five dollars. She huffed exasperation, knowing full well it was a stupid bank error.

A glance at the figures in her checkbook confirmed her view. She was right and the bank was wrong, but that probably wouldn't save her from the bad-check fee. Or another fee from the store where she'd written the check. Stupid computers. Nothing like a dumb machine to make a bad day really rotten.

She smiled, thinking about Chris. Nothing like a genuinely good man to make all the rottenness insignificant.

The message light blinked on her answering machine. A rise of hopefulness tightened her breast. Emmett King calling to say he'd made a dreadful mistake? Then his condemning face filled her vision, and she flinched. He was unhappy about her opening her own store; that supposed complaint was probably the excuse he'd been looking for.

She pressed the playback button.

A man said, "Dragons lurk, Cookie. Beware! I wield your banner. By *your* own words I am your chosen knight. *Yours!* Resist the knaves with flattering tongues and false promises. Any dastardly blackguard who defiles you must *die!*"

Chapter Six

Chris listened to the phone message a second time. All traces of humor and boyishness had disappeared from his face. Glaring at the answering machine, he looked like a cop—or a street fighter with a score to settle.

"That is so sick," Melanie said. She hugged her elbows and wavered between feeling scared and feeling foolish. All her earlier brave words—all that talk about not being a victim—felt like sawdust in her mouth. After hearing the message she'd raced like a spooked rabbit to Chris.

"Is it Larry?" he asked.

She lifted a shoulder. "It doesn't sound like him. And the accent..." The caller had the slightest trace of a southern accent; it nagged at her memory. "He could be disguising his voice." She looked up and swallowed against the dryness. "He never threatened to kill anyone before."

Too tired for this, she slumped against the kitchen counter. "No matter how many times I changed my phone number, he always found me. It got so I unplugged the phone at night. I know he got me fired. I know it. Now this?" She shuddered—that low voice had sounded so angry.

"What does he mean by Cookie? And banners and knights?"

She turned her palms upward in a helpless gesture. "That's the weirdest thing. I dated a boy in high school who called me Cookie, a pet name. We wrote a lot of letters, but I didn't save them. I sure didn't tell Larry about them. He was too jealous.''

"Are you sure it's Larry? Could it be your old boy-friend?''

Her and Doug's long, steady relationship had been a combination of puppy love, mutual interests in movies and novels, romantic notions, convenience and habit. ''I seriously doubt it.'' She told Chris about the letter and the notes on pink paper. ''The first one I thought was from Doug. But the notes on my door? And this call?''

Chris removed the cassette from the answering machine. ''Could it be another man? Someone you told about Doug?''

She drew a total blank. ''I don't know any other men. Doug was the only boy I ever dated before I met Larry. It has to be Larry.'' She tapped her fingers rapidly across the countertop. ''Maybe that private investigator found out about Doug.''

''Private eye?''

''Tim Service. He followed me everywhere, took pictures of everyone I talked to.'' She chuckled. ''I think some of the neighbors are convinced I'm wanted by the FBI. But it won't do any good to ask him. Larry keeps him on retainer.'' Her stomach tightened into familiar knots. ''I'm so sorry for dragging you into this.''

He waved a hand absently in dismissal. ''You have a re-straining order against Larry.''

She nodded. ''He's not allowed within a hundred feet of me or this house. He isn't supposed to call.'' She jutted her chin at the cassette. ''But how can I go to the police? He'll deny it.''

Chris scowled thoughtfully. ''Do you have Doug's phone number?''

''No, why?''

''Find out if Service asked him about Cookie. Ask him if he's willing to tell a judge.''

"Will that do any good?"

"If Doug talked to Tim Service and Service is in Larry's employ, then a judge should have no trouble making the connection."

"He'll deny it. You don't know how good he is, how believable." The old bitterness washed over her, and fighting it down left her shaky.

Chris tapped the cassette on the counter. "If he knows you're on to his game, he'll quit. Especially if a judge is on his back."

It made as much sense as anything else. Except she had no idea where to look for Doug. She tried directory assistance for Columbus, Ohio, but they had no listing for him in the city or any of the outlying suburbs. She tried her mother.

Weighed down by sudden guilt and regret, and knowing her mother was still angry about the divorce, Melanie resisted the urge to explain her situation. Larry was her mother's dream of the perfect son-in-law: wealthy, well educated, urbane. Throughout her marriage, Melanie had been too ashamed to tell her parents the truth. After Larry had beaten her, she called them from the hospital. Her father's first words had been "What the hell did you do to make him so mad?" It still hurt.

Melanie asked about Doug Harland. Her mother replied coolly that she saw no sense in digging up the past.

"Mom, this is important. Do you know where he lives now?" Melanie caught her pleading tone and winced.

"If you had thought your marriage was important, you wouldn't be having to look up old boyfriends. Really, Melanie, I don't understand you. I spoke to Larry. He's brokenhearted. He can't understand why you're doing this to him. Frankly, I can't, either."

Her eyes burned. Poor brokenhearted Larry, pouring out his tale of woe—probably with Phyllis sitting on his lap. "Thanks a lot, Mom. I gotta go." She hung up without saying goodbye. Her parents were still on friendly terms with Larry? It made her feel sick.

Melanie tried directory assistance again, asking for an Elvin or Marjorie Harland. The operator checked, and then an electronic voice came on the line with a phone number.

She called Doug's parents. Mrs. Harland answered, and Melanie introduced herself.

A long silence ensued, and then there was a chuckle. "My goodness! Are you in town, dear? How long has it been?"

Melanie engaged in a few minutes of chitchat, but kept her answers short and vague. Finally she asked about Doug.

Another silence followed, then Mrs. Harland said, "He's married now, dear. A delightful girl. Her name is Helen. They live in Virginia." She grew bubbly as she told Melanie about Doug's three children and his new house and his partnership in a construction contracting firm. She gave Melanie Doug's phone number.

After hanging up, Melanie groaned and rested her head against her hand. "I just know it wasn't him. Oh, God, I don't want to call him."

Chris nudged her arm. "Go on, get it over with."

Taking a deep breath, Melanie dialed. While the phone rang, she silently cursed Tim Service, a sleazy little character who dressed like a "Miami Vice" cop and mangled the English language. He acted very familiar with Larry, never seeming to notice Larry's distaste. Larry called him Peeping Tim.

A woman answered the telephone.

Melanie said, "Mrs. Harland? I'm Melanie Rogers, an old friend of Doug's. Is he—"

"*Melanie?* He's told me about you."

Unsure whether that was good or bad, Melanie licked her lips. "I hate to bother you, but I have a problem. May I speak to Doug?"

"He's out of town." Her voice was cool. "Business."

Melanie's scalp prickled. "I see. Is there any way I could reach—"

"No."

Jealousy came through loud and clear, and Melanie wondered exactly what Doug had told his wife about his old high school sweetie. "May I leave a message? I need to talk to him." Mrs. Harland replied with a sound open to interpretation, and Melanie gave her telephone number and said Doug should call her collect.

She sighed deeply as she hung up. Larry using the name Cookie had to be a fluke... except that that first letter had been so strange. The same tone, the same words, the same purple-prosed exaggeration she herself had once used. Cookie? Larry never used pet names.

She blinked rapidly. Pink paper? It looked just like the popular dime-store stationery she had once claimed as her own—pink paper decorated with little hearts and bows, and matching envelopes. Very girlish, very silly, very... pink.

Coincidence, it had to be some sort of weird coincidence.

"Well?" Chris asked.

"He isn't home. He's away on business."

"Uh-huh," Chris grunted. "Are you positive it isn't him?"

Exasperated, she looked askance at him. "He's married. Three kids. He lives in Virginia." She thumped a fist on the counter. "This is what Larry is good at! Mind games. Forget it, Chris. I'll unplug the phone."

Chris played with the cassette tape. He pressed the pads of his fingertips against the plastic as if he could absorb the truth from it. "I don't want to scare you. Maybe you know this already... I think you do. Ex-husbands can be extremely dangerous. Some men would rather destroy something than let it get away."

He tossed the cassette between them, and it rattled on the counter before coming to rest. "It's too damned easy to ignore this, Melanie. This is a threat. I've seen too many dead women, most of them killed by men who could not let go."

Suddenly Chris was one of them. The police officers who told her how to protect herself, then, in the same breath,

said they couldn't do anything unless Larry actually hurt
her. The counselors with their statistics on domestic violence and guidance through the legal system and their apologies for lacking solutions. Her parents, who thought a
beating was a fair price for an intact marriage.

"Thanks a lot for the words of wisdom, Chris. But what
am I supposed to do? You tell me that! He beat me up and
I had him arrested and it took him a whole hour to get out
of jail. I pressed charges, I signed a complaint, I stood up
in court. And the judge listened to good old Larry. I swear
to God, he was winking when he lectured Larry about
chastising his wife. That's the word the judge used. Not beat
me up, *chastised* me. He's such a nice guy, he didn't really
mean to throw me down the stairs."

Chris looked shocked. "Melanie, I—"

"Damn it, you can't know! You can't! I know he's sick
and sadistic. But what am I supposed to do? Huh? Change
my name, get plastic surgery? Move? Spend the rest of my
life looking over my shoulder, wondering when he's going
to show up?"

"I didn't—"

"You can't know how terrible this is. You can't know
what it's like to be scared of a ringing phone or always
searching parking lots to see if he's there. Getting up in the
night five or six times to make certain the doors are really
locked." A taste like tenpenny nails filled her mouth.

"He sends scuzzy-looking men, and they say, 'Larry
sends his love.' They show up in restaurants, follow me to
the mall. Once a strange man sat next to me in a movie the-
ater and said if I went home Larry would forgive me.

"I'm not living like that anymore! Hiding, afraid to leave
my house, afraid to talk to people. Don't you get it? You
come in here with your advice, but I know! I can't stop him,
the police can't stop him, and the courts won't stop him.
The only thing I can do is stop being scared. It's the only
thing I can control."

Chris's eyes darkened. His brow furrowed, and his hands rested on the counter in white-knuckled fists.

Melanie sucked in a shuddery breath. The outburst left her drained, and ashamed of flinging her anger in Chris's face. "See why I didn't want to say anything? I'm sorry, so sorry. Maybe you'd better go home, Chris. This isn't your problem."

"You mean that? You want me to leave?"

She nodded her head.

"I understand, Melanie. A lot more than you think."

She clung to the sincerity in his voice. He couldn't know, no one who hadn't lived it could understand, but she heard genuine sympathy.

"I even got a gun last year. I went to classes and shot at targets that looked like people. I hate that thing! It's so ugly, and it smells so bad. I'm not a gun person, but that's what he wants to make me. Some kind of animal." She lifted her head and found him calm, his gaze even. "I can't stop Larry from hurting me, but I can keep him from turning me into an animal. Can you understand that?"

"Yeah," he said, his voice very soft. "I understand."

Her eyes burned, and her throat swelled painfully. She scrubbed one eye with a knuckle. The rubber tip of Chris's cane squeaked on the bricks as he came around the counter and into the kitchen. He smoothed hair from her brow.

"I'm on your side. And I do understand. Want me to stay? Keep you company?"

She rested a weary gaze on the cassette tape. "I do... but I don't. I don't want your pity. I don't want a guard."

He tipped her chin. "Then how about a friend?"

"Are you sure you want to do this?" Melanie asked as Chris closed the car door. "This may turn out to be really boring."

"I've got cabin fever so bad that even Winston is getting on my nerves. Besides, Vic is cleaning house and making it plain I'm in the way."

Thankful for his company, Melanie backed the Beretta out of the garage. Chris had spent the weekend on her couch. She felt guilty, and it felt strange having a man in her house. Yet she felt safe, too. "Consider yourself warned."

She closed the garage door. "I have to stop by the bank first. I called, but they gave me the runaround. Their computer—"

A bright square of pink caught her eye. "Damn it," she muttered, putting the car in neutral and pulling up the emergency brake. She got out and stomped to the gate. A pink envelope made her furious.

She went back to the car and flung the envelope at Chris. "A Cookie letter." She slammed the car door and fastened her seat belt.

Scowling, Chris opened the letter as Melanie drove out of Camellos Court.

"Is this supposed to mean something?" Chris asked. He read the letter aloud. "'Dragons and darkling witches lurk in the shadows, but I am your knight, your arm. Beware of dragons, their smell is sweet, but their corruption runs deep and their smiles hide many sharp yellow teeth.'" One side of his upper lip lifted. "'The darkling witch sought me, but my armor is strong and my wiles are many. The wicked wretch sought your slander, but I can see the monster no matter how comely the form. They cannot fool me. Let them try! Let them all try! In your name and upon the chalice filled with the purity of love...' Jesus, there's two pages of this crap."

"Throw it away." Melanie put on her turn signal and stopped at the intersection.

"Single-spaced." Chris turned the letter over, his scowl deepening as he again asked, "Is this supposed to mean something?"

Mean something? It sounded insane. "Sure. It means Larry's a nut." She snatched the paper from his hand and crushed it into a ball. She wanted to toss it out the car window, but couldn't bring herself to litter. She tossed it in the back seat.

"Is he on some kind of King Arthur kick? Play Dungeons and Dragons games?"

"Please, forget it." He started to say something else, but Melanie gave him a hard look and said, "Please? It's a gorgeous day. Let's enjoy it." Then it hit her; Chris wasn't carrying his cane. She asked him if he needed to go back for it.

"Don't need it. Gave it to Carmen. Give her something to chew on besides me." He reached back and grabbed the crumpled pink ball. He smoothed the paper.

"Chris."

"It's evidence."

"Chris!"

He folded the paper and stuck it in his pocket. "Okay, okay. But I'm a cop. Indulge me." He settled into the bucket seat and faced forward, blinking innocently. "So, what kind of place are you looking for?"

She admitted that she didn't know exactly. Her appointment with the real estate agent should give her ideas about available stores and how much they cost, and about commercial zoning in Albuquerque. She wanted a small store with a generous glass front but not too much automobile traffic. An indoor mall would be perfect, but she didn't want to open a place in Winrock or Coronado Center. Too expensive and too impersonal. She envisioned a small but loyal clientele.

Chris asked, "Is there good money in exotic birds?"

"Yes and no. Well-trained birds are valuable. But I don't expect this to make me rich. I may become famous in bird-fancier circles, but I doubt any gigolos will ever pursue me."

"How about cops?"

Keeping her eyes on the traffic, she grinned tartly. "That depends on which cop it is." She turned into the bank parking lot. "Want to wait or come in?"

"I'll suffer with you," he said, and opened the door.

She covertly studied his gait as they entered the bank. He limped, but he didn't appear in much pain. Amazing, considering the damage it must have taken to create that scar.

Melanie waited for the accounts manager. She studied her bank statements, deposit slips and checkbook. Despite what that snippy person had said on the phone, her checking account was in fine shape. If she heard, "The computer says..." one more time, she would scream.

The accounts manager finally invited her into his office. Melanie handed over her paperwork and checkbook. The manager hemmed and hawed, working out figures on a calculator, then typed commands into a computer terminal. He scowled at the screen.

"Well?" Melanie asked.

"Our records show your account has been cleared."

"What does that mean?"

"The account is no longer active."

"There's been a mistake. I didn't close my account." She closed her eyes, wondering how many more bounced checks would show up in her mailbox. "You people do keep written records, don't you?" She cut a glance at Chris, not appreciating his speculative frown.

The accounts manager handed back her checkbook but took her statements. "Excuse me for a moment, Miss Rogers. I'll find the problem."

As soon as he left, she turned on Chris. "I know what you're thinking. But I can't blame this one on Larry. He doesn't have access to my checking account."

"I wasn't thinking that at all," he said, with a too-innocent smile. "I was thinking about a buddy who got a paycheck for almost forty thousand dollars. He gave it back, but it took him six months to convince the computer to stop docking his paychecks for the overpayment."

"Thank you ever so much for the encouraging words." She laughed, feeling better.

It took forty-five minutes for the manager to return. Melanie called the real estate office to reschedule her appointment. A secretary promised to leave a message.

The manager wore a sheepish smile. He gave her back her statements and a sheaf of papers. "My deepest apologies, Miss Rogers. A computer error. If I can get you to fill those out, I can clear this matter for you."

"What about the bounced checks? Am I responsible for the extra charges?"

"I'll take care of that."

By the time they left the bank, it was nearly eleven o'clock. Melanie said, "What a way to spend the morning. Sorry you came along yet?"

Chris entwined his fingers with hers. "Nope."

"The least I can do is buy lunch. The realty office is on Menaul, not far from a place with stuffed sopapillas worth dying for."

"It's a date."

They spent little time in the realty office. The agent, Julia, had a listing prepared, but she had another appointment. She apologized for being unable to advise Melanie on zoning regulations on such short notice. Her advice was to call the city's planning department. Armed with the listing and Julia's card, Melanie left the office.

She drove up the street to the Little Burro restaurant.

It was a new place, very in with the chic crowd, even though it looked more like a truck stop than a hot spot. The decor consisted of plastic booths, tacky plastic ferns of gigantic proportions, and wooden cutouts of burros and howling coyotes in pastel colors. Waitresses in short shorts and puffy-sleeved blouses bustled about.

"Crowded," Chris said as they followed the hostess to a booth near the back. All around them, men in three-piece suits and women in tailored dresses engaged in earnest conversations.

"It always is." Melanie slipped into a booth and caught the admiring once-over a waitress gave Chris. He wore jeans and a polo shirt that revealed bulging biceps and sun-golden, corded forearms. The leggy waitress gave him an inviting smile and handed him a menu.

One of the hazards, Melanie thought philosophically, of falling for a man with gorgeous blue eyes.

"Annie talked me into coming here when it first opened. I thought, oh, no, what am I doing in a place like this? But the food is terrific."

Over a lunch of sopapillas stuffed with chicken, olives, sour cream and green chilies, Chris entertained her with police stories. His tales were funny, and time slipped away quickly. As they stood by the register to pay the bill, Melanie handed over her credit card and discussed with Chris which store to inspect first.

"Uh, excuse me, miss," the young man behind the counter said. He wore an apologetic expression, but held his shoulders stiffly.

"Yes?" Melanie held out her hand for the card.

The cashier drew the card close to his chest. "I can't accept this."

She glanced at the cash register. Stickers announced they accepted all major credit cards. "Why not?"

"They said I have to cut it up." He snatched a pair of black-handled scissors from behind the counter and stepped back.

"Cut it—?" One good snip, and her card was destroyed. "Why? What? Why did you do that?" People behind her in line hushed their conversations, watching her and the cashier. Her cheeks burned. Chris put a hand on her shoulder. "That card is perfectly good! Why did you do that?"

"They told me to." He cut his eyes right and left, looking as embarrassed as she felt. "It's stolen."

Melanie dug through her wallet and flung her driver's license, library card, insurance card and credit cards on the counter. "Why would I steal my own credit card? Where's the manager?"

In her ear, Chris said, "Forget it. He'll call the police."

She shrugged away from Chris's hand. "He cut up my credit card!"

Now belligerent, the cashier said, "You have to pay for your meal."

"Forget it. You can get another card." Chris pulled out his wallet, laid a twenty-dollar bill on the counter, then scooped up Melanie's cards. He hustled Melanie out the door. Heads swiveled to follow their progress.

Furious, Melanie spun on him. His expression cut off her angry words. She stalked to her car. Limping, Chris caught up with her and said, "I can't afford a scene right now. You can get another card."

Great, just great. Humiliated in a crowded restaurant, and now Chris was playing mystery man. She opened the car door, unlocked his side, then slumped behind the steering wheel. "First Larry, now computers. Gee, Miss Rogers, you aren't paranoid, everyone *is* out to get you."

"I'm sorry," Chris said.

"Quit saying that. It isn't your fault." She fumbled the key into the ignition. "I use too much plastic anyway. It's a habit I need to break."

She rebelled at the idea that Larry was behind this. Because if he was, then it meant he had access to her personal affairs. It meant he could strike anywhere, anytime, and there was nothing she could do about it.

"Melanie?"

"Don't say it, Chris. There's no way Larry can get my credit card numbers. No way! So back off!"

He clamped a hand over her arm and leaned in close. His eyebrows nearly met in the middle. "Don't talk to me like I'm the enemy," he growled.

Fear closed her throat. She was going to drive Chris away, make him so sick and tired of her chronic problems that he'd throw up his hands and decide she wasn't worth the bother. She licked her lips. "I'm sorry," she whispered.

His eyes softened, and he caressed her arm. He opened his mouth as if to say something, then frowned slightly. She searched his eyes, finding warmth and understanding. Trust filled her, relaxing her. She pressed a soft kiss to his mouth then settled back on her seat.

He smoothed hair away from her cheek. "It's just a credit card."

She nodded and started the car. Striving for normalcy, she said, "What's the address of the place over on Wyoming? I don't think it's far. We can look at it first."

She had almost found her good mood again when flashing blue lights filled her rearview mirror. She glanced at the speedometer. A steady thirty-five. The police car loosed a short blast of siren.

Chris told her to pull over. He slouched on the seat, chin down, eyes forward. Melanie stopped the car. Pulling her purse across her lap, she rolled down the window. With silvered glasses hiding his eyes, a policeman approached cautiously.

"Is there a problem? Was I speeding, Officer?"

He looked up and down the length of her car. "Are you aware that you don't have taillights or a license plate?"

"Excuse me?" She shot Chris a startled look, then pushed open the door. The policeman jumped, his hand locked on his gun holster. "This is a brand-new car!"

She hurried to the rear of the car, and her mouth dropped open. The rectangle for her plate was empty and both taillights were smashed. Jagged pieces of red and yellow plastic clung to the empty frames. Even the bulbs were broken. She blinked rapidly, trying to remember the last time she'd noticed the back of her car.

Head down, hands in his pockets, Chris joined her. "The car was fine when we left the house."

Sick dread made Melanie sway. Lunch danced nauseatingly in her belly, and a shimmering sensation of unreality made the world swim.

In a dull, detached voice, she said, "It was fine when I left the house this morning. It must have happened at the Little Burro. Or maybe at the bank, or the real estate office. I don't know." She looked at the policeman. "What do I do? Somebody stole the plates and smashed my car."

Chris fingered a jagged piece of plastic. "This wasn't from somebody backing into you. No scratches on the finish. No scuffs on the bumper."

"You need to fill out a report, ma'am. I need your registration." The policeman walked to his patrol car.

Numb, Melanie nodded. Larry. Getting even for the BMW? Getting even for Chris? And the bank, her credit card? How? He didn't know her account numbers. They were new, all of them postmarriage and under her maiden name. It wasn't possible.

A sick little voice tugged at her ear, saying nothing was impossible for Larry.

Chapter Seven

"Service won't talk to me," Melanie said, tugging at her skirt.

With her hair piled on her head in a loose knot and a yellow dress clinging to her slender figure, she looked stunning. Thinking only a blind monk could resist her, Chris studied her profile as she stared at the door to Tim Service's office.

"If he doesn't, so what? You aren't any worse off than before." Chris nudged his dark glasses higher on his nose. "But my guess is he'll cooperate."

Melanie blew out a long breath and squared her slim shoulders. She took a step, then stopped. "Sure you can't come in?"

He touched her shoulder lightly. "Better not." He couldn't tell her he feared the private eye. The odds that Osterman had chosen Service to keep an eye out in Albuquerque were a thousand to one, but Chris couldn't take the chance.

"Tell him you'll file a complaint with the DA. He'll jump." At that, she quirked a skeptical eyebrow. He added, "The worst he can do is throw you out."

"Oh, all right. But this won't do any good." She pulled a face, then went inside the office building.

Chris sat in the car. He absently massaged his right leg. It ached like fire this morning. Spending yesterday in line at

Motor Vehicles, then waiting around on the concrete at the car dealership while mechanics fixed the taillights, hadn't done it any good.

Melanie was probably right. Even if Service admitted he knew about "Cookie," would a judge consider it proof that Larry violated the restraining order?

Melanie returned in five minutes. Her knitted brow and pursed lips said Service had refused to talk. She got in the car and slammed the door. "He is such a little creep. He told me he had a gravid responsibility for client confidentiality."

"A what?"

She rolled her eyes and started the car. "Service has a vocabulary problem. It's nearly impossible to listen to him without laughing. He doesn't even wear socks!"

"Gravid responsibility? Doesn't gravid mean—?"

"Pregnant. Never mind." She gripped the steering wheel with both hands. Her chin trembled. "But you know what's sitting on his desk? A computer. Larry said once that Service is some sort of computer genius. He's sleazy enough to mess up my bank account and credit card."

"Computers," Chris said with a groan.

"Should I call the police?" she asked, an edge in her voice. She looked ready to cry.

"What else did he say to you?"

"Nothing," she mumbled, and put the car in reverse.

Clamping a hand over hers, Chris said, "Yes, he did. What did he say?" He got the distinct impression that she **was avoiding** looking at him. "Did he make a pass at you?"

"It doesn't matter."

"Like hell!"

She cringed. "Don't. I can't handle jealousy. It doesn't matter, it happens all the time. It's me, Chris. I don't know, maybe I look weak. Please don't act like this."

He worked down the anger, squeezing it way down until it settled in the pit of his belly and would go no farther. He said calmly, "You aren't responsible for sleazebags. And I'm not jealous."

She cut her eyes at him.

"I'm not. I'm mad at myself for making you go in there. I should have known it wouldn't do any good." He smiled, hoping it wasn't as fake-looking as it felt. He squeezed her hand, then released it. She flashed him an appreciative smile that made him feel small enough to crawl under the car seat. He was jealous, and what he really wanted to do was rip out Service's tongue.

"Breaking into the bank computer is against the law, isn't it?" she asked.

"It's nearly impossible to prove."

"So good old Larry gets away with it again."

"We'll see." He sagged on the seat, wishing he didn't have to worry about Osterman.

ENTERING THE KITCHEN, Melanie asked, "Is the coffee ready?"

Chris lowered his newspaper. She wore a ruby-red dressing gown belted tightly around her slim waist. Her skin glowed pink from the shower, and her hair was bound up in a towel that was like a turban. The thin robe clung to her damp breasts, revealing their high roundness. Her nipples gave him a pert hello through the fabric.

He gulped coffee and scalded his tongue. "Think I made it too strong," he said, then worked his stinging tongue against the roof of his mouth.

There were dark shadows under her eyes, and her mouth had a pinched look. Last night he'd awakened on the couch and seen her gliding from door to door, checking locks. She'd been doing that for several nights now.

She held a comb in one hand and opened her other hand to show him a clump of dark hair. She chuckled, but the laugh held a disgusted note. "My hair is falling out. Animals do that when they're frightened. It's a survival reflex—they drop a bunch of hair and the scattered scent confuses their enemy." She dropped the hair in the trash can, then poured a cup of coffee.

She started for the bedroom, but stopped and gave him a hard look. "I still cannot believe that son of a bitch canceled every one of my credit cards." She disappeared into the back.

Chris's jaw ached. Stress was eating her alive, and he felt like excess baggage.

Melanie's undiffused adrenaline was building to intolerable levels. Larry was killing her in little ways, by doing things like canceling her bank accounts and reporting her charge cards stolen. There was no way to fight that kind of harassment, no way to act. More so than her, Chris knew that as long as Larry didn't physically violate the restraining order, it was no use calling the police. They couldn't prove he'd authored the notes or made the phone call or called the pet store. There was no way to prove he'd vandalized her car or invaded her financial records. Larry was getting a lot of harassment value at little cost.

Chris took a testing sip of his coffee. The tip of his tongue recoiled, but it was bearable. That letter about the dragons and witches nagged at him. Was Larry on some sort of knight-in-shining-armor kick? Melanie said it didn't mean anything to her. Why did Larry think it did?

He stared at the phone. His boss, Captain Oliver Daws, was a genius at reading people. He might offer some insight about stopping Larry. But until Daws sent a Western Union telegram—their prearranged all-clear signal—Chris dared not call anyone. Larry was sick, but Osterman was worse.

Melanie came out as he finished a second cup of coffee and the sports section. Her hair hung in loose waves; he liked the way curly tendrils sometimes fell over the side of her face. With her big amber eyes peering out, the look gave her a mysterious air. A purple blouse and skirt showed off her curvy hips and slender legs, and the hot-pink belt cinching her waist matched dangling bead earrings. Artful makeup disguised her tired eyes.

Chris wondered if sexual desire ever proved fatal.

Pushing wooden bangles up her arm, she asked, "What'll it be for breakfast?"

She sounded more like herself. Maybe she was right. Chris had heard somewhere that punishment didn't work because it attacked the problem backward. To stop behavior, remove the rewards. Refusing to acknowledge the harassment removed the rewards. Larry had to tire of it.

Unless Larry grew frustrated and decided on some final retribution.

He hoisted his coffee cup. "I'm fine. No need to cook."

Raking him with a teasing gaze, she arched her fine brows. "You don't look like you enjoy missing meals."

"Are you trying to tell me I'm fat?"

Her smile turned unmistakably flirtatious. "Healthy. Eggs?" She opened the refrigerator and began pulling out food. She started bacon and sausage frying on an electric griddle. "I've gained three pounds since I met you. I don't know how you do it. By rights, you ought to weigh four hundred pounds."

"Exercise. Join me. We can have some fun, and it works off the tension." He winked. "And I can look at you in a bathing suit."

She passed off the latter comment with a haughty sniff. "I better do something. I won't be able to fit my clothes." She tied an apron around her waist.

He watched her bustle around the kitchen, and his thoughts drifted to old-fashioned courtship. Making love with their minds and words instead of their bodies. Learning the nuances, the way her voice dropped when she teased, the prim way she curled her lips inward as if to stop a not-quite-ladylike smile, the way she said some things, then waited, wide-eyed, judging his reaction.

A friend had once complained, "It's too damned hard to be friends after you've been to bed." Maybe that was the key to a lasting relationship? Friendship first?

While they ate breakfast, the phone rang. Letting it ring four times before answering, Melanie said a cautious hello. She smiled and handed over the phone. "Victor."

"I hope you're minding your manners and remembering to put the toilet seat down," Vic said.

"Yeah, yeah." Chris shook his head. Vic would have made a great father. "What do you want?"

"I'm not interrupting anything?"

"Breakfast."

Vic made a satisfied sound. "I spoke with Taylor—never mind, you don't know him. I need to go to Chicago."

"Already? You just got home."

Vic laughed dryly. "Some of us have extravagances that must be paid for. Besides, this sounds like a terrific job. I think I'll be allowed to do something besides pastel coyotes and cloth cacti. Do you mind keeping Winston and Carmen entertained for about ten days? They love you so much."

Especially Carmen. "No problem, Bro."

"Good. I need to catch a plane at three o'clock, which is barely enough time to make arrangements with Ernesto and pack my bags. Do you feel up to driving the Saab? Ernesto is swamped with paperwork."

"Hold on." He covered the mouthpiece with his hand. "Will we be back before two? Vic needs to catch a plane."

"Another trip? Sure."

Chris assured Victor he'd drive him to the airport, then hung up. "Off to Chicago," he told Melanie. "Ten days."

He looked at Melanie's gray parrots. Abelard was the smaller one, the friendlier one. Sometimes Chris felt a tug on his pants leg—Abelard asking to have his head scratched. Heloise stuck to the perch. Not bad, for birds. Ten days with Carmen? Oh, well, did he really need all his fingers?

Melanie swung her head toward the door, head cocked, listening. She dabbed her lips with a napkin, then pushed away from the table. "Shoot. I forgot the garbage."

Chris started to rise. "I'll get it."

"Finish your breakfast." She went to the door, then paused and turned him an inviting smile. Her eyelids lowered provocatively. "I may let you take out my garbage...someday." Then she dropped one eyelid in a slow wink.

That simple statement held volumes of juicy promise.

LISTENING TO THE RUMBLE of the garbage truck, hoping it didn't pass her by, Melanie mentally hurried the garage door. She tugged her garbage cans outside.

A splash of white caught her attention. Frowning, she stood transfixed by rainbow sparkles on clear cellophane. Sunshine illuminated a bouquet of white roses propped next to her gate.

The garbage truck swung around to her house. She stepped aside as the sanitation worker jumped off the back and grabbed cans. She half heard his greeting, half heard the rumble of the truck's compacter.

What was Larry up to now?

The truck rumbled away. Melanie stood staring, loath to touch the flowers. Behind them, upright against the gate, was a manila folder.

"Hey, did the garbagemen kidnap... Melanie?" Chris strode out of the garage. He touched her arm.

Her flesh quivered. "He's at it again." Emboldened by Chris's presence, she picked up the bouquet and the folder. It had a label with the typed notation 901-CON, L. Connalley. She shoved the folder at Chris, then grimaced at the flowers.

Chris opened the folder. His eyebrows lifted, then lowered into a stormy frown. It held photocopies of Melanie's bank statements and credit card receipts. On a sheet of paper torn from a legal-size yellow pad was a note scrawled in penciled script.

I, Timothy James Service, do apologize. I apologize very very much and I am so sorry for hurting Melanie Connalley. I promise and do so solemnly swear I will never ever use my computer again to hurt her or do her harm or steal her money and I am sorry. I will never follow her again or take her picture without her permission or in any other way invade her privacy or allow others to invade her privacy. I swear. Timothy James Service.

Then, at the bottom, in stingy block printing:

Craven varlets cringe before the sword of your avenging knight!

Melanie squinted at the note as if staring very hard would make it make sense. "What is going on, Chris?"

"Maybe your chat with Service got through his thick skull." But he didn't sound as if he believed it.

She shook the roses, and they rattled in the cellophane wrapping. "This came from Larry. He always sends white flowers. What do you think it means?"

"You tell me." He wore his cop face, hard-jawed and glowering.

Bristling, she jerked off a garbage-can lid and stuffed the roses inside. "It doesn't make any sense."

"A stuffed-shirt lawyer who thinks he can buy what he wants in life is trying to win you over with this crap? What aren't you telling me?"

She gaped at him, seeing Larry with his hateful gray eyes and sneering lips. She heard Larry's cutting accusations. The past crowded her, choking her, fogging her reasoning.

Her voice low and clipped, she said, "I am not going to be accused and judged guilty because of someone else."

"I never said—"

"You want to play that game! Then go home! Get out of here!" She spun on her heel and stalked through the garage.

"Melanie, what—?"

She flung over her shoulder, "I've had enough of jealous men to last a lifetime! Get lost!" She stomped into the house and slammed the door.

Abelard and Heloise squawked and flapped their wings. She blinked at them. Anger turned cold. Chris was the best thing that had ever happened to her. Was Larry destroying that, too?

"Oh, God," she breathed, aching with fear. She ripped open the door. "Chris!"

Arms crossed, he leaned against her car. "Why are we fighting?"

She fiddled with the doorjamb. "I don't know. I think I was fighting with Larry. I'm sorry, so very sorry. I don't know what came over me."

He brushed her arm with his fingertips. "You're shook up," he said, "and I'm ticked 'cause I can't do a thing to help you." He hung his head and scuffed the garage floor with his sneaker. "Okay, I admit it, I'm jealous. But not like you think. I care about you. I care a lot." He lifted his head, and his eyes held frustration. "And I can't get close because Larry is in the way. I want to help you, but I don't know how."

She swiped her eyes. "I wish I could kill Larry. Erase him." She played her hands over his dark red shirt, hesitantly at first, then, as his expression softened, more boldly. "I'm trying so hard... Don't hate me, Chris." She blinked away the burning in her eyes.

"Never." He huffed a self-deprecating laugh. "I'm feeling sorry for you being stressed out, and I'm the one acting like this. I'm used to solving problems, not sitting back and watching." He nudged her lightly, and she moved inside.

They reclaimed their places at the table. Her coffee had cooled, but Melanie sipped it anyway. Tasteless.

"Now," Chris said, his face mild but his eyes chilly. "We need to talk." He laid the folder on the table. "Why would Larry send this?"

Wanting to drop the subject, she shrugged. "An apology?"

He flicked the yellow paper with his finger. "This sounds like something out of King Arthur. What's that club called where everyone dresses up in medieval—"

"The Society for Creative Anachronisms, and no, Larry does not belong." She studied the folder. "The first letter sort of made sense. It sounded like a rehash of something I might have written ten years ago. But I don't understand this."

Chris said, "Psychology isn't my forte. But one thing I know, when a perp sends threats, they're worded very clearly. At least, to whoever he's threatening." He passed a hand over his eyes. "This sounds as if he forced Service to write that apology. Are you absolutely certain this is Larry? What about Doug? Was he ever violent?"

Defensiveness stiffened her spine. She clamped it down, knowing that Chris was trying to help her. "It is not Doug. He's two thousand miles away."

"What about that guy you dated?"

"What guy?"

His eyes narrowed. "That day I met you, you said you had a date. What about him?"

She blinked, uncertain what he was talking about. Then it dawned, and she shook her head. "Roddy? No."

"Why?"

"One, we didn't date. Two, I don't know him and he certainly doesn't know anything about me. And three, he doesn't live here anymore. He went to Arizona or Texas or someplace. And four...well, there's probably a million more reasons. I'm telling you, Chris, crazy as it all sounds, this is definitely Larry.''

Then she remembered Tony Ornales. The locksmith who had made the keys to her house. Tony couldn't know about Cookie or Tim Service, but a shudder rippled down her spine anyway.

But then, they could always make a list of half the world's population—the male half—and work from there, she mused. They all seemed like likely suspects.

''I know what it is. I'm supposed to call Larry and thank him for getting Service off my back.'' She made a face at the folder, then laughed wryly. ''Don't you get it? Now Larry can say Service did it on his own initiative. I'm supposed to be grateful he's protecting me from the bad old private eye.''

Chris grunted. ''Service must have called Larry as soon as you left.''

Melanie leaned forward and grinned. ''Knowing Larry... I'll bet anything that Service doesn't know about this. Larry scribbled that note. One of his stupid games.''

''I see,'' Chris murmured.

''I'm supposed to get excited and go to the police. Then Larry looks like the good guy.''

''He'd do that to Service?''

''He'd do it to anybody. People are a dime a dozen to him.'' She cocked her head hopefully. ''You're the expert. Is there any way we can use this legally? Can we prove anything with it?''

His expression, a blend of disgust and thoughtfulness, told her what she didn't want to know. ''We can't prove this came out of Service's office, or that he wrote the note. As far as evidence is concerned, this is garbage.''

She refilled her coffee cup. ''For my eyes only...again. This is so frustrating—'' The morning paper caught her eye. Chris had left it folded neatly, and she read half the headline: Missing gi— The accompanying photograph stunned her.

''Oh, my God,'' she breathed.

She stared at a high school photo of a pretty black-haired girl with a wide smile and luminous eyes. Annie Guererro. The full headline read Missing girl found.

"I know this girl." Her chest tightened, and her breakfast congealed into a leaden lump. "Chris, this is awful. She's been murdered."

The accompanying story said Annie had gone to meet friends and never returned home. Her mother had reported her missing. A boy looking for aluminum cans had discovered her body by the Rio Grande. The police called it homicide.

Chris slipped an arm around her shoulders. "Good friend?"

"At work." A thrill of horror left her shaking. She folded the newspaper and shoved it away. "That poor kid—only nineteen. She was so bouncy, so full of life. She had about a million friends, used to date a different guy every night. I can't believe she's dead." She leaned against Chris's strong chest and listened to the beating of his heart.

She wanted to go back to bed and pull the covers over her head, to shut out the world. Annie had liked everybody; everyone had liked her. Melanie remembered warning Annie, "You can't go out with every guy who asks. There's some really creepy men out there."

Annie had merely laughed. "I got great radar. I can spot a creep a mile away! Don't worry about me, I only date the nice ones."

Nice . . . Melanie threw a glance at the newspaper. *What happened to your radar, Annie?*

Her own problems suddenly seemed small. "Let's get out of here. I'll clean up the kitchen later."

Driving through town, Melanie tried her best to concentrate on the real estate listing and the empty properties. She kept seeing Annie—with her snapping gum, her love for animals, her unceasing cheerfulness and her nonstop chatter with the customers. Melanie wished they had been better friends. She didn't even know where Annie lived, only that she lived with her parents—had lived with them. Murdered and dumped by the river. The world was a mean and threatening place.

Chris jerked his thumb at an orange-and-white fast-food restaurant. "Let's get a Coke."

She pulled into the parking lot.

"You're in no mood to look at stores," he said. "You're not even seeing them." He placed a hand over hers. "Is it your friend? I can sympathize, honey. I know what it's like. Want to talk about it?"

Melanie shook her head. "Nothing to talk about, really. I mean, we weren't close or anything. I worked with her. I didn't even talk to her after I was fired. It's so...unfair." She clucked her tongue and sagged. "Unfair..."

Chris patted her knee. "Call it a day. Let's go loaf around the swimming pool."

"Why do you put up with me?" she asked.

"I assure you, my intentions are strictly dishonorable, Miz Rogers," he said in a hokey southern drawl. He teased a smile from her.

She checked her watch. Only a little after eleven. It felt much later. She checked the listing. "Okay. There's a place not far from here. Let's look at it, then play hooky."

"Want a Coke?"

"Diet 7-Up."

While he went inside to get the drinks, she studied the real estate listing. Melanie had made a mistake with Julia. The woman didn't seem to grasp what Melanie wanted. Or did she herself really know what she wanted? She felt thick and stupid, unable to control her thoughts.

Chris returned with the drinks, and they headed north toward Fourth Street.

The store for lease was in the older section of town, surrounded by established neighborhoods and dotted by mom-and-pop-type businesses.

Melanie drove into the parking lot of an L-shaped strip mall built in the spare, square lines of the 1960s. It held a supermarket, a used furniture and antiques store, a copy shop and an art supply store. The parking lot was clean, and the storefronts were well maintained, with clean windows and bright signs.

Melanie's mood lifted when she noticed that the empty store sat in the crook of the L.

Chris joined her on the wide sidewalk. "Kind of off the beaten track."

"Exotic birds aren't impulse buys. I'm not really after the walk-in trade." She studied the cars driving through the parking lot. The traffic patterns pleased her. People seemed to prefer driving straight across the lot, rather than taking the turn through the L. She cupped a hand against the glass and peered into the shop.

Electrical outlets showed bare wires. Nuts, bolts, and pieces of display fixtures littered the bare concrete floor. It was long and narrow with a door in the rear. A little big, but she could lower the ceiling and build partitioning walls.

"Let's go next door."

They entered the art supply store. An elderly man was framing a painting. Melanie introduced herself and learned he was Paul Lutz, the owner.

Melanie asked about construction and the reliability of the heating and the air-conditioning, and how the mall owners were about maintenance. Paul answered readily, emphasizing that he'd been in this location for almost thirty years and had never had any real problems. Aside from good-natured complaints about the rising cost of insurance, the location pleased him.

Melanie noticed Chris sorting through containers of sable-hair brushes. After thanking Paul for his time, she asked Chris, "Ready?" His interest in the art supplies amused her.

"Uh-huh," Chris said absently, replacing a Speed-O-Graph pen. He trailed his fingers over stacks of boxed pastels.

She teased. "Don't tell me you're an artist?"

He grinned. "I studied commercial art in college." As if noting her incredulity, he added, "I haven't picked up a paintbrush in years."

This new facet of his personality fascinated her.

On the way home, he explained, "I always liked to draw, but Dad gave me such a hard time about it I switched over to engineering. Math is not my strong suit. So I dropped out before I flunked out, and joined the police force." His smile twisted. "I always figured someday I'd go back to school. Never have."

Her fascination increased. "Do you like being a policeman?"

"I'm good at it." His gaze wandered, then settled on a billboard announcing The Albuquerque Dukes! Baseball at its best! "Funny how much I don't miss it." He winked at her. "Could be the fine company I'm keeping."

Warmth encircled Melanie's heart, and she felt better about the day. "Do you mind if I drop you off at Victor's? I want to talk to Julia."

"No problem."

Melanie spent the next few hours finding out how much the property cost to lease and who managed it. She arranged to meet Lupe Ortiz, the mall's management agent, at the store. Lupe had a prepared packet of rental terms, insurance requirements and what mall management was and was not responsible for. She was brisk and efficient, but friendly.

Melanie measured the interior and front window, thumped the walls and envisioned the store layout. She studied her estimates of projected costs. She started to tell Lupe she needed estimates first on renovations, then decided to go for it. "It's perfect, Lupe. When can I sign the papers?"

Lupe's black eyes sparkled. "That's what I like. A woman who knows her own mind." She handed over a business card, then made notes on the clipboard she carried. "I'll draw up the leasing agreement.... How about my office, tomorrow morning at nine?''

A sense of being very adult and responsible filled Melanie. She saw herself from the outside looking in, seeing an honest-to-goodness businesswoman, making decisions and setting the course of her own life. It felt both silly and satisfying.

It also struck her how much work she was committing herself to.

Slightly dazed, she went home. She parked her car, then hurried to Victor's to see if Chris was back from the airport.

"I did it!" she told him. "I sign the papers tomorrow."

"Congratulations." He hooked his arm with hers, and they strolled across the street to her house. "This calls for a celebration, honey. Champagne."

"Oh, I have a million things to do now. I have to find a carpenter and an electrician. I have to get a business license and permits. I need to contact my suppliers. And a window washer, don't let me forget to hire a window washer."

They entered her house through the garage. Melanie's smile turned into a gape as she eyed the pink and yellow pottery on the floor. Her shocked gaze slowly traveled across the room, taking in a knocked-over chair, and the table centerpiece, crushed and scattered on the floor.

Chris caught her arm. He pulled her back and fumbled in his jeans pocket. Keys jingled. He whispered, "Get out!" then pushed her through the door and garage.

"What happened to my house?" she cried.

Chris steered her toward Victor's. Inside, he planted her next to the couch. "Stay here." His voice brooked no argument. He went back to a bedroom, then quickly returned. He held a pistol in his right hand—a big, shiny, ugly, deadly-looking gun. He held it close to his shoulder, the barrel pointed skyward.

"Stay here," he ordered, and then he left.

The closed door snapped her out of her stupor. She realized Chris thought whoever had broken into her house was still there.

Chapter Eight

"When the cops get here, don't expect me to answer questions. I'll stick around, but I need you to do the talking."

Too shocked to question Chris's strange request, Melanie nodded. She crooned at Heloise and Abelard. The sensitive parrots were upset, but unharmed. She told herself she could handle anything as long as Heloise and Abelard were okay.

Hugging her elbows, she surveyed her bedroom. The linens had been ripped off the bed. The closet door stood open and clothing littered the floor, and bureau drawers had been pulled out and the contents scattered. A cloying reek of mingled perfumes came from broken bottles in the bathroom.

"Is anything missing?" Chris asked.

She shrugged helplessly. Everything seemed vile, tainted, soiled. She forced herself to open her jewelry box. Her sapphire ring was still in its velvet box. It felt as if someone had reached inside her and pawed over her innards. She tried to rub away the crawling feeling on her arms.

"You need to file a report, Melanie," Chris said gently. "Any other valuables?"

She drew a deep breath, then checked the closet for her camera. Still there. She wandered through the house. Her stereo, television and VCR were all still there, and the silver had been left untouched. Her Moseby Harrison intaglio still hung on the wall. The broken dishes came from the table, swept to the floor and trampled on.

She returned to the bedroom and wondered if she could ever sleep in her bed again. She stood in front of the armoire. Belts, scarves and purses littered the floor. She nudged through winter sweaters with the toe of her suede pump, then crouched and sifted through the jumble of colorful wool, angora and cotton.

"My gun is missing, Chris. It was in here. In a black box. It's gone." She pawed through the sweaters and accessories, but the .32 Llama was missing.

The doorbell rang. She swayed, her mouth dry with the fear that Larry had her gun—the gun she had once felt so sure she could use to protect herself. Did he mean to kill her? Or did he want to make certain she couldn't defend herself the next time he broke into the house? Chris steadied her. Holding his hand tightly, she answered the door.

Two uniformed policemen waited in the courtyard. Melanie invited them inside. Chris sat on a bar stool, his gaze focused on his hands, which were folded before him.

The police went through the house, checking the doors for forced entry, surveying the damage and making notes. When Melanie told them her gun was missing, the policemen exchanged a hard look. She found her permit, registration and bill of sale.

"I know who did this," she said. "My ex-husband, Larry—I mean Lawrence Connalley." She spelled the last name for them. "I have a restraining order against him, but he's harassing me anyway."

"He have a key to the house?"

She shook her head. The sick feeling worsened when she remembered her missing parrot earrings. Should she report that, too? "I don't know how he got in. I'm very careful about locking up." She gave them Larry's home and office addresses.

"We can talk to the neighbors." The officer studied the patio door. "Trouble with these places is they're too secluded."

"You'll talk to Larry?"

"If we can find someone who saw anything."

"Can't you take fingerprints?" She looked to Chris, pleading with her eyes for him to speak up, to force these men to take her seriously.

Looking alarmed, Chris shook his head vehemently.

"I can get a fingerprint kit, Miss Rogers, but I don't think it'll do any good. A lot of rough surfaces. Wood, these walls, none are conducive to prints."

"The furniture in the bedroom is smooth. You can take—"

"Melanie," Chris said. He beckoned with one hand. His eyes held something hard and full of warning. She went to his side, and he whispered in her ear, "Drop it, please."

She cut her eyes at the policemen. "I know it was him!"

"Drop it."

Too upset to argue, she dropped the subject. The policemen finished their report, promised to talk to the neighbors, and left. As soon as they were out of earshot, Melanie turned on Chris. "What is wrong with you? I know it was Larry. They—"

"They might lift my prints. You can't know how sorry I am, but I can't let them run my prints through the computer."

His eyes had darkened, and tense lines strained his mouth. He clenched his fingers. Melanie sagged onto a bar stool and buried her face against her arm. Everything was such a mess—flowers from Larry, file folders, poor Annie murdered and dumped by the river, Chris refusing to help her catch Larry. Helplessness swamped her.

"You never lock the door to the garage," Chris said.

Melanie lifted her head. He was her friend, more than a friend, but he'd let her down. Was he afraid? Who could she depend upon if even he was afraid? "It's a push lock. Besides, I always close the garage."

He swung around on the stool. "And you lost the other remote unit."

"The car dealer guy said it was thrown away. How could Larry get it?"

"Do you have a picture of Larry?"

She shook her head, then stopped. "Yes, but it's not a good one. Why?" She found a photo album.

She'd thrown away all her wedding pictures and other pictures of Larry, except one from their vacation in Acapulco. She'd kept it because of the beautiful flamenco dancer who'd enticed Larry onto the dance floor. She showed it to Chris. Larry was in three-quarter profile, his white shirt and trousers formless in the poor light.

"He's about twenty pounds heavier now, about one-eighty or eighty-five. But he still wears his hair pretty much the same." She watched Chris as he studied the photograph. What was he hiding from? She'd almost forgotten his secrets, but now they leaped back to the fore.

Chris tucked the photograph in his shirt pocket. "Let's go over to the dealership. Lock your garage when we leave."

WAITING for a traffic light, Melanie asked, "Why didn't you say anything when the police were at my house?"

The question didn't surprise Chris; if anything, it surprised him it had taken her so long to ask it. Her eyes were dark gold with suspicion.

He studied the photo of Larry, a tall, good-looking man with thick dark hair and proud features. Melanie had divorced Larry, but he still owned her. Larry occupied her thoughts, ruled her actions, distracted her. Jealousy burned a hole just below Chris's diaphragm and filled his mouth with an acid taste.

Worse, he knew he had let her down.

When the car moved, he said, "Being a cop does something to you. I can pick out another cop from twenty yards. Hard to hide what you live."

"Are you in . . . legal trouble?"

He shook his head. "Wish it were that simple." He looked out the window, seeing sunburned shrubbery and litter in the streets. "Never even bucked a traffic ticket."

She stopped for another traffic signal, then looked at him. Her face was thoughtful, perhaps a little sad. "Then what difference can your fingerprints make?"

"I told you I was in trouble." He wanted to shout, to tell her to mind her own business, that he was doing the best he could, damn it, that this wasn't easy for him, either. Her eyes slid away from him. She gripped the steering wheel as if it might fly away. A new emotion added to the jumble inside him: heartbreak. It struck him that secrets were a form of abuse. He had abused Melanie's trust, and she was hurting because of it.

"I'm going to help you catch Larry. If the car dealer recognizes him and we can prove Larry has the remote, then you can go to the DA."

She nodded, but clamped her lips and focused on the road ahead. She was sliding away from him, drawing the conclusion that he was undependable.

He said quietly, "I can't let them take my fingerprints, because a man is trying to kill me."

She sucked in a sharp breath.

"I've been running an investigation on him for several years. I hurt him, hurt his organization. He blew me up, Melanie. He set a trap for me, a bomb. It killed a cop and crippled another and nearly killed me. I got lucky once, but he isn't going to screw it up the second time. That's why I can't let the police lift my fingerprints."

He crossed his arms and slouched, staring at his knees. "Anything they lift from your place will run through local and national computers. This man can tap them. He would hurt people to get at me, Melanie, maybe Vic or you. I can't take that chance."

Her hand trembled as she worked the gearshift. The car bucked at her sudden clumsiness on the clutch.

"It's killing me that I can't help you. You mean the world to me, and I want to stop Larry. If I thought it would do any good, I'd go after him myself. But compared to the guy after me, Larry's a bug."

"My God," she breathed. Her face paled. "I'm so sorry... I've been so caught up in my problems that I—"

"There's nothing to be sorry for. Look, we'll get what we can and pull the plug on Larry's game. But a lot of cops know me and know about me, so we need to keep the police out of it as much as possible."

At the Chevrolet dealership they found Jim. The salesman was guarded. "I hope there aren't any second or third thoughts, Miss Rogers," he said. "It's sold."

Chris bristled. Didn't Jim believe in friendly customer relations? He looked to Melanie. "It's about the garage-door opener," she said. "Have you found it yet?"

"After you came by, I asked all the men in maintenance, but no one remembers seeing it."

Chris showed him the picture of Larry. "Did this man look at the BMW?"

Jim studied the picture, then shook his head.

Melanie offered, "He's about twenty pounds heavier. Big shoulders. He would have been wearing a business suit."

"I don't recognize him."

Chris asked, "Could you describe the man who bought the BMW?"

"It wasn't the gentleman in the picture. I'm certain of that." Jim frowned, his gaze gone distant. "There was a man who came in very soon after Miss Rogers left that day. He was interested in the BMW. It was before we took it back to the shop. I thought he was going to buy it."

"Do you remember what he looked like?" Chris asked. "White, Hispanic, black? Young, old? Did he look like the type who would buy a BMW?"

Jim let out a long breath and crossed his arms. "Now that you mention it, I guess he did." He glanced at Melanie. "Customers I remember. Almosts, sorry." He darted pointed glances at a couple who were studying a minivan.

Chris thanked the salesman, hooked his arm with Melanie's and walked her to her car. He opened the car door and had a sudden thought. "What does Larry drive?"

"Usually the Porsche. He has a Rolls, but he never drives it. It's an antique—thirties or forties or something. He also has the Fairlane. He calls it his slumming car."

Chris's cop tingle tickled the back of his neck. "A Ford Fairlane? What color?"

"White. All his cars are white. Why?"

Chris hoped his face didn't reveal his anger. He hated being followed. "I want to ask Jim one more question." He went back to the salesman and waited until he finished with his prospective buyers. He asked Jim if he remembered a white Porsche or Fairlane.

"What are you? A cop?" Jim asked with a chuckle.

"It's important that we find that remote unit."

"I'd like to help, the lady did me a big favor. But nope, sorry." He scowled, again distant. "Wait a minute. The man who was so interested that day was driving a white Ford. I can't remember if it was a Fairlane. But, yes, it was a white Ford. Late-model. Good condition."

"Can you think a little more?"

Jim rubbed his jaw. "I can't guarantee it, but I think he was maybe in his late twenties, early thirties. White, well dressed. That's it. I really can't remember."

When Chris returned to the car, Melanie asked, "Learn anything?"

"Jim has a weird attitude."

She started the car. Her smirk intrigued him. At his questioning look, she giggled, softly and self-consciously.

"Jim must think I'm strange. I traded him the BMW for this Beretta. Even. No cash involved."

He gaped at her. No wonder Jim seemed so edgy. He was probably waiting for Melanie to cry foul.

Her laughter held a cracked note. "Don't ask me to explain it, Chris. I can't even explain it to myself. All I know is I had to get rid of that stupid car."

He chuckled. "If you get the urge to trade your house or something, let me know. By the way, it was probably Larry. Jim remembered the Ford."

Her smile turned strained. "What do I do?"

"Fix the garage door."

She put the car in gear, then froze, her hand on the gearshift. Her hand trembled. "I'm sorry, Chris. I get so worried about myself, and . . . I didn't think . . ."

He folded his hand over hers. "Some top guns are looking out for me. As long as I play things quiet, it's okay." He smiled to reassure her. "The last thing I want to do is play one-up about who has the biggest problem. So let's drop it and fix what we can fix and worry about the rest of it when we have to."

"Larry is a minor problem," she said. "Stupid letters, a few broken dishes. We can handle him."

The look she turned him, a mingling of regret, fear, trust and steeliness, undid him. He knew then that he was in love. Nothing had ever scared him like this; nothing had ever felt so good. He eased a tendril of silky dark brown hair from her cheek. "Everything is going to be okay, honey. Trust me."

Back at her house, Chris swept up shards of broken stoneware while Melanie called a garage-door company. After hanging up she looked pleased. "No big deal. I don't have to replace the whole thing. They'll send out a man tomorrow with new remotes and he'll recode the receiver." Then her face registered annoyance. "I just remembered, I have to meet Lupe tomorrow. Would you mind waiting for the repairman?"

"The only thing I ask is that you take Vic's car."

A little twitch shook her, but she didn't argue.

They cleaned the dining area. Chris offered to help in the bedroom. He caught the way she shuddered as she gathered her bed linens. She carried everything to the laundry room while he replaced the drawers in the bureau, dresser and armoire.

He glanced down the hall, then picked up a lacy hot-pink garter belt. He wanted to whistle. He didn't go through her underthings, but he was tempted. The colors intrigued him—blue, green, yellow, red and patterned bras and panties. Silky little teddies in jewel tones. Matching slips. Nothing neutral-colored or sensible.

Melanie's soft throat-clearing made him lurch and drop the garter belt. "Really, Mr. Glenn," she said dryly. "Those are personal."

Those are damned sexy, he silently corrected, and sheepishly turned to the bed to straighten the mattress. Then he went into the bathroom. Mingled perfumes made his eyes water as he swept broken glass into a dustpan.

"Damn it!" Melanie said. He stuck his head out of the bathroom, and she glared at him. "That creep stole my underwear."

"You sure?"

"I'm sure." She flung down a pair of panties and stalked out.

Chris found her standing in the middle of the living room, head down, crying into her hand. He folded his arms around her and rested his chin on the top of her head. Every racking sob cut straight to his heart.

"It'll be all right, honey. Shh, it's gonna be all right." He rubbed her cold arms. He didn't believe for a minute everything would be all right.

"HOW RARE IS RARE?" Chris asked.

Melanie looked up from her paperwork. She sat cross-legged on a beach towel next to the swimming pool, wearing a green one-piece swimsuit, cut very low in front and very high in the legs, revealing luscious thighs that would have put a sixteen-year-old to shame. Her skin was pale, creamy, glistening with sun block.

She sniffed at the grill. "Make sure it's hot and no longer mooing." She went back to making notes on layout plans for her store.

Chris started to place the steaks on the grill, but paused, transfixed by the narrow expanse of her back and her bare neck. Tendrils of dark brown hair escaped from the knot on top of her head. It had never occurred to him how sexy a neck could be. Hers was slender, with a curve—a swan neck. No wonder old novels rhapsodized about necks.

He went behind her and eased himself to the ground. He scratched the scar on his leg. As long as he didn't push it, he didn't limp much. But the scar felt tight; as he rebuilt his muscles, it stretched, and itched. He settled himself as comfortably as possible and peered over Melanie's shoulder.

He studied the peach fuzz below her hairline. It looked like baby hair atop baby skin. She didn't acknowledge him, but he knew she knew he was there. He kissed her neck above the knob of her spine. Her skin was sun-warmed, and the sun block tasted like soap.

"All this work on planning the store. I've been ignoring you, haven't I?" she asked. She graced him with an over-the-shoulder, sideways look, both innocent and knowing.

His muscles felt like gelatin. He nuzzled her neck. "A little," he whispered in her ear. "Let's take a before-dinner swim."

Shaking her head, she said, "Poolside is close enough, thank you."

"C'mon." He rubbed her arm slowly with his hand, absorbing the warmth, aroused by the slick feel of sun block. She smelled faintly of coconuts. "When am I going to get you in the pool?"

She gathered papers into a pile and set them aside, then turned around. "I don't know how to swim." She looked away, and her cheeks colored. "I'm scared of water."

"You don't swim at all?"

She shook her head slowly, then turned her face to the shimmering turquoise water. "It's a kind of phobia with me."

"The best way to get rid of a phobia is to face it. I won't let you drown."

She kissed him, a diversionary tactic he found quite acceptable. She tasted of mint and smelled of coconuts and sunshine. With a hand against the back of her neck, he laid her down, following with his kiss, shifting on the rough towel and stretching out his legs. Her response made his blood roar, pounding against his eardrums.

Cradling her head on his arm, he lifted a few inches to stare into her eyes, wanting to drown in their velvety depths. He kissed her again, loving the soft fullness of her lips, the erotic slipperiness of her tongue. He caressed her flat belly.

She worked her arms around him, and her small hands explored his back. With teasing touches she played her fingers over his spine and his shoulder blades. Her nails raked lightly against his skin. He worked his hand upward, finding the mound of her breast, the erect tautness of her nipple through the silky Spandex. She made a tiny sound deep in her throat, then stiffened and clenched his shoulders. Confused, he lifted his head. Wariness filled her eyes and she smiled uncertainly.

"Uh," she said throatily, "can I ask you a personal question?"

He hoped it was something personal, something he could answer. "Sure."

"Well . . . it's about other women."

He rolled off her and sat up. He crossed his chest with a finger. "I swear, I'm not married."

"I know that. It's just that . . ."

Her blush made him feel doltish and thick. Then his head cleared with a snap; he knew what she was asking. Nasty stuff went around these days, and love could be deadly.

He helped her sit up, then got to his feet. Good old frustration nudged him hello. "I better get those steaks on." Shifting the fit of his jeans, he went to the grill. He focused on the steaks, not wanting to blow this by embarrassing her.

"Truth is, I'm pretty old-fashioned. I believe in monogamy." He hoped he hadn't misread her question.

"I don't want all the sordid details." Her downcast eyes belied her words.

Flames leaped, and he doused them with water from a squirt bottle. He was too old for cuteness, and he was going to sleep with her eventually. That was as certain as sunrise—even if it meant going the legal route. It was an idea, he found to his surprise, that didn't bother him in the least. Frustration died away. He was the last person to ever discount the pleasures of sex, but he hungered for something more.

He said, "I don't chase hookers, and I don't sleep with women I don't know."

She nodded.

"They ran enough tests on me in the hospital. Somebody would have said something."

Her blush deepened. He fought the urge to laugh or tease. She said, "Larry is the only one . . . but he wasn't faithful. It used to chill me, thinking what he might bring home." She turned her head enough to look at him. "I had myself tested about a dozen times last year. I felt certain he gave me an awful disease. This is a disgusting subject. I'm sorry. I don't mean to keep shoving you away."

He turned the steaks. "It's the times. Can't be too careful." He winked at her. "In case you haven't noticed, you're special to me."

She arose and pulled on a short terry robe. She looked over the table, then lifted her gaze.

"Look, Melanie, sweetheart, you want me in your bed, say the word. But if you want to wait, hey, that's okay. I admit to a certain amount of discomfort, but I can live with it."

She covered her eyes. Her laugh came out so low it was more of a shaking of her shoulders. "I don't know if I can handle this much honesty."

He hadn't meant to be funny. He'd wanted her to understand. Gently pulling her hand from her eyes, he said, "I mean it. I want more from you, from us. When you're ready." He pulled out a chair for her, and the wrought-iron legs scraped the tile.

She sat, but looked troubled. In a barely audible whisper, she said, "It's been so long since anybody cared about me. I don't know how to act anymore."

He poured beer in her glass, then called Winston. The Lab yawned and stretched, then trotted to the table. Chris gave him the beer can for deposit. He looked down at Melanie and wanted to tell her he loved her, but he didn't know how.

Winston started for the house, then froze in his tracks. He barked, and the beer can clattered on the tile. He skittered a few steps to one side, barking.

"What's wrong with him?" Melanie asked.

Winston's barking acquired a deep and threatening note. Raised hackles gave the gentle Labrador a dangerous demeanor. Winston ran to the north side of the yard and leaped against the fence. Chris caught a flashing movement on the roof.

"Somebody's up there," he said. "Get in the house. Lock the doors. Keep Winston with you." He hurried through the house to the front and out the gate.

He swept his gaze over the flat rooftops of the connected garden homes. The adobe walls were nearly eight feet tall, but presented no obstacle to anyone determined to climb them. From any wall it was only a short jump to the roof.

He jogged toward the street. Each time his right foot struck the ground, pain drummed through his hip—he'd pay for this later. He looked up and down the street. A gaggle of teenage girls in a Camaro honked and waved at him. A woman was watering her front yard a few houses down. He crossed the street and asked if she'd seen anything. She eyed him suspiciously and shook her head no.

He remembered that he wore no shirt and no shoes—perfect for questioning strange women. He limped back to the house.

Opening the door cautiously, Melanie asked, "Was it Larry?"

"Probably kids horsing around. Larry doesn't strike me as the type to mess up his clothes crawling around on a roof. Let's go eat."

The steaks were overdone. They tried to resume the conversation, but it was strained. Neither mentioned Larry, but he intruded anyway. Melanie kept glancing at the roof.

Since Chris had cooked, Melanie washed dishes. Rubbing his aching leg, he headed for the living room to catch the baseball scores.

"Why do they call the local baseball team the Dukes?" he called, wanting to hear her voice. He wondered if she loved him.

She stuck her head out the kitchen door. "This is the Duke City, named after the Duke of Alburquerque. He was...um, viceroy of New Spain. This is one of the oldest cities in America."

He flipped through the channels to find the news. "How old?"

"What is this, a history quiz?" She grinned whimsically and shrugged. "Early 1700s. That's as close as I can get. Hey, you've been so good about helping me, how about we play tourist? Maybe ride the tram? I've never ridden the tram up to Sandia Crest. I hear the restaurant up there is very good."

He found the news and thought, she does love me, she cares and enjoys my company. Again he felt the urge to tell her he loved her. *Say it, Chris Cool, blurt it out and watch her face.* "Sounds like fun." The news caught his attention.

"The police have no leads in what appears to be a senseless murder." A picture in the corner of the screen showed a weasel-faced man. A caption said Timothy Service.

Melanie said, "Or if you feel up to it, we can go out to the volcano—"

Chris waved for silence and turned up the volume.

"...local private investigating firm. His secretary found the body in his office."

A field report showed a tired-eyed man identified as Detective William Whiteford. The reporter shoved a microphone in the detective's face. The question was garbled. Whiteford answered, "I can't give you any details on that."

Holding a dish towel, Melanie stood behind Chris. "Are they talking about Tim Service?"

The newscast broke for a commercial. Chris silently cursed television news. "I think so."

The next morning they read the newspaper and learned that Tim Service had been murdered in his office. His secretary, a part-time worker, had returned from a short vacation, grown worried about the locked office and her boss not answering the phone, and called the police. The coroner estimated Service had been dead two weeks.

"How gruesome," Melanie said. "Didn't anybody miss him? How can someone be dead two weeks before anyone notices?"

The cop part of Chris's brain grabbed suspicions and made connections. Two weeks ago Melanie had visited Service, and then the folder had shown up on her gate. It had to be a coincidence. Larry had no reason to kill Service, did he? The appearance of the white roses and file folder was certainly fishy. Coincidence...that Melanie knew two murder victims?

Melanie had talked to Chris about Annie Guererro. Annie, he gathered, had been a flirt who refused to settle down with one boyfriend. Although Melanie insisted Annie had

PLAY
ONE MILLION
BIG BUCKS
ONE MILLION
AND YOU COULD WIN THE
$1,000,000.00
PLUS JACKPOT!
YOUR PERSONAL GAME CARD INSIDE...
HARLEQUIN

WHY WE GIVE FREE BOOKS AND GIFTS There's no catch! We give away FREE BOOK(S) and a FREE GIFT to interest you in the Harlequin Reader Service®, but you are under no obligation to buy anything . . . EVER! You may keep your FREE BOOK(S) and gift and return the accompanying statement marked ''cancel.'' If you do not cancel, approximately a month after you receive your free book(s), we'll send you 4 of the newest Harlequin Intrigue® novels and bill you just $2.24 each plus 25¢ delivery and applicable sales tax, if any.* You may cancel at any time by dropping us a line or returning any shipment at our expense!

* Terms and prices subject to change without notice. Sales tax applicable in NY.

been a nice Catholic girl who didn't cruise bars, Chris guessed Annie wasn't above dating a man she'd picked up in a shopping mall or met at a concert. Melanie agreed, sadly, that Annie had trusted her judgment far too well.

But Annie hadn't known Tim Service or Larry—or had she?

When Service had investigated Melanie, had he spoken to Annie? Had the girl said something important—something now missing from the file folder? Had Larry met the girl, perhaps using her to learn the best way to get Melanie fired, then killed her to shut her up?

That reached too outrageously into the realm of paranoia, and it was a ridiculous line of reasoning anyway. Larry would want to boast about his exploits, to prove to Melanie that he could reach into her life and manipulate it. Trashing her house proved it. What possible motive could cause Larry to murder an innocent girl? Or his own private investigator?

He looked at Melanie.

Her face was bewildered. "Chris," she said quietly, "I talked to him two weeks ago."

"It's a coincidence." Chris tried his damnedest to make himself believe it.

"You said that letter looked as if Service was forced to write it. We have to call the police. What if Larry killed him? What are we going to do?"

He faltered, torn. In hiding or not, he was a cop. His own skin wasn't supposed to matter. Yet Melanie's did. What if she put the police on Larry's trail and it turned out to be a coincidence after all? What if that was the match that finally lit Larry's fuse?

He loosed a heavy breath. "We have to do something."

"Something" turned out to be what Chris hoped the gatekeeper in cop heaven would forgive him for—an anonymous tip. He called the police from a pay phone and said, "I have a tip for you about the Service homicide." He winced, then forced himself to say, "I can't tell you my name."

The officer's skepticism telegraphed clearly over the line. "Give it anyway," he said.

Chris ignored him and said, "Timothy James Service had a client named Lawrence Connalley. If you go through Service's files, you'll find out that Connalley's file is missing. Do yourself a favor and check it out."

Chapter Nine

Ringing jangled Melanie out of sleep. Grunting, she groped for the phone and picked up the handset. "Hello..." she mumbled. She blinked at the clock. Was it really 2:00 a.m.?

A woman said, "You little bitch. I hate you," then snuffled.

"Huh?" Melanie scooted against the sheets. "What?"

"It's always Melanie this and Melanie that. I hate you. I'm going to marry him. Leave him alone!"

"Phyllis? Is that you, Phyllis? Jesus, do you know what time it is? Are you drunk?"

"He'll marry me, you'll see! Do the decent thing and let him go. You lost, I won! Leave him alone." Her snuffling worsened. "You leave him alone or I'll kill you, bitch!"

"Oh, for pity's sake, Phyllis, you're welcome to him." Melanie hung up, then fumbled around the back of the phone and pulled the plug.

A soft rap sounded on the bedroom door. "Melanie, honey? Who was that on the phone?" Chris asked.

"Wrong number," she muttered, then rolled over and went back to sleep.

CHRIS STARED at the newspaper. It crinkled under his fingers.

"Chris? Are you ready to go?" Melanie called. She came into the dining area, looking radiant in a bright yellow blouse and tight blue jeans. She swung a large bag—her portfolio, she called it—and bits of paper stuck out the top. She stopped in midstep, her eyes round and alarmed. "My God, what's wrong?"

"Huh?"

"Your face . . . it's dead white. Has something happened to your leg? Did you fall?" She flung the bag on the counter and hurried to his side.

He shook his head. "The feds busted Osterman," he whispered.

She sank to a chair and peered into his eyes. "Who?"

He pointed to the article and photograph. "Peter Osterman. They finally busted him." He tapped the white-haired man wearing dark glasses in the photograph.

"Is he—?"

Chris nodded, too numb to smile or feel relief. "They finally got him. They're taking him in for arraignment."

"Then you're safe? You don't have to hide anymore?"

He shook his head. "I'm laying low until he's put away. I have someone who'll tell me when it's all clear." He grinned. "I don't believe it."

"Are you sure you're okay?" Melanie rubbed his arm. "What did he do to you?"

Staring at the photograph, he said, "He's an arms dealer. He hijacks shipments and rips off National Guard armories. He even hits factories. I got on to him by accident. I was working narcotics and we raided a crack house. I found a case of M-16s, military rifles. We traced them to an armory break-in in Tucson.

"Then the perp I busted, turns out he'd stolen the rifles from the people who'd stolen them from the armory. He wanted to deal with us, go into the witness protection program. He gave me Osterman's name. Said he was the buyer, the big guy. Only before we could turn him over to the feds, the snitch had an accident in jail.

"Trouble was, Osterman's a big guy legitimately, too. Politics, charities, big business. No one wanted to peek into his affairs because he was so squeaky-clean on the surface. Everyone was afraid of him. So me and my partner, Billy, we started a little investigation on the side." He gave her a knowing look. "Nobody kills my witnesses and gets away with it."

He managed a wan smile at the memory. That "little investigation" had taken hundreds of hours of uncompensated overtime and turned him and Billy into Osterman trivia experts.

"It took nine months before we got lucky again. But we hit the jackpot. We intercepted a shipment headed for South America. Major hardware—LAWs, grenade launchers, you name it. We busted one of Osterman's lieutenants and he had a book. It was in code, but the feds broke it, and it gave us damned near everything. Only thing missing was Osterman.

"The department loaned me and Billy to a special ATF task force—"

"What's ATF?" Melanie asked.

"Alcohol, Tobacco and Firearms. The feds. By the time Osterman figured out his lieutenant had been stupid enough to lose the book, we'd made a lot of busts and confiscated a lot of hardware. By then, the FBI, foreign governments and police departments all over the United States were in on the act—all of us after Osterman."

Chris shook his head and held his finger and thumb a fraction of an inch apart. "He always stayed this far away from the dirt. Witnesses always had accidents. He was wrapped up in a blanket of money, and we couldn't get to him. Then he found out about me and Billy. He figured out we'd started it all."

Memories shook him, and his nostrils worked against the phantom stink of burning metal. He stared at the photograph for reassurance. "Billy was driving, but I forgot my radio and I got out to go get it. Billy started the car, and this voice comes out of the glove compartment. 'Detective

Glenn, Detective Scopes, the fox who outfoxes himself ends up with his fur decorating a wall.'"

Melanie's eyes widened, and her fingers played a nervous tattoo on the tabletop.

"Everything happened so fast. I yelled at Billy to get out of the car, and I ran. Then it blew up. Billy didn't make it. The explosion caught a uniform cop who was walking through the lot, too."

"Oh, my God," Melanie whispered.

"Yeah." He traced the photo with a fingertip. "He's hurting, and he knows I started it. While I was in the hospital I got a get-well card. It said, 'Lucky once, never twice.'"

She searched his face. "But now he's going to prison. You're safe."

He shook his head. "Not yet. This is only an arraignment. He can beat the charge, or make bail. Now is not the time to get sloppy." He winked at her. "But this is a pretty good start."

"When will you be safe?" she asked, looking confused.

Although he was itching to call Captain Daws and find out everything, he knew he couldn't. Osterman might be busy, but he had plenty of people to see to his interests.

He closed the paper. He said, honestly, "Maybe never. Right now, though, Osterman's got too many problems to worry about me. I can live with a reprieve. Let's go to work."

He drove Vic's Saab. As usual, he kept an eye on the traffic behind them. There was no sign of a white Ford. Apparently, Chris mused, Larry had finally given up on tailing them. He hadn't seen the white Ford in days. Maybe Larry *was* involved in the Service homicide and knew the police were watching him.

Occasional Cookie letters arrived, plaintive little pink messages. Melanie refused to read them—or even touch them. Chris found them very strange. Aside from the weird talk about knights, dragons and fair maidens, Larry seemed to think Melanie should be grateful for something. Some of the notes had a boastful air, as if Melanie should congratulate him for the terrific job he was doing. He kept begging her to be thankful for her castellan. Chris had looked up the word *castellan* in the dictionary—it meant governor or warden of a castle. That information only confused the issue.

He drove into the parking lot on Fourth Street and parked in front of the shop. Melanie pressed her fingertips to her lips, then transferred the kiss to the sign that read Coming soon! The Bird Lady—Parrots and other Exotics. The name of her store tickled him. She had originally meant to name it Southwest Exotics, but decided Victor's moniker said it best. Chris followed her inside.

The place smelled sharply of paint and raw wood. The walls gleamed with diagonal stripes of vibrant green, blue, pink and yellow. It matched the scattershot design in the industrial carpeting. "Birds love color," she'd explained. "It stimulates them and keeps them happy."

Melanie hunched over the service counter frame with her elbows on the plywood top and one foot idly waving. She studied a list. Melanie loved lists.

"What's up today, boss?" he asked.

"The sad realization that I'm going about everything backward and upside down." She sighed, heavily. Then she grinned, and her eyes sparkled with winsome light. "I don't know why I'm doing this. I don't know a thing about business."

"What you don't know, you can make up. What's the problem?"

She gave him a happily hopeless look. "Nothing big. I have to file all this paperwork, and I need an accountant. I've forgotten that I need a cash register, too. I also need a van." She held up a sheaf of pink papers. "Considering delivery costs, it'll pay for itself. I'll need something to transport birds. How about if, after the carpenters get here, we go down to the courthouse to see what else I need to do? Then we could shop around for a good used van.''

What he really wanted to do was make love to her, right here, amid the stacks of lumber and cans of paint. He hadn't thought about sex this much since he was eighteen. Touching her drove him crazy; not touching her drove him crazy.

Last night he had coached her in working his three-pound dumbbells. As she bent at the waist, lifting the weights to tone her triceps, he'd watched the half moons of her buttocks peeking below her swimsuit. Unable to resist, he'd filled both hands with their delectable roundness, their irresistible softness.

She'd jumped. At first she had grinned, her eyes wide and merry, even devilish, but then her smile faded and her eyes had slid away, darting over the roof and fence. He'd known exactly what she was thinking: *Larry's watching.*

Chris wished she had yelled at him for acting obnoxious—anything other than the vulnerable tremble of her baby-bow mouth and fright in her eyes. Anything other than the raging jealousy that burned his gut.

"Sure," he said. "A van."

"Good," she said. "I don't know anything about cars. Can I trust you to keep me from buying a clunker?"

"Yes, ma'am."

He satisfied himself with enjoying her excitement and enthusiasm. It was infectious. He was beginning to think opening day was as important to him as it was to her.

More and more he considered quitting the force. Only television producers thought cops lived glamorous lives. Police work was nine-tenths drudgery and frustration. During these days at Melanie's store, Chris had learned that he liked walking into a place and having people be glad to see him, willing to talk to him, happy to be of service. That the majority of people were honest and hardworking was easy for a policeman to forget. Melanie made it easy to remember.

They spent the morning running errands. Most of the time they went from one floor to another in the courthouse, trying to find a clerk with a straight answer about the additional paperwork Melanie needed. At the car dealership, Chris spotted a six-year-old van with a stripped interior. While Melanie puzzled over why anyone would cover the dashboard and armrests with fuzzy purple bathroom carpet, Chris checked out the engine and undercarriage, declaring them sound.

"The carpet has to go," Melanie told Chris in an aside. She promised the salesman she'd be back in a day or two after she looked around some more.

Back at the shop she sorted paperwork while Chris went to the grocery store for lunch fixings. Hearing the door open, she said, "Did they have blueberry bagels today?" She glanced up. It wasn't Chris.

Her heart seemed to thud into her belly, then bloom into a choking mass. It was the creep who had tried to give her a message at the shopping mall. His cowboy boots scuffed the carpet. Melanie heard the carpenters at work in the back and knew she should shout or scream or something, but she couldn't make her throat work.

He stopped in the middle of the floor and looked around at the half-built fixtures and bright paint.

Mustering her courage, she said, "The store is not open for business. I'm afraid you're in the wrong place."

"Nice," he said. "Lots of pretty colors." He smiled and cocked his head. "I saw your boyfriend leave, Mrs. Connalley."

She swallowed the growing lump in her throat. "Get out of here."

"Larry says get rid of the boyfriend and you can keep the store. He wants to work out your problems. He misses you. He needs you."

She groped blindly for the telephone. "Get out. I'll call the police."

"Look, lady, go home to him. He loves you. You're breaking his heart. You can work your problems out." His smile widened. "He really misses you."

Laden with a grocery bag, Chris walked in and stopped short. For a moment he stared, puzzled, at Melanie. Then his face darkened and his eyes snapped, glittering like icy sapphires. "Store isn't open, man," he said. "Beat it."

Nonchalantly the man turned his head and said, "My mistake." He started for the door.

Her voice low and clipped, Melanie said, "Larry sent him, Chris. He has a message."

Chris sidestepped, blocking the door. The big man stiffened, drawing back his beefy shoulders. "I don't know no Larry." He took a bold step for the door.

Chris dropped the bag, and something crunched wetly. He shot out a hand and caught the man's thick wrist, then darted in with his body and shoved, spinning the surprised man around and jerking up his arm. Chris kept shoving, and boards and paint cans clanked and clattered. The creep stumbled to his knees. He shoved the man's arm until his hand nearly touched his neck. The man squealed.

Shocked by how fast Chris moved and horrified by the black fury on his face, Melanie gasped. She held out a hand and whispered, "Stop it—Chris?"

"Larry sent you, huh?" Chris growled, jamming his knee into the creep's back.

The man grunted. "Hey, it's just a message, man! To his wife! You're ripping out my arm!"

"I'll do more than that." With his lips pulled back, his eyes glittering and his neck and shoulders swelling, Chris looked like a madman. "Here's a bulletin for you, smart guy. She ain't his wife. You want to pass messages? Here's a message. You tell Larry if he doesn't back off I'm gonna rip out his heart. Got it?" Veins popped out on his forearms, and his cheeks knotted. He jerked the man's arm, earning another squeal. "Got it?"

"Yeah, yeah, I got it," he gasped.

Chris sprang backward and hoisted the man to his feet. Melanie's eyes widened. The man was huge, but Chris maneuvered him to the door as if he were a puppet. He shoved him outside and the creep went sprawling to the sidewalk.

In a glacial voice, Chris said, "If I ever see you around here again, I'm gonna make a necklace out of your teeth."

Boots scraping, the man scrambled to his feet and sprinted away.

Gee, I wish I could do that, Melanie thought inanely as she gaped at Chris.

He picked up the grocery bag and peered inside. Without looking at her, he said, "Oops, busted the yogurt." His chest heaved. "Did he touch you, honey?"

"No." She knew she should be scared, or outraged, or indignant, or something.

"You all right?"

"Larry knows about you," she said. "Is it ever going to stop, Chris?"

Chris turned his head slowly. His eyes held a wild and fearsome expression. "If he gets anywhere near you, I'll kill him."

VICTOR COCKED HIS HEAD, one eyebrow lowered, the other raised, as he studied the store in progress. "Melanie," he said, "your color sense is exquisite, but a trifle overbearing."

A wisp of disappointment twinged inside her. "You don't like it?" It had cost so much to get the finest materials and workmen; was she deluding herself? Victor would know. His taste was impeccable.

"I never said that." He nudged her with his elbow. "I imagine all these colors will pale once this place is filled with birds. I merely meant this half-finished effect is a little hard on the eyes."

She relaxed. "That's my intention. Not to hurt your eyes, but to make a backdrop for the birds."

She hooked her arm with his and led him on a tour, explaining that the circular frames would soon be bird islands, and how the walls would be lined with cages for budgerigars, cockatiels and lovebirds. He made approving noises about the PVC pipe perches. The plastic pipe was clean, variable in size, and resistant to powerful psittacine bills.

Victor studied the carpentry. He jiggled corners and examined joints. "Nice work." He watched the carpenters hammer together the framework for the wall dividing the store. "Where ever did you find these men? True craftsmen."

"Paul—he owns the art store next door—he recommended them. And yes, they are good. Very reasonably priced, too."

"You're not bad for an amateur." Victor winked at her. "So, Chris has been helpful?"

"I don't know what I'd do without him."

"Hmm. Do I hear a hint of the literal sense in that statement?"

Melanie played her fingers over the service counter's freshly laminated surface. "Perhaps."

"Now, now, don't be coy. Is there a chance my brother intends to settle down?"

"We haven't discussed it." Did they need to? With Chris she felt a sense of belonging, of rightness. Picturing a life with him was easy; picturing it without him, impossible. She grinned. "Okay, Victor, no coyness. How come he never married?"

Victor held his palms upwards. "You ask the wrong man, my dear." He graced her with a lopsided grin. "It is most likely that Chris is, shall we say, a workaholic. This is his first vacation in five years, or so he tells me." He patted her arm. "Are you really thinking about marriage?"

A jumble of ambiguity shifted her insides. Larry had made himself scarce lately, but she still felt him out there,

still felt watched. Half-finished effect, Victor had said....
That described her life too well.

"I don't know," she answered honestly. "I haven't had
much luck in that department."

He chuckled. "Well, rest assured, you could do far worse.
Despite Chris's rough exterior, therein beats the heart of a
true gentleman."

"Why, Victor," she teased, "you're matchmaking."

"No, dear, I am merely conspiring with *you* against
him."

Chris entered the store with a box of donuts, three cof-
fees and a two-liter bottle of Pepsi for the carpenters.
"Pretty impressive, huh, Vic?" He swung a flat white paper bag onto a counter.

Melanie and Victor both clamped their mouths shut and
swung their heads to look at Chris. He looked from one to
the other, then drew his head stiffly aside. "What's going on
here?"

Melanie stifled laughter and busied herself with a pile of
paperwork. Blinking innocently, Victor asked, "So tell me,
when is the grand opening?"

Melanie lifted a shoulder. "If everything goes on schedule, in about a month. At least I hope so. I've arranged with
my suppliers to deliver the birds then. This place had better
be ready for them." Sniffing, she wrinkled her nose. She
hoped the paint and carpet fumes would be gone by then.
She definitely didn't need sick birds, or her house turned
into an aviary.

"There are so many details," she continued. "I never realized how much went into it. Suppliers, deliveries, the
business license, permits, an accountant. The list is end-
less."

Victor tapped his chin with a finger. "That should tell you
why I don't open an office. All those rules and regulations!
But you are doing a terrific job." He hugged her shoulders.
"And I'll be your first customer."

"You want another parrot?"

"A hyacinth macaw, or a blue-and-gold. I'll leave it up to your expert judgment to find a suitable companion for Carmen. I feel guilty leaving her all the time—a friend for her would be nice."

Melanie caught Chris's glower. She had explained to Chris that Carmen's bites and screeches were merely instinct, and nothing personal. He needed to catch her in a naughty act, grab her upper mandible and scold her properly. But she'd nipped him so many times, he was shy of that huge white bill. She could almost see him thinking, "Terrific, *two* of the damned things."

Victor glanced at his watch and sighed. "And speaking of business, I have to go over the latest slog of paperwork with Ernesto. Quarterly taxes." He gave her a significant look. "You'll know about all that soon enough."

After Victor left, Melanie wrapped her arm around Chris's lean waist. She leaned her head against his shoulder. "He likes it. At least I'm getting the decor right."

"Why shouldn't he like it? It's going to be great."

She sighed, gripped again by a scared-excited feeling. "Everything is so much more expensive than I imagined, and it'll take years to build a solid client base, and it's so much responsibility."

She shivered, thinking about how much money she had invested. It meant a tight budget for the next few years. No more shopping binges at Winrock or Fashion Square.

"And I don't know if I'm ready to be a boss. I've never had to tell anyone what to do before."

Chris stroked his jaw. "You're pretty good at ordering me around."

She gave his waist a playful pinch; she could barely find enough skin to grasp. A little thrill of sexual desire coursed through her. She'd started working out with him in the evenings. Regular exercise made her feel better—plus, it was fun ogling his glistening muscles. "You know what I mean."

"Ah, someone other than a doting slave."

"Yeah." She laughed and pushed away. "Now come, slave, we have islands to paint."

He placed his hands together and bowed at the waist. "Yes, mistress."

Despite the scariness of a new business venture, Melanie felt alive. Not even Larry dampened her spirits—too much. She liked to imagine Chris scared him. Part of her felt a little stupid. She was a modern woman, a business owner, but she still didn't feel completely safe unless Chris was around.

And she was in love with him. She wanted to be with him, wanted to savor every moment of his companionship. She wanted to...marry him. She gazed at his hair, wanting to play with it as he knelt to paint a bird island. Sun-streaked and growing shaggy, it increased his boyishness.

Mistress and doting slave? She didn't think so. They were merely two adults who happened to work very well together. Chris's easygoing nature meshed well with her slight hyperactivity. When she got excited, he waited patiently, grinning, until she wound down. He had a knack for listening, and he allowed her to verbalize her indecisiveness without jumping in with an instant solution.

She wondered if she was as good for him as he was for her. Self-doubt arose, snakelike and cold in her breast. What if they married and some flaw in her, one she wasn't aware of, caused him to hate her?

Squelching that negative thought, she picked up a paintbrush. The sack Chris had tossed on the counter caught her eye. It was from Paul's Art Supply next door. "What's that?" she asked.

He shrugged lightly. "A sketchpad and some pencils."

"Thinking about a career change?" she teased.

"Maybe." He dipped his brush in electric-blue enamel. "I could get used to this easy life."

His answer caught her off guard. Far back in her mind she worried about what Chris meant to do when Osterman was finally locked up in prison. Go back to where he came from? He had a home, family, friends, a career, a life.

Maybe it was time for them to have a serious discussion about their relationship and where it was headed. Time to banish the doubts.

Soon, she thought. They'd talk soon.

A few days later, Melanie sat at her kitchen counter. Chris had taken Victor to the airport to catch an early flight. Poor Victor. An emergency in the Chicago project demanded his personal attention. "Alligators up to my hind end," he'd explained. Melanie sympathized. Readying her store had taught her plenty about being up to one's tail in alligators.

She ate cereal and read the business section of the newspaper. Abelard nipped her shoe, and she slipped him a sliver of cantaloupe.

"Poor baby," she murmured. "I've been neglecting you."

The Gray nibbled the melon, not looking particularly neglected. Her floors did, though. She wrinkled her nose at the dust balls collecting in the corners. Her gaze went to the couch. Linens and pillows draped the cushions.

Poor Chris, sleeping on the couch.

Guilt gnawed at her, followed by dark anger at Larry. Every time she kissed Chris, the back of her neck prickled as if Larry were watching. Every time she began to relax, began to feel normal, another Cookie letter arrived, or something else would remind her that Larry had ordered her to get rid of "the boyfriend."

She loved Chris, and sensed he loved her. Yet Larry was like a pane of glass between them.

Chris must be as sick of her couch as she was of seeing him there. Melanie marched to the bedroom and opened the closet. In the very back hung a scarlet peignoir, never worn. She held it up to the light. Sheer silk gossamer ruffled slightly with her movements. Bits of lace and flimsy straps formed the bodice, and the skirt was a scarlet cloud.

Melanie smiled. "Go to hell, Larry. I've got a life." Sunday, she determined. She'd make reservations at La Hacienda in Old Town, then they'd stroll the plaza hand in hand and admire the old church and the store windows.

Her eyelids lowered in sensual imagining. When they came home, she wouldn't say anything to Chris as she went to her bedroom and changed into the peignoir and dabbed perfume between her breasts and behind her knees. Nor would she say anything as she walked into the living room, lit candles, opened champagne and turned on soft music. Chris's eyes would glow, and his grin would be anything but boyish. Add some coconut oil, perhaps, to massage his back?

The phone rang, startling her out of her reverie. She hung up the peignoir and hurried to the kitchen.

She stared at the phone. She'd unplugged her answering machine, so it rang insistently. Fear roughened her breathing. Larry? Did he know that Chris was gone? Tensed to hang up at the first ugly word, she picked up the phone.

Paul Lutz apologized for calling so early. But he didn't sound apologetic, he sounded . . . sick.

"What is it, Paul?"

"There's a big mess down here, Melanie. I came in and . . . I had to call you. It's a fire. I'm afraid your store is damaged."

She closed her eyes and swayed, then caught the edge of the counter. "How bad is it, Paul?"

"Bad. It started in your place. The damage is very bad."

Chapter Ten

Paul had said the damage was bad; he'd failed to mention that Melanie's store looked like a war zone.

Melanie approached the police line, where yellow tape warning Do Not Cross had been strung. A large crowd had gathered to watch the fire trucks. Traffic slowed on Fourth Street as drivers rubbernecked at the flashing lights, firemen and smoke.

Melanie watched firemen lugging a huge fan into Paul's art store. Another fireman came out of her store. The big windows were gone. Safety glass littered the sidewalk in thousands of blackened pebbles. The window frames were twisted black fingers of misshapen steel beckoning to the bustling firemen. The lowered ceiling had been burned away, making the interior look like a coal mine.

Sullen gray smoke hung over the parking lot, and Melanie worked her tongue against the hot, charred taste in her mouth. The bands about her rib cage were so tight they made each breath agony. What was she supposed to do now?

Paul Lutz, the purplish bags under his eyes pronounced, touched her arm with a trembling finger.

"I'm so sorry, Paul," Melanie whispered. "How much damage is there in your store?" She watched a fireman on the ground talk into a walkie-talkie and wave at a fireman on the roof.

"Not bad," he said. He ran his fingers over his head as if he had hair to smooth. "Water and smoke damage, mostly. The fire didn't break through the wall."

She swallowed the choking lump in her throat and thought of the electricians who had rewired the sockets and light fixtures in her store. Seeking any sign that he blamed her, she asked, "Was it electrical?"

"I don't know," he said. "All I know is it started in your place around six this morning. At least the man I asked said so. A policeman saw the flames and contacted the fire department. Very lucky." He started and shot her an anguished look. "I mean, the entire mall—"

"I know what you mean." She blew out a long breath. "I need to call my insurance company."

Melanie saw Lupe Ortiz. The property manager was speaking to a fireman and making notes on a clipboard. Melanie touched Paul's arm, gave him a wan smile, then went to see Lupe.

"Ms. Rogers!" Lupe cried. She looked as crisp and efficient as Melanie remembered. "This is terrible, just terrible! The insurance rep isn't here yet, but it looks as if the property is completely destroyed. Oh, my dear! All that wonderful work you've done. Terrible, just terrible!"

The fireman swung his attention to Melanie. "You're Miss Rogers, the tenant?" he asked.

She nodded, then realized she'd forgotten her purse. She felt slightly naked without identification.

"Excuse me, Miss Ortiz, I'd like a few words with Miss Rogers." Lupe glanced at her watch, said something about phone calls and hurried away.

The fireman introduced himself as Officer West. The "officer" threw Melanie, but her mind was too dull to question it. Making notes in a black three-ring notebook, he asked her how long she had leased the property, what type of business it was, who her insurer was and what type of loans she had. Watching the firemen break up smoldering wood, she answered.

Slowly it penetrated that his questions seemed very personal. Officer West? She tore her gaze from the gaping maw of her ruined store and blinked at him. "Why are you asking me about all this?"

"It's standard, ma'am." His eyes were cold, piercing. "I'm an arson investigator."

Another fireman approached. His hands were greasy black, almost shiny in the morning sun. He scratched his chin and left a sooty mark. "Back door looks like someone used a hammer on it," he said to West.

West scribbled in his notebook. Then he looked at Melanie and said, "Did you have an alarm system?"

She gaped at the other fireman. "What do you mean someone used a hammer?"

"Did you have an alarm system, Miss Rogers?"

"The security company is coming next week.... Someone broke in? Are you saying this is arson?" Her voice rose to a squeak. Her legs felt like jelly, and she staggered, hugging her elbows and pressing her arms tight against her roiling belly.

West nodded. Some of the coldness left his eyes. "I'm afraid so. Someone broke in through the back door, dumped gasoline and lit it. You can still smell the gas."

She whipped her head about, searching the crowd, searching parked cars. Where was that bastard? *Get rid of the boyfriend and you can keep the store.*

"Larry did it," she said, her voice now firm and bitter. "Lawrence Connalley. My ex-husband. He's been harassing me for over a year. I have the restraining order to prove it. He threatened to do this. He burned down my store."

Officer West wrote swiftly, flipped a page and wrote more.

Her voice rose. "Insurance? Larry knows all about insurance. He knows they'll cover the materials, but probably not the labor. He knows this will drag out into another big legal hassle. He's driving me crazy! He threatened me, said he was going to do this!"

Officer West tried to take her arm. "Miss, do you need to sit down?"

She wrenched away and cried, "Don't you see what he's doing to me?" Her face felt hot and wet. She pressed the heels of her hands to her cheeks and found tears.

Officer West spoke softly into his walkie-talkie. A female police officer soon arrived. She put her arm around Melanie's shoulders and led her to a patrol car. Melanie sobbed out the story of the messy divorce, the harassment, Larry's tricks, the way he'd vandalized her house. The policewoman murmured sympathetically, and Officer West took notes.

Officer West moved out of earshot and conferred with a pair of police officers and another fireman. Cried out, her eyes raw and burning, throat aching, Melanie slumped on the seat of the patrol car. She stared at the ruins of her store.

Bands around her rib cage squeezed, hurting—Larry wasn't getting away with this. The firemen could sift for clues through the ruins of her store until doomsday, but they'd never touch Larry. He'd probably hired some kid to do his dirty work. A few gallons of gasoline? Untraceable. Larry knew too well how to hide his tracks.

Melanie lurched out of the patrol car. Larry wasn't winning this one. He might knock her down, but he couldn't crush her. She stomped to her car.

"Miss Rogers?" the policewoman called.

Melanie jerked open the car door. The bastard, the sleazy, arrogant bastard. He wasn't getting away with this. She jammed the key into the ignition and started the engine with a roar.

The policewoman pounded on the car window. "Miss Rogers! Please, we need you here."

Melanie shoved the stick into reverse, grinding gears. Letting out the clutch too fast, she burned rubber. The policewoman waved her arms and shouted for Melanie to stop. Melanie jammed the gearshift into first and aimed for the street.

Driving fast up Menaul, she headed east, driving faster after she passed I-25 and Menaul widened into Montgomery. She cut through yellow lights at intersections and whipped in and out of traffic. Aching fury seared her soul and ripped her sensibility to shreds.

At Tramway Road the tires squealed around the turn. She missed Antonito Road, and the Beretta bucked, the rear end slewing as she made a U-turn, then gunned the engine. Heedless of the narrow, twisting road rimmed by towering boulders, she sped high into the foothills. She passed private roads with wrought-iron or adobe gates and expensive cars moving sedately down into the city. Blind to everything except rage, she reached Larry's house, pulled into the circular drive, brakes squealing.

Fists clenched, she glared at the three-story adobe mansion perched on an outcrop of red rock. Towering curved windows offered a panoramic view of Albuquerque. She imagined Larry standing before a window, a brandy snifter in his hand, smirking at the billows of smoke rolling off her ruined dreams.

She raced up the terrazzo-tiled walkway and pounded on the front door with her fist.

"Larry!" she screamed. It echoed off the rocks. "Come out, you coward!" She beat the door with both fists until her hands turned red and aching.

The door opened a crack and a wary blue eye peered out. It was Edith, the housekeeper, her broad German face pale and worried.

"Where is he?" Melanie demanded.

"Ah, Mrs. Connalley... Ah, Mr. Connalley, he is not—"

Melanie slammed both hands against the door. Edith was a big, raw-boned woman, but Melanie shoved her aside. "Larry!" she screamed.

Her gaze swept over the wide foyer. She wanted to rip away the whitewashed plaster with her bare hands, smash the two-hundred-year-old credenza, leap upon the crystal lamps and rip them from their sconces and stomp them to dust beneath her feet.

"He is not here!" Edith insisted, lapsing into a thick German accent. "Please, Mrs. Connalley, he is not here. Here you should not be!"

Melanie spun on the woman. "Do you know why he hired you?" she shouted. "Do you? You're so damned grateful to him. He pays you slave wages, and you're so damned grateful. He's the one who wrecked your immigration status in the first place!"

Edith's expression crumpled. Melanie gasped, appalled. Larry had handled Edith's divorce from an air force officer. With the subtle threat of having her deported, he kept Edith practically an indentured servant. Edith had always been kind, and Melanie felt sick about causing the hurt betrayal in Edith's eyes.

She fled the house.

She drove west and picked up the freeway. Murderous rage simmered and seethed. Larry was a demon, despoiling everything he touched. All he knew was how to hurt.

She took the downtown exit. Tires screaming, she turned off Central and into a parking lot. She glared at the bronzed windows hiding Larry's office—the demon's lair. She almost smiled at the image of storming into his office and letting his staff and clients hear what a foul monster he truly was.

She saw him.

Melanie stomped on the brake, forgetting the clutch. The Beretta lurched and died. She pushed open the door and almost fell in her haste. Her heels clattered on the asphalt.

Larry walked with another man toward the underground parking lot. She called his name, and both men stopped short and looked at her. She focused on Larry—the jowly face, the cool gray eyes, hard as little marbles, the thousand-dollar suit tailored to emphasize his broad shoulders and disguise his paunch, the dark red tie, the immaculate shirt. He looked like a lawyer, a man of wealth, breeding and prestige. He was a monster.

Larry glanced at his companion, then at her, and dared to smile, his expression smug. He drew back his shoulders and stroked his lapels. His hands were large and soft, the fingernails gleaming.

"Go ahead and stand there with your lily-white hands," Melanie said, her voice low, trembling. She clenched her hands into fists to stop the shaking. Hate burned holes in her stomach. "But you aren't getting away with it, Larry. You aren't. I won't let you. Maybe the police can't catch you, but I will."

He stood between a Lincoln Continental and a red sports car. He glanced behind him, quick and wary, a trapped animal. Melanie flattened her lips in a snarl.

He said mildly, "If you wish to talk, we can go elsewhere."

His coolness made her falter. "I don't want to talk. I want you to leave me alone."

"If you're having problems, we should definitely talk."

She shook her head. His steady gaze bored into her, and the old fears crept in. Forcing her shoulders back, she cried, "I'm warning you! You've gone too far this time."

He cut his eyes at his companion, then shifted his stance. For her ears only, he said, "I always knew you were too inept for any type of business venture. Now is a good time for you to admit it to yourself." His eyes narrowed. "I'd say this is what you deserve for acting like such a slut. I know all about that cheap lover of yours."

Swaying, she stared at him in sick horror. He had done it, he'd admitted it . . . and he knew he was going to get away with it.

He took a half step closer to her and lowered his head. "Get rid of him. I'm willing to start with a fresh slate, Melanie. I'm willing to forgive you. Think about it."

He turned away and touched the other man on the shoulder. They started back between the cars.

"You aren't getting away with burning down my store!" she called.

He glanced over his shoulder and smiled, but kept walking. A wail of pain and anger quavered from her mouth, and she launched herself at his broad back. She hit him squarely between the shoulder blades. The blow ricocheted to her shoulder; her entire arm went numb and tingling.

Larry grunted and lurched, catching himself on the hood of the sports car. He whirled on Melanie. His face was twisted, crimson, and his eyes were glassy flints. Melanie saw him draw back his arm, saw the back of his hand aimed at her face.

The blow caught her fully across the mouth. A starburst of pain exploded in her head. Tears blinded her, and blood filled her mouth. She slammed against the Lincoln and struck the sideview mirror. Her back burst with fire. Reeling, she flailed for balance, stumbled, and crunched her knee against the rim of the wheel well. With a cry of agony, she fell. Her hands and knees scraped the asphalt.

"You saw it!" Larry exclaimed. "That woman attacked me! You're a witness."

Through a blur of tears, Melanie saw the other man nod. His shocked gaze fixed on her, and his mouth hung in an idiot gape. Her knee and back throbbed. Her hands burned. She swallowed blood, nauseated. *Don't cry, don't let him see you cry...*

Larry shook a finger at her. "Don't push me, Melanie. I give you chance after chance, but you're pushing me." He rubbed his right hand against his chest as if scrubbing away dirt. Then he caught his companion's elbow and walked away.

CHRIS'S FRANTIC CONCERN transferred to Winston. Sitting protectively on his Frisbee, the big dog crouched in a corner. He emitted low whines and cringed each time Chris's pacing drew him close. Carmen hunched on her perch, nervously preening.

Where was Melanie? Chris had returned from the airport to find her gone. Then he had driven to the store. He clutched the back of the couch and squeezed his eyes shut. Paul Lutz had told him about the arson investigators and the police, and about how Melanie, her face a shocked white mask, had driven away.

Chris had checked her house, called and listened to her phone ring hundreds of times and driven through the city for hours searching for her. He looked at his watch. Nearly seven o'clock. Sick anguish sapped the strength from his limbs.

The doorbell rang.

His right leg thudded with a dull ache as he raced to the door. The bell rang again. He peeked through the security peephole, then ripped open the door. "Jesus Christ! Where the hell have you been? I've been worried sick...."

Her eyes were enormous, dull and hollow, ringed by puffy brown smudges. Her face was deathly white and streaked with dirt and blood. Her lower lip was split and swollen to twice its normal size. A bruise darkened her cheek, her hair hung in tangled strings, and dirt and splotches of rusty blood soiled her blouse. Her shorts were filthy.

"Oh, baby," he breathed, drawing her gently inside and closing the door.

Her mouth opened, but nothing came out. Her wide eyes, tarnished mirrors reflecting nothing, scared Chris. He guided her to the liquor cabinet. She limped and held her side as if she were sore and tender inside. Fright turned to pity mixed with anger. Chris wasn't certain he wanted to know what had happened.

He steadied her with one hand and found a bottle of bourbon with the other. He poured a hefty shot in a tumbler and pressed it into her hand. Like an automaton, she woodenly lifted the glass to her mouth. Her slender throat worked as she drained the bourbon.

Chris wondered if he should take her to a hospital.

Color burst on her cheeks, and sweat slicked her upper lip. Her eyes teared, and she jerked forward, coughing violently. Chris held her, patting her back. Clammy sweat and grit covered her bare arms.

The coughing spell ended, and she wiped her mouth gingerly with the back of a hand. "Trying to kill me?" she gasped.

"Need another?"

Recoiling from the cabinet, she shook her head.

He guided her to the couch and they sank onto the cushions in tandem. He held her and stroked her arms and hair and urged her to talk.

"He burned down my store," she said, in a dull little voice that sounded very young, very frightened. She clutched the front of his T-shirt with both hands, her fingers curled into the fabric. She stank of sweat and dust and blood.

"I know. I spoke to Paul."

"I found Larry."

"Jesus..."

"It's so...humiliating. I hit him—so stupid. I don't know what happened to me. I went crazy. I hit him, I wanted to kill him, I wanted him dead. He burned down my store. I think I'm crazy, Chris."

"*Shh,* you aren't crazy. Did he... did he hit you?"

She nodded against his shoulder. Chris squeezed down the aching anger, forced away images of Larry hurting her.

"I can't win. I went to the river. I sat on the sand and watched the water go by. It's still high, still fast and wide. It'll go down in August, shrink, grow muddy. I wanted to die... walk into the water and just go away." She laughed hollowly, and it turned into a sob. "I'm too scared of drowning to drown myself."

Heart aching and heavy, Chris arose and pulled her upright. She'd never felt so fragile. Her pain shook him.

"Don't make me drink anything," she pleaded.

"Come on." He led her, limping and stumble-footed, to the bathroom off Vic's bedroom. "Take a shower. I'll fix you a cup of cocoa. With marshmallows. Okay?" She nodded as if wind instead of muscle were moving her head. He used the flat of his hand to urge her into the bathroom. "Take a nice hot shower, honey." He pulled the door shut and waited until he heard the water start to run.

"Larry, you bastard," he muttered. This wasn't the first time in his life he'd wanted to kill someone, but it was the first time he had ever really considered it.

She stayed in the shower a long time. Chris waited on Victor's bed, and when the water stopped running he found, with detached amusement, that he was afraid. He stared at the skylight and saw himself walking up to Larry Connalley, introducing himself, then giving him a taste of what he'd dished out to Melanie. Vivid imagery filled his mind, of fists crunching bones, splitting flesh, of hearing the breath rush from Larry's lungs, of seeing fear in his eyes. He heard himself saying, "And this is for her mouth and this one is for her banged-up knee and this one is for the trapped-animal look in her eyes . . ."

The door opened. Wrapped in an oversize bath sheet, with her hair hanging in wet ropes over her shoulders, Melanie looked like a child. Water dribbled off the ends of her hair and ran in fat beads over her bare shoulders.

Then he saw her mouth. He looked away and scrunched the velvet bedspread in his fingers, remembering her saying, "He's heavier now, about one-eighty or eighty-five...." What did she weigh, maybe an even hundred after a good meal?

"It hurts, Chris," she murmured.

He arose and, avoiding looking at her, went to the dresser. "Want me to take you to the hospital?" He picked up the mug of cocoa. The marshmallows had melted into foam.

"They can't fix what hurts," she said simply.

In a low, clipped voice, he told her, "I want to kill that son of a bitch."

She made an odd noise, and her shoulders hitched. "He's the devil. Nothing ever hurts him." Sighing deeply, she shifted the towel. "I don't have any clean clothes."

He gave her the hot chocolate. "Where are your keys, honey?" He wanted to touch her, hold her, but he feared hurting her, feared she'd flinch in revulsion and his heart would break.

She shook her head. Her hands trembled, and she wrapped them around the mug, her knuckles whitening.

"I'll get you something to wear." He strode out into the living room and stood in the middle of the room, trying to find her purse.

You're not a killer, Glenn, he told himself. Not a vigilante, not a rogue cop looking to settle scores. You believe in law and order and going through channels.

He's heavier now . . . It hurts, Chris. . . .

He stomped out of the house. Her car was parked at an angle in the middle of the compound. Light came from the interior, and the driver's door was ajar. A wispy squeal came from a buzzer, warning that she'd left the keys in the ignition. He got in the car and pressed the garage-door opener.

He parked her car in the garage, then went to her bedroom. Once there, he had no idea what she wanted or what to get for her. Finally he collected a pair of panties, a T-shirt, jeans and her hair comb.

Abelard whistled plaintively, and Chris muttered, "It's okay, guys, I'll take care of her."

When he returned, he found her sitting on Victor's bed, one leg curled under her, the other dangling over the foot of the bed. Her knee was swollen, scraped and purpling with a bruise. "Good cocoa," she said.

"Thank Carnation." He laid her clothing on the bed, regretting having always been too busy to take the department-sponsored courses on crisis management and victim support. He planted his fists on his hips and stared at the floor. "I don't know what to do, Melanie," he confessed.

She wiped her mouth and winced. He winced with her. Her lower lip was twice its normal size, and the cut gaped. "I can't pretend he'll go away. He isn't going to stop—ever."

"Let's go away, honey. We'll go somewhere safe."

Expression bleak, she shook her head. "There is no safe place. You know it, too." Her eyes grew shiny. "He admitted burning my store. He laughed in my face, because he thinks I can't prove it. But I will prove it . . . somehow."

He touched her arm lightly, hesitantly.

"I'm not giving you up, Chris. Not you, not my freedom, not my life. I love you. You're the best thing that ever happened to me, and I'm not giving you up. I am not running away."

Gingerly, watching her for any sign of pain, he sat on the foot of the bed.

"I was looking at the couch this morning, and I thought, I love him, why is he sleeping on the couch? Why is his razor in the guest bathroom? Why isn't it in mine, where he can fuss about my stockings while he shaves?" She blinked slowly, and fat tears rolled down her cheeks. "And there's this scared little voice in my head saying, 'Because Larry might be watching.'"

Chris exhaled, long and slow. She brushed his forearm, and he turned his head, an unaccustomed burning sting in his eyes. "I love you, Melanie. I think I fell in love with you the first minute I saw you." His throat ached. "I don't know what to do. Everything I want to do goes completely against the grain."

She leaned far forward and placed the mug on the floor. Then she took his hand in both of hers. Her flesh, still warm and damp from the shower, was like satin. She drew a deep breath, and the towel slipped, revealing a half inch of her breasts. Feeling like a heel for being aroused, Chris looked away. She touched his chin and forced him to look at her.

"Are you angry with me?"

He shook his head.

"I think the worst thing he did to me was destroy my ability to..."

"Trust?" he offered.

She shook her head. "Not that—maybe that, I don't know exactly. I couldn't depend on him...I couldn't need him. Whatever I desired or wanted he used as a weapon, so I stopped wanting anything. That's what I'm doing to you, isn't it? I feel guilty and afraid for needing you. Do you want me to need you?"

"I need you." He nodded. "I need you to need me."

Wonderment, tinged with disbelief, filled her eyes. The corners of her mouth twitched as if she wanted to smile but could not quite do it. "While I was in the shower, all I could think about was you. I wanted you to hold me and love me and—" she dropped her head, and her fingers tightened on his hand "—make me feel alive again."

He suspected this conversation had less to do with the two of them than with her need to make sense out of what had happened today. She'd lost her store, her dreams and her dignity, and pain surrounded her like a sickly aura.

He said, "I was about sixteen and mad at the old man. And I'm grousing at Mom and she's bustling around and letting me rant. Then I says to her, 'Why do you put up with him? All he does is use you, treat you like a slave.' It was a stupid thing to say and I knew it even then, but I was mad. Only, instead of getting mad at me, she sort of smiles and nods. She said, 'He uses me because he loves me and trusts me enough to take me for granted.'"

He entwined his fingers with hers. "I think what she was telling me was that it was okay, because she could use him, too." He shrugged. "They've been married nearly fifty-three years. They must be doing something right."

Her tears stopped, but her cheeks glistened. He used his thumb to wipe away moisture. "If I can't give you what you want, honey, I'll tell you. But I'll never hate you for wanting it."

"I need you," she whispered. "But I don't know if it's for the right reasons."

His heart ached with each thudding pulse. "Do you love me?"

"Yes."

He kissed her eyelids, then her forehead. "Then it's the right reason."

She pulled away and lowered her head. "I want to go home," she murmured, so low he could barely hear her. "Let's go home."

"Okay, honey," he said. "Let's go home."

He walked out of the bedroom, and she watched him go. She limped to the bathroom to dress. Chris had forgotten a brassiere, and the pink nylon T-shirt left little to the imagination. She slipped on her sandals, recoiling from the sand in them, and picked up her dirty clothes, hugging them to hide her bralessness.

Chris locked up Victor's house, and they crossed the street. She went directly to the laundry room and dropped off her dirty clothes, then stood wavering. She wanted Chris to love her, make love to her... but why? To prove something to Larry?

She wanted everything perfect, but didn't know where to begin or what to do. It had been so long since she'd slept with a man, and guilt gnawed her at the thought that she was using Chris to ease the pain of loss. Should she invite him into the bedroom? Slip into something comfortable? Offer him a drink?

"Need some help, honey?" Chris said.

She started. He leaned a shoulder against the doorjamb, looking beautiful and strong. One eyebrow quirked, and his gaze locked on her bosom. She cut her eyes down and saw her nipples straining against the thin fabric. Fighting the impulse to cross her arms, she leaned back against the washer.

"Do you really love me?" she asked. The way he looked at her as if she were the only fine sight in the universe made her insides feel mushy.

"I really do." His grin turned crooked, and he shuffled a foot idly.

"Why?"

His smile faded. "I need a reason?"

She gave it some thought. Did one need a reason to love? Or was the reasoning too deep, too complicated, for words?

"In sickness and in health," he said, frowning as if he were examining what he said. "Richer or poorer. I don't need a reason. Reasons go away, but I never will." He stretched out his hand.

She touched his fingertips, studying the muscular fingers and blunt nails. Safe, gentle hands. She whispered, "I want you to make love to me. . . . I need you."

"Want me to kiss anything and make it feel better?" he asked politely, closing his hand over hers.

She lifted her gaze and found nothing polite in his smile or his dark and smoky eyes.

"Everything hurts," she said.

"I can take care of that."

She loosed a shuddery sigh, then pushed away from the washer. Hesitating, she looked away. "I feel guilty, like I'm using you. Trying to prove something."

"So maybe you are. There's nothing wrong with that."

"There isn't?"

He shook his head. "You have a phobia, like your thing with water. You have to beat the fear, or it beats you." He tugged her gently, drawing her close. He laid his hand against her cheek. "I love you, Melanie. I'll always love you."

Those soft words were all she really needed to know.

Chapter Eleven

Melanie stared into the darkness and listened. She heard crickets. Beside her, Chris breathed deeply. He lay on his side, one arm draped over her breast. Shivers gripped her and she snuggled against his heat, seeking security.

For precious hours she and Chris had been the only people in existence. Problems set aside, world forgotten, they had affirmed their love. For precious hours Melanie had stopped being afraid.

She squeezed her eyelids shut and concentrated on the comfort of Chris against her side and the soft, slightly raspy sound of his breathing. She nestled her nose against the sheet, inhaling the sweet-sour scent of their lovemaking.

Stealthy thumping tensed her muscles. She stared at the ceiling, straining to see the vigas. It was not quite a noise, more a vibration she felt in her bones.

Fear tightened her throat. Gently she eased from under Chris's arm. He mumbled and smacked his lips. The sheets rustled as she slipped off the bed. The bricks were cool under her feet, but a deeper chill caused the gooseflesh prickling her skin. She groped at the foot of the bed for her robe.

Favoring her sore knee, she padded to the door and with one finger eased aside the drapes. Her backyard, illuminated by a sliver of moon and starlight, was tiny, flat and bare. She searched the shadows against the fence. Hoping she wouldn't awaken Chris, she tested the locks.

Heart pounding, she went to her office. She knocked her hip against the desk and bit the inside of her cheek to stop a cry. Rubbing the sore spot and silently cursing one more ache atop all the others, she checked the door.

She crept into the living room. Standing in the middle of the room, she held her breath and listened. Her scalp prickled, and hammers tapped her nerves. He was out there, watching, waiting. She felt it—felt Larry. She curled her hands, wishing she had her gun, wishing he would show his hateful face and she could pull the trigger.

Staring at the door, she knew that if she silently turned the key and eased the knob around and jerked the door—

"Melanie."

Hot breath rushed from her throat. Gasping, she spun and staggered backward.

"Melanie?" Chris said. His shadowy arm reached for her.

"Oh, God, you scared me," she whispered.

"Can I turn on a light?"

"Uh-huh." She shielded her eyes, as he turned on the light over the dining-room table. Blinking, she saw that he was wearing white briefs and holding his gun. He made a strangely endearing sight. She smiled. "What are you doing?"

"Wondering what you're doing." He rubbed one bleary eye with a knuckle. "What's the matter?"

She shook her head. "Please put that thing away. It's...monstrous. It makes me nervous." Oddly, knowing that he was nervous, too, made her nervousness disappear.

He cut his eyes at the big pistol, then shrugged and disappeared back into the bedroom. She sank onto a chair and dangled her hands between her knees. The light disturbed the birds. Heloise chuckled irritably and tucked her head under her wing.

What was she doing? Her reason for getting out of bed grew vague.

Smacking his lips, Chris walked into the living room. She focused on his legs. In spite of the scars, they were great legs.

The hair was so sun-bleached it was practically invisible. His calves were knotted with muscle. He stood next to her and she stroked his thigh. The hairs were crisp and curly, springy under her light touch. She tested the scar with her lips and tongue. It was like tough satin.

"What's the matter?" he asked, stroking her hair.

"Nerves. Guess I had a nightmare. I thought he was watching us. I thought I . . . felt him."

He ruffled her hair. "Let him watch." He winked raffishly. "Maybe I can teach him a thing or two."

She chuckled. When he grasped her hands, she rose willingly. He brushed a feather-soft kiss over her bruised mouth, then cocked his head. His smile turned impish. He tugged the tie of her robe and worked his hands inside the silk, rubbing the peaks of her breasts with his palms in slow, delicious circles. Her nipples tightened, and a shudder rippled through her knees.

"Exercise is a sure cure for insomnia," he said.

She leaned into his hands, filling them with her softness. She worked her hands under the waistband of his briefs and caressed his buttocks. He was muscular even there; the differences between them made her slightly dizzy.

"How old did you say you were?" she asked throatily, sighing under the kisses he planted on her cheeks.

"Thirty-four. I'll be thirty-five in August."

"I think you're lying." Feeling sexy and desirable, she worked her hips sinuously against the bulge of his erection. "You don't act a day over twenty."

He chuckled deep in his throat. "Must be love. I don't feel a day over twenty."

"You have great buns," she whispered.

"Oh, yeah? Come on back to bed and tell me what else is great. I love compliments."

She showed him instead.

They slept late the next morning. Melanie groaned when she saw that the blue numbers on her digital clock read half past ten. Movement made her groan again. Her body ached.

Her face felt as if someone had removed it, used it in a quick game of racquetball, then put it back. She was afraid to look at her knee.

Chris opened his eyes. They were sleepy, but luminous. "Hey, gorgeous," he mumbled.

She kissed him. Love made all her aches and pains bearable. "I'll put on coffee and fetch the newspaper," she said, and stroked his hair, hating to leave him, even for a second.

She found her robe in the hallway where she'd dropped it. Tying it around her waist, she frowned to find Abelard on the kitchen counter helping himself to some grapes. He squawked cheerfully and waddled out of reach. "Get off, you bad bird." Not that she minded, but birds were impossible to housebreak. She caught him and set him on the floor. He busily explored the undersides of cabinets.

She started coffee brewing, then found her keys. Her joints creaked as she unlocked the front door. Glancing toward the bedroom, she grinned. No doubt Chris knew exactly the right therapy to make the aches go away.

A spot of white caught her eye.

Her breath caught in her throat, and the too-familiar bands of fear squeezed her lungs. A strange sound filtered to her ears, and it took several seconds for her to realize that she was whimpering.

On her doorstep, marked by pearls of dew, lay a single, perfect white rose.

MELANIE EYED the jumble of paperwork spread across the countertop. "I don't know where to start, Chris. I lost so many records in the fire. It's hopeless."

He poured fresh coffee in her cup and pushed it to her. "Call everybody who sold you anything and get duplicate records. The insurance company will accept them."

His optimism annoyed her. Nothing had gone right since the fire. She'd spent hours with Officer West, detailing Larry's threats. She'd given the arson investigator a description of the man Larry had sent with a message. She'd even showed him some of the Cookie letters, but he'd said they weren't evidence of anything.

Because of the arson investigation, her insurance agent couldn't, or wouldn't, adjust her claim. He promised to take care of everything in a reasonable amount of time. But reasonable to the insurance company and reasonable to her might prove two different animals. And there was the matter of the installed fixtures versus the raw materials. The claims adjuster promised good faith in estimating replacement costs. What did that mean?

Shame filled her about her annoyance. Chris had worked as hard as she on the store. Sometimes she imagined it meant as much to him as it did to her. Losing it hurt him, too. Unlike her, though, he wasn't a big baby. She straightened her shoulders and scowled, determined to show a little backbone.

She picked up the phone to try the carpenter again. She hoped he kept adequate records. Hearing no dial tone threw her for a moment, until she remembered she had unplugged the phone. She rapped her head with the handset, hating how stupid and thick she felt.

The doorbell rang.

Melanie stared at the drapes over the sliding-glass doors. Two shadowy figures lurked in her courtyard. Unable to make herself move, she swallowed convulsively. Her heart thumped in her chest.

Chris answered. A man asked for Mrs. Connalley. Steeling herself, Melanie went to the door.

One man wore a brown suit, the other wore a sports shirt and slacks and a turquoise necklace around his throat. The way they looked at her made her press closer to Chris. Larry's goons, sent to get even for the fight in the parking lot? Larry hated scenes.

The man in the suit reached into his breast pocket and pulled out a leather wallet. He flipped it open, revealing a gold badge. "I'm Detective Sergeant William Whiteford," he said. The other man showed a badge, too. "This is Detective Grange. Are you Mrs. Melanie Noreen Connalley?"

Relief swept through Melanie. She waved a hand in invitation. "It's Melanie Rogers now. I changed back to my maiden name. Please, do come in. I've been expecting you...sort of."

Exchanging a look, the men wiped their feet on the sisal mat before entering. They looked over the living room and dining area. Whiteford focused on the birds. Abelard used his bill and claws to climb down the perch.

"Coffee?" Melanie offered, relieved that Officer West had finally taken her seriously enough to involve the police. Pouring coffee into mugs, she said, "I know you've come to ask about Larry. Ask away. I'm more than happy to answer your questions."

She smiled at Chris; he seemed puzzled. Knowing his uneasiness around the police, she said, "I can talk to these gentlemen, then meet you at your house?"

Chris shook his head and perched stiffly on a bar stool.

Melanie urged the policeman to sit at the table. She gave them the coffee and offered cream and sugar. Grange asked for sugar. Whiteford stared at a framed print of a pair of macaws. Was he a bird fancier? Prepared to like these men, she sat and wrapped both hands around her coffee cup.

"Well, what can I tell you that Officer West didn't? Larry went too far this time, didn't he? I can't believe he thinks he can get away with it."

"Get away with it, Mrs.—Miss—Rogers?" Whiteford asked.

"The arson. He probably hired somebody. But he's still guilty."

She looked from man to man. Whiteford had a nondescript face, even-featured, his eyes and hair as brown as his suit. Grange was moon-faced, and so weather-beaten his skin looked like mahogany leather. His dark eyes were slits lost in crinkled flesh. Neither looked friendly nor helpful in the least. Short hairs lifted on the nape of Melanie's neck.

"You are here because Larry burned my store? That's it, isn't it?"

Whiteford asked, "You're married to Lawrence Eugene Connalley of—" he glanced at a notebook "—9612 Antonito Road?"

"Divorced." She looked to Chris, seeking answers. His blue eyes were cold and hooded, expressionless. "You are here to talk about the arson, aren't you? I'm telling you, he did it. He even said he did it."

Whiteford cleared his throat. "Lawrence Connalley is dead, ma'am."

Melanie tightened her fingers on the coffee cup, and heat seeped through the pink stoneware. She slowly lowered the cup to the table. Fuzziness filled her, shifting colors in the room. Larry was the devil; he couldn't die. "Pardon?"

"Your husband died three days ago. You haven't heard, seen the news?"

She shook her head, numb. "I've been busy. He's dead? Are you sure? I mean, you're positive?" She fingered her lower lip. The swelling was gone, but the cut was still tender. A pang of guilt shot through her at the thought that her hateful wishful thinking had caused Larry's death. "Did you notify his sister? She lives in Boston, his only family."

She slumped and closed her eyes. Vera Connalley, a professor at Boston University, was as sweet as Larry was—had been—cruel. Larry had alienated her, too.

"What happened? A car accident? Heart attack?" Part of her wanted to be glad he was dead, but she felt too numb.

Whiteford answered, "He was murdered."

She jerked, then leaned forward, searching. Was he kidding? He wasn't. "Oh." She drew a shuddery breath. "I see." A rise of gooseflesh gave her chills.

"I knew it. He's such a creep. You wouldn't know it to look at him, but he really is—was. His practice dealt with a lot of bad people, drug dealers and pornography distributors. And immigration cases. He was terribly cruel to those people. He'd charge poor people thousands of dollars." She stared at her coffee cup. Larry, murdered? "I hate to speak ill of the dead, but whoever killed Larry probably had a very good reason."

Whiteford nodded. He reached into his shirt pocket and brought out a notepad and a pencil. The pencil had teeth marks in the yellow paint. "You say your husband had enemies?"

"Ex-husband." She sipped her coffee, but it was tasteless. She tried to shake off the sensation of being caught in a made-for-television movie. She half expected a short, fat guy with a megaphone to run into the house, screaming, "Cut! Do it again, with more feeling this time!"

"I spoke impulsively. He never discussed business with me directly. All I know is what I overheard or learned through gossip. I'm sorry, I can't give you any names."

"Your divorce wasn't amicable?"

She barked a short, bitter laugh. "Larry hates to lose." She lifted a shoulder. "Looks like someone did me a favor."

Grange made a soft noise. Melanie started and looked from man to man. "I don't mean to sound coldhearted. It's that . . . Larry is a cruel man. He's been harassing me. He vandalized my house and car. He burned down my business. I filed police reports."

Chris cleared his throat, loudly. She looked at him, and his eyes held a warning. She frowned a question. He shook his head; it was a twitch, stealthy but emphatic.

She turned back to the detectives. "I'm sorry. It's been a very upsetting week." She drew a deep breath. Monster or not, Larry didn't deserve murder. "What can I do to help?"

Whiteford asked, "Where were you on the night of the fourth and the morning of the fifth?"

"The fourth?" The fourth was three days ago, the day her shop had burned, the day she'd found Larry. "I was here. Why?"

"All night?"

Her cheeks burned. Chris said, "She was with me. All night."

Pencil poised, Whiteford grunted. "And who are you?"

"A friend. I live across the street."

Whiteford raked his gaze over Chris, studying the powerful arms exposed by a blue tank top. "Have a name, friend?"

Chris drew a deep breath, and his lips tightened in a stubborn line. He met Melanie's gaze. A wave of panic swept her. *I can't let them take my fingerprints because a man is trying to kill me.* Even dead, Larry endangered them.

"Christopher Glenn."

"Anyone else here?" Whiteford asked.

Chris shook his head.

Melanie looked at Grange. He was watching her with impassive black eyes, as contemplative as a cat studying a sparrow. A prickling sensation tightened her skin.

"Ma'am, do you own a handgun?"

She gaped at Whiteford. She shoved away from the table and stood, clutching her elbows. "My God! You think I killed him! How dare you?"

Whiteford lifted an eyebrow.

She laughed her incredulity. Chris tried to take her arm, but she twisted away from him. "I don't believe this! Am I under arrest?"

Chris said, "Relax. Answer their questions. It's okay."

"It is not okay!" She flung her arms wide. "Where were the police when I needed help? What did you guys do for me when he beat me up and trashed my life? 'Change your phone number, ma'am. Move, ma'am. File a complaint, ma'am, but unless he actually kills you, we can't do a thing.' You want the truth? I'm glad that bastard is dead. I hope he suffered. I wish I had killed him. I wish—"

"Shut up!" Chris grabbed her arm. His roughness startled her into silence. "Excuse us a minute." He jutted his chin at the sliding-glass door. "We'll be right there." He jerked open the drapes, then went around to the front door and all but shoved her through.

"What do you think you're doing?" she demanded.

He shut the door, then caught her shoulders in a steely grip. "Cool it, Melanie. Right now. Get a grip on yourself."

"That man made my life a living hell for seven years and now he's doing it from the grave! They think I killed him."

His fingers tightened. The detectives watched them intently through the glass door. "No, they don't. If they thought you did, you'd be under arrest. They are conducting an investigation. If you don't cooperate, they will find a way to find out what they want to know. You don't want that. I sure as hell don't. Now cool it."

Reality slapped her. Chris was in terrible danger. Osterman, a man who could use the police to find him, wanted to kill him. Chris should disappear, leave, run away. He was staying because he loved her. It sobered her. Now was not the time for falling apart.

Drawing a deep, steadying breath, she nodded. "I'm sorry. I'm so scared, so confused. What do we do?"

"Answer their questions. And quit carrying on about how much you hate Larry." He laid the flat of his hand along her cheek. His expression gentled. "Okay?"

She nodded.

"That's my girl." They went back inside.

Unable to meet the eyes of either detective, Melanie sat at the table. She toyed with her coffee cup. "I apologize for losing my temper. I'll answer your questions."

Whiteford gave Chris a considering look. Melanie thought it a very dubious look. Was Chris a suspect, too?

Whiteford asked, "Do you own a handgun?"

"Larry stole it. I filed a police report."

"Can anyone confirm you were here on the night of the fourth?"

"It was a private party," she said icily. She lifted her eyes to the detective. He has a job to do, she reminded herself.

Larry's murderer had to be caught. Still, anger seethed, fueled by incredulity that he dared believe she did it. She cut her eyes at Grange. His watchful silence gave her the creeps. "Larry was here."

Whiteford perked. "You spoke to him?"

"No. He climbed over the wall or something. He left me a flower."

"Flower?"

She looked at her hands and mumbled, "A white rose. While we were married, he gave me white roses as apologies. It used to work. I used to believe he was sorry."

He grunted and flipped back through his notebook. "Do you know a Mrs. Edith Honnecker?"

"Larry's housekeeper." She stared at her hands, knowing what was coming next.

"Mrs. Honnecker claims you came to Mr. Connalley's residence on the morning of the fourth."

"Uh-huh. And you probably already talked to people who saw us fighting downtown. He burned down my store. I was angry—no, I was furious. I confronted him." She caught herself tracing the bruise on her cheek and lowered her hand. "It turned physical. But I didn't kill him."

A nasty inner voice reminded her of what she'd told Edith that day. She clamped her lower lip in her teeth to keep from blurting it out. No, she denied vehemently, not Edith. Could Edith murder—?

Again, Whiteford went through his notes. "Do you know Timothy Service?"

That question came from so far out in left field, it took Melanie completely by surprise. She blinked, blank for a moment before remembering Service was dead, too. "He's a private investigator. He worked for Larry."

"Are you personally acquainted with him?"

"I met him a few times." A squeaking noise startled her. She looked down and saw her fingertips grinding on the coffee cup.

White roses and a file folder.

"Have you ever been in Timothy Service's office?"

She nodded, then looked to Chris, but his hard face told her nothing. "I saw it on the news about his murder. I...thought Larry might have something to do with it."

If her words shocked Whiteford, he didn't show it. "Why?"

"Because Larry sent me a folder. I didn't know Service was dead, but the newspaper said he'd been dead about two weeks and...I talked to him around then. I think the folder came from his office."

"Why didn't you come to the police?"

"I was scared. I left Larry because he beat me up. He was always after me, holding the restraining order in contempt. I was afraid if I got involved, it would make Larry mad." Hearing the weakness of both words and reasoning, she tried to cover for Chris. "I made an anonymous tip. I told the police about the missing folder. I thought if Larry were arrested, I could come forward."

"Do you have the folder?"

Chris said, "I do. My place." He stepped off the stool.

Grange stood. "Why don't you get it for me, Mr. Glenn? I'll go with you."

Chris narrowed his eyes. "Sure." He touched Melanie's shoulder and his eyes held reassurance.

As soon as Chris and Grange were out the door, Whiteford's demeanor changed. He relaxed; he smiled. "Why didn't you give the folder to the police?"

Made wary by the change in the policeman, Melanie lifted a shoulder. "Chris said it was circumstantial evidence. It didn't mean anything unless Larry was arrested. Do you think he killed Mr. Service?"

He glanced at his notes. "Do you know Anne Marie Guererro?"

Caught off guard again, she clenched her coffee cup. "Yes."

"You worked together."

"About seven months, yes. I didn't kill anybody."

Whiteford cocked his head, his eyes unreadable. "I'm not saying you did, Melanie. I'm just looking for information. Anything you want to talk about?"

She wanted to crawl under her bed and hide. She glanced at the door and willed Chris to hurry up and return.

"Are you and Mr. Glenn dating?"

She nodded. "He doesn't have anything to do with any of this. He never knew Larry."

"Does he know Larry beat you up?"

She wanted air. "It happened over a year ago. I had Larry arrested."

"You did the right thing."

"It didn't do any good, though. While we were separated, he kept after me. Even after the divorce was final, he wouldn't leave me alone. He burned down my store and vandalized my house. He stole my gun."

"How long have you and Mr. Glenn been dating?"

"A few months. I met him the day my divorce was final."

"He seems like a nice guy. What did he say to you out there?"

The way he kept jumping around unnerved her. Did he mean to? "He told me to control my temper and cooperate."

"Must have been rough on you to have to put up with abuse. My wife always tells me, 'Go ahead and get mad, Will, but if you ever hit me, you're never sleeping in this house again.'" He chuckled softly. "I believe her. I bet you were willing to do almost anything to make Larry stop."

"Not murder." She looked up. "Why did you ask me about Annie?"

"A little strange that one person knows three homicide victims. Don't you think that's strange?"

"I don't know what to think anymore."

"You seem nervous, Melanie. Let's take this conversation down to the station. I'll get a tape recorder—"

"Are you arresting me?"

He shook his head. "No, nothing like that. But you have a lot of good information. I don't want to miss a word of it."

CHRIS WALKED with Grange out of Victor's house. Grange was a cool customer, the kind of cop who knew how to let silence dangle so that a suspect would fill it. He asked innocent-sounding questions. Chris answered in monosyllables, knowing Grange would be comparing notes with Whiteford later.

Chris had questioned countless suspects; it felt strange as hell being on the receiving end.

Melanie came out her gate. She looked tiny next to the slope-shouldered detective. Chris quickened his step.

She said, "Detective Whiteford wants me to go down to the police station. He wants to record what I have to say."

"Routine," Whiteford said.

Chris turned a glare on the detective. "I'll drive you, honey. We can both go."

"No," she mouthed.

"It's all right."

"Chris," she whispered, "you can't."

He wrapped an arm around her shoulders, taking no pleasure from the thwarted frustration on Whiteford's face. Unless they arrested Melanie, they could not compel her to talk. However, it was the oldest tactic in the world for the police to pretend that a person did have to talk.

He sized up the homicide detectives. They looked like honest cops—they felt honest. Chris knew his options hovered between bad and bad. He could either not talk and have them run a full-scale investigation into who he was and his connection to Melanie, or bring it out up front and hope for the best.

"No problem," he said. He glanced at his watch. "We'll meet you gentlemen downtown in about fifteen minutes."

"I think it's best if Miss Rogers—"

"Package deal, Whiteford."

The hard look in Whiteford's eyes told Chris he'd run out of options. Whiteford knew he was dealing with a fellow cop. The only thing left was damage control.

PARKED BEFORE the police station, Chris said, "You aren't obligated to talk. If questions make you uncomfortable, shut up. Whatever you do, don't lose your temper. And keep your feelings about Larry to yourself." He eyed a row of patrol cars. Right at this moment he didn't feel at all proud of being connected to law enforcement. "They're going to split us up."

She looked startled, her amber eyes wide and vulnerable. "Why?"

"Inconsistencies. They want us to implicate each other. They'll make insinuations, maybe subtle threats." He tapped the steering wheel. "Maybe you should call your lawyer."

To his surprise, she laughed. It held a helpless note. "Right. No one wanted to go up against Larry in court. I had to settle for a bumbler struggling to meet his utility bills. I was lucky I didn't end up paying alimony to Larry. Forget it. I didn't do anything wrong."

Her courage shamed him. Despite the little-girl tremor in her full lips, despite the scared width of her eyes, she was tough. Love made his heart heavy.

"What about Osterman, Chris? You can't go in there with me."

"Too late, honey. Trust me on this." He slipped on dark sunglasses.

Hand in hand, they went inside. Melanie wore a red sundress and her arms gleamed like ivory under the harsh fluorescent lighting. She looked tiny, fragile and frightened.

Whiteford and Grange shared a cubicle surrounded by pegboard walls. Chris urged Melanie to sit.

Chris sized up Whiteford. He was around forty, sharp-eyed, with a testy pull to his mouth. He wore a gold band on his left ring finger and a steel-rimmed watch. No flash, no glitter, but a wealth of shrewd intelligence.

Chris said, "Here's the deal—"

"I don't make deals," Whiteford said. One corner of his mouth twitched.

Fighting down the impulse to start giving these two a rundown on his and Melanie's rights, Chris crossed his arms over his chest. "Where's your interrogation room? I want to talk to you two in private. Off the record."

Whiteford waited a beat, then rose. He beckoned for Chris to follow.

Chris entered a narrow, bare-walled room furnished with a metal table and two folding chairs. Grange closed the door.

"Have a seat," Whiteford said.

Chris removed his dark glasses and perched on the edge of the table. "You've got a nasty murder on your hands," he said. "Rich man, motivated suspects crawling out of every corner. Possible connection to another murder."

"Go ahead," Whiteford said.

"Beautiful ex-wife with a grudge."

Whiteford lifted his eyebrows.

"One problem—she didn't do it. Another problem—if you keep after her and me, you'll end up with a few more stiffs."

"You a cop?"

Chris chuckled mirthlessly. "Why the question?" He pulled out his wallet and handed it over to Whiteford.

The detective studied the gold shield and identification before handing it to Grange. "Yeah, I thought I recognized you. You're quite a hero, even here. What the hell are you doing in my town, Glenn?"

Chris relaxed, trusting his instincts. Trusting Whiteford. "Trying to stay out of trouble."

Whiteford blew air through his teeth. "Impossible for some folks."

"If my face hits the papers or my name shows up in computers, then Osterman is coming to Albuquerque."

Mumbling a curse, Whiteford leaned forward and rested his hands on his knees. "You bought yourself a truckload, Glenn. My gut says agree with you. She didn't do it. Trouble is, there's a lot of money at stake here. Connalley's estate is worth over six million dollars, and your girlfriend is his heir. That's enough money to make my gut wrong for once."

Chris stiffened. "What?"

"She forgot to mention that? Seems Connalley never got around to changing his will. She inherits everything. And according to Connalley's fiancée, there was some hanky-panky going on. She's saying Miss Rogers had some sort of knife at Connalley's throat. Who knows, blackmail?"

Nasty thoughts whirled through Chris's brain, sickening him, but no matter how he tried, they wouldn't go away.

"This wasn't a robbery or a crime of passion," Whiteford said. "Connalley was tortured. Tied up, his right hand mutilated, shot three times and left to bleed to death. It's revenge. And here's a nice touch. We found an earring at the scene." He held his thumb and forefinger about three inches apart. "Wooden bird. A parrot. It was on his chest. She likes parrots, doesn't she?"

Chris swallowed, hard. He'd never forget the first time he saw Melanie. The bright tropical print blouse, her shining hair... big parrot earrings.

"There's more. Connalley employed Service to investigate his wife. Service's secretary said Miss Rogers spoke to Service in his office the day before his murder. Now you show up with the file out of Service's office. Funny, Service was tied up, just like Connalley. Same rope, same knot. Called a bowline. Fishermen and sailors use it. Very distinctive.

"Now let's put another angle on it. We picked up the body of a girl. Only she's all tied up the same way. And she knows Miss Rogers, too." Whiteford propped a foot on a chair and crossed his arms over his knee. "Ever work homicide, Glenn?"

Numb, Chris nodded.

"Ever work a serial killer? First one's always practice, then they get good at it. Gets to be like a hobby. Only I think this one's different. I don't think that first killing was practice. I think it was a prelude, the start of something big."

Grange said quietly, "Six million dollars big."

"Too farfetched for you?" Whiteford asked.

"Yeah," Chris said, his throat dry and voice weak. "Too farfetched." Still, he knew how much Melanie despised the man.

Whiteford said sadly, "Hate to see a cop go bad. But you're a hero, Glenn. Turn in your lady friend and maybe I'll change my mind about making deals."

"She didn't do it. She doesn't have anything to do with any of it."

Quietly Grange said, "Bad thing about being a cop is everyone looks suspicious. But it's worse when a cop believes in innocence. A lot worse."

Chapter Twelve

Chris shut the car door, then sat staring numbly at the police station. On one level he admired Whiteford and Grange. They were good, knowing what questions to ask, how to inject the right amount of sympathy in their tones, knowing when to shut up. But mostly he was angry and shaken. They suspected him? Chris Glenn, a squeaky-clean cop with an impeccable record and citations for bravery? Now a suspect in three murders?

He clutched the steering wheel, afraid to look at Melanie.

No evidence, he told himself firmly. If they had hard evidence, they'd make an arrest. They'd issue search warrants for Victor's and Melanie's homes.

Through his teeth, he asked, "Why didn't you tell me about Larry's will?"

Melanie turned her head slowly. Her face was paler than usual; brown smudges marred the flesh under her eyes. Whiteford and Grange had interrogated her for nearly three hours, recording every word. She looked exhausted, scared and angry.

Suspicion gnawed him, making his belly ache. Tim Service—what had he actually said to her in his office that day? Who had actually written the Cookie letters? She said Larry had beaten her, abused her, harassed her.... Had he? What about that clown in the store? Melanie said Larry had sent him.... Had he? Why was Annie Guerrero dead?

"It doesn't make any sense," she said. "There's no reason in the world why Larry would leave anything to me."

Dull knife blades sawed through his heart. He loved her! When his gaze locked on her hands, hands that were slim and pale, with oval nails, Chris knew those were not a murderer's hands. They were gentle hands, animated hands, loving hands.... He loved her hands.

Six million dollars... enough money to make my gut wrong for once....

Chris started the car, but before he put it in reverse he asked, "Where are your parrot earrings? You wore them the day we met. I haven't seen them since." The words left a vile taste in his mouth.

The line between her eyebrows deepened, and she lifted her upper lip. Her eyes sparked flinty gold. "What do they have to do with anything?"

The murders had absolutely nothing to do with Melanie. "Where are they?"

"They were stolen."

He slammed a fist against the steering wheel. "Jesus Christ! What the hell does that mean?"

She cringed, tiny and vulnerable, curling into herself. But her eyes smoldered, dark and hateful. "Larry stole them. That night when the birds were so upset, when we went to Conchita's? I didn't think anything was missing, but when I looked for them they were gone. They're three-dollar earrings, Chris. They don't mean anything!"

Unpleasant wetness filled his mouth. "You should have told me."

"It doesn't make any difference. What is this? Why are you acting like this—like a cop? I didn't kill him!" She scrubbed her eyes with her balled hands.

"Damn it, Melanie! Whiteford found an earring at the murder scene."

"Larry stole them."

"It was on his body!"

Color drained from her face. Her breast rose and fell as she panted through her mouth.

Suddenly she flung open the car door, snatched up her purse and leaped out of the car. She raced away, her flat heels clattering on the asphalt.

"Melanie!" Chris shouted, but she darted between parked patrol cars and around the building. Stunned, Chris heard the accusation in his voice—saw himself through her eyes.

"You got a stellar reputation, Glenn," Whiteford had said. "Be a real shame to blow it letting a woman make a patsy out of you."

Chris gripped the steering wheel so tightly that he could see the veins pulsing on the back of his hands. He swallowed the lump in his throat. He was doing exactly what Whiteford wanted. Whiteford's patsy.

He backed out of the parking space, then drove around the block and up and down the streets, but Melanie was gone.

WISHING she'd never met Larry Connalley, wishing she'd never heard of him, Melanie perched on the edge of the leather chair and tried to digest what Henry Vandegraf had told her.

As Larry's former law partner and the executor of Larry's estate, Henry had made the funeral arrangements and contacted Larry's sister. According to him, Vera had displayed not the slightest interest in Larry's death.

Melanie remembered an old saying: If you want to know who your true friends are, die.

True friends . . . She blinked back tears, trying to banish images of Chris's face. So wild, yet so cold, his voice harsh with accusation. *Chris, oh, Chris, how can you believe I murdered him?* Black despair grayed her vision; crushing loneliness wounded her soul.

Henry said, "No offense, Mrs. Connalley, but I advised Larry to change his will. Several times. The truth is, he thought he could reconcile your marriage."

"After what he did to me?" She traced the yellow and red stripes on her straw handbag, bewildered that Larry could delude himself so thoroughly, entertain for a second the idea that she would ever resume that colorless, fearful existence. Didn't he have Phyllis? His wealth? His reputation? Why would he want her?

She lifted her gaze to the attorney. "I'm in a lot of trouble, Mr. Vandegraf. The police think I murdered Larry."

He shifted papers on his desk. "I'm afraid if you require representation, I do not handle criminal cases. I can however, recommend a colleague—"

"I didn't kill him."

He nodded. "During the divorce proceedings I advised him to allow for a measure of graciousness. He was not a gracious man." He wrote on a business card, then pushed it across the desk to her. "Stephen Jones is a very good attorney. Call him. I recommend his presence before you speak to the police again. And I will speak to Detective Whiteford, and explain the situation on your behalf."

Larry was not a gracious man? she thought, and swayed with the urge to laugh. Vandegraf had uttered the understatement of the year. Did he know the extent of Larry's cruelty? Did anybody? Would anyone ever believe her? "Thank you, Mr. Vandegraf. Thank you very much."

"I am obligated as executor to proceed cautiously in this matter. It may be some time before you take control of the estate."

She turned the business card in her hand. A criminal lawyer...*criminal.* Even dead, Larry couldn't leave her alone. "All I want is for the police to stop thinking I killed him."

The attorney said, "I will allow you considerable time to think before you decide to sign a quitclaim." He placed a thick sheaf of papers inside a folder and handed it over the desk, waiting patiently until Melanie took it. "A listing of his holdings. If you have any questions, feel free to contact me either here or at my residence. And if I could get your phone number? I've been unable to contact you."

She gave him her phone number as she slid the folder inside her purse, then stood and extended her hand. "Thank you, Mr. Vandegraf."

Her exhausted mind whirled as she left the office. During their marriage she had assumed Larry's wealth was as much a sham as his cultured veneer, his holdings based on credit, a carefully juggled paper empire. Larry had indulged those assumptions. When she'd filed for divorce, she'd learned the truth. Real estate, stocks, bonds, partnerships in corporations—a mind-boggling list.

Riding the elevator down, she stared at the papers peeking out of her purse. Even in death Larry plagued her. What was she supposed to do with his estate? The doors opened and she faced Phyllis Rath.

Melanie gasped. Without makeup, Phyllis's face was haggard. Huge brown circles marred the flesh under her eyes. Her blouse was oddly wrinkled; it took Melanie a few seconds to realize it was buttoned improperly. Her hands trembled, and black hair hung in strings over her shoulders.

The elevator doors closed, and Melanie flinched at the brush of air against her back. She stared at Phyllis's shoes. One was taupe, the other bone.

"You," Phyllis whispered hoarsely. "Come to pick his carcass?"

Horrifying realization hit Melanie. Phyllis had actually loved Larry. Now she was suffering, grieving.

"He loved me. He was going to marry me. But you couldn't leave him alone."

"No, Phyllis, you don't understand—"

"I understand," she hissed, and clenched her hands, raising them slowly. "Always Melanie. Little bitty precious Melanie." She drew her head aside, her haunted eyes narrow and full of bleak suspicion. "Was he with you all those nights? He was, wasn't he?"

People were beginning to stare. Unable to stop looking at Phyllis's ravaged face, Melanie edged past her. Phyllis slammed her hand against the elevator button. "He loved me! *Me!* For five years, he loved me! He laughed at you, called you a nasty little cold fish. He loved me."

Melanie groped along the wall toward the public phones. She didn't breathe until Phyllis disappeared into an elevator. She called a taxi from the lobby, then stood on the sidewalk waiting for it, staring dully at the afternoon traffic. Poor Phyllis. Melanie imagined Larry's cruel voice mocking her, speaking of other women, taunting her for the crime of loving him.

She saw the taxi and waved.

She opened the door, then froze, her gaze locked on a white Ford Fairlane parked down the block and across the street. Sunshine silvered the windows, concealing the occupant. The driver in the car behind the taxi honked his horn.

"Miss?" said the taxi driver.

Melanie slipped into the taxi and shut the door. Watching the Ford, she reeled off her address. The Ford cut into traffic. A whispered groan trickled past Melanie's lips. Larry was dead! He was dead!

"You all right, miss? Aren't taking ill, are you?" the taxi driver asked.

"I'm fine." *Quit!* He's dead. She massaged her aching temples with her fingertips.

As the taxi turned north on Rio Grande, Melanie glanced out the back window, and her heart thudded, seeming to drop into her belly. Three cars behind them was a white Ford.

Now might be a good time to renew her acquaintance with the psychologist who had helped her when she was married, Melanie thought. Did she really imagine Larry's ghost was chasing her? In a Ford, no less.

The taxi stopped at Camellos Court. Melanie paid the driver, then stared at her gate, remembering that Chris had her car and her keys.

"Chris," she breathed, heart aching. Why couldn't he trust her? Why did he look at her as if she were a murderer? She couldn't face him.

He was the one decent thing in her life, and now... Everything crashed down on her head—anger, fear, grief over her store, her dreams, her privacy, Chris. Desperately she tried to muster the strength she had once had, when she'd walked out on Larry, when she'd won her divorce, her freedom, her self-respect, but she wanted to sit on the street and bawl like a baby.

"Melanie?"

She lifted her head. Chris stood in her gateway. It hurt too much to look at him. He said, "I heard a car. I hoped it was you. Where have you been?"

"What do you care?" Harsh words echoed in her mind. *Why didn't you tell me about Larry's will? Where are your parrot earrings?* His blue eyes cold with accusation, cold, so cold...

He opened the gate wide. "I'm sorry, Melanie. I got scared and took it out on you. I'm really sorry."

Head down, she pushed past him into the courtyard. He'd hurt her so badly, but she loved him so much. She walked blindly into her house.

"Melanie."

"I need some time alone. To think."

He caught her arm.

"Don't," she said wearily. "I thought you trusted me... loved me. How can you think I killed him?"

He smoothed his hand across her cheek, brushing back her hair. Melanie choked on the knot in her throat, longing to believe the pain in his eyes. He curled his fingers around her neck and drew her close.

He whispered, "I'm not stupid."

Hypnotized by his intensity, she murmured, "You think I killed him."

"No, I don't." He kissed her.

She stiffened and tried to draw away, but he persisted, claiming her mouth with his. Hesitant, she touched his back lightly, then firmly, embracing him. His love flowed over her, filled her.

"I love you, Melanie," he whispered against her cheek. "It's ripping me apart knowing I hurt you." He rubbed slow circles on her back. "It was stupid letting Whiteford get to me. I love you and I know you didn't kill Larry. Say you forgive me, Melanie. Give me another chance."

She could save him. She could reject him, throw him out of her house, fling his words back at him and send him away. And he would go far away, far from her taint and troubles. He'd be safe, no one could hurt him. She heard the vindictiveness in her head, envisioned him slinking away to lick his wounds and live another day.

She whispered, "I love you, Chris. Don't leave me."

A HEADACHE CONCENTRATED behind Melanie's left eye. A wicked hammer tapped the eye socket, making it jangle. She lay on the couch with pillows under her head and an afghan covering her. The house was dark and silent except for the television, the volume turned down low.

Smacking her gummy lips, she propped herself on one elbow. Chris sat on the recliner with a beer in one hand. Winston lay in front of the fireplace.

The newspapers they'd been too busy to read since the day of the fire were stacked on the floor.

"What time is it?" she asked.

"A little after nine. You all right?"

She sat up, then closed her eyes against a wave of dizziness. "I'm starving."

"I made chicken salad. Or I can heat up some soup." The recliner creaked as he lowered the footrest. He crouched beside her and rested a hand on her knee. "Do you forgive me, honey?"

She smoothed his hair. "I shouldn't," she said. "I should make you go away. Osterman will find you. If they arrest me, they'll arrest you, too, and he'll find you. You should go away, Chris." She swallowed hard, forcing bravery. "I can take care of myself. I didn't do anything wrong, but you have to go away."

He shook his head, his manner mild. "You aren't getting rid of me that easy."

"Chris, I'm endangering you."

He tugged her wrinkled skirt. "Look at you—you're a mess. Go change into something comfortable and I'll rustle you up something to eat."

"Chris."

He caught her hands and squeezed lightly. "Listen up. If you think for a minute that I'm running away and letting that son of a bitch Whiteford hang a murder rap on you, you're crazy. So, baby doll, love of my life, beautiful girl of my dreams, shut up." He grinned and rose, pulling her to her feet.

"You're crazy."

"Crazy about you." He urged her toward the bedroom.

She changed into her robe. When she went back to the living room, Chris waited with a chicken salad sandwich and a cup of soup. She ate gratefully.

He cracked open a beer and, beside her on the couch, stretched out his long legs. "We need to talk."

"Are they going to arrest me, Chris?"

"I'm a more likely suspect. They'll keep after us. Find a lawyer. I don't want you talking without one."

Thinking about the card Vandegraf had given her, she nodded. "I can't help thinking I'm involved somehow. It's too weird. My earrings, Tim Service, and Annie?" She sipped the soup. Chicken noodle, exactly what she needed. "I spoke to Henry Vandegraf today. He was Larry's partner. He said he'll tell the police that I didn't know about the will."

He glanced at the newspapers. "Going by what the cops said, and the newspapers, there's no way you could have done it alone. You're too small. So here's the deal. They don't have any hard evidence that links you or me directly to the crimes. I figure right about now they've got transcriptions of our interrogations in front of a judge. If he thinks they have anything, they'll be here soon with search warrants."

"There's nothing to find. I didn't do it. Is somebody setting me up?" She darted glances around the room. "What if the killer planted evidence? Could it have to do with the will?"

"You said he has a sister?"

She nodded. "If the will goes into probate, she gets everything. But she lives in Boston. I can't imagine her involved in this. She's a very sweet lady."

She closed her eyes, seeing Phyllis's mismatched shoes. Overwhelming grief or maddening guilt? She said, "Larry's mistress—oh, my Lord, she did call." To Chris's questioning gaze, she said, "A few weeks ago I got a strange call in the middle of the night—it was Phyllis. I thought I dreamed it. Then I saw her today. She was a mess, falling apart. She accused me of having an affair with Larry. Maybe she did it and then put my earrings there so I'd take the blame."

Melanie shook her head. "I think he treated her the same way he treated me. He probably boasted about sending me flowers, probably talked about reconciling our marriage. It may have driven Phyllis over the edge. And he stole my gun. Phyllis may have found it. Maybe she had help." She drew a ragged breath. "I was angry, upset... I didn't mean to tell Edith about Larry." She explained how Larry had bullied the housekeeper into working for him with the threat of having her deported. Then, her voice lower, torn by shame, she added what she had told the woman.

Chris rolled his eyes. "Didn't anybody like Larry?" A rhetorical question. "Trouble is, what does this mistress or the housekeeper have to do with Service? Or Annie?"

Melanie stared blankly at the soup, feeling as jumbled as the loops and tangles of skinny noodles. "If Phyllis believed Larry and I were in the process of reconciliation, maybe she went to Service to find out? No, that doesn't make any sense. None of this makes any sense."

She gave him a hopeful look. "We gave them the file folder, the letters from Larry."

Chris shook his head. "Bushy-haired stranger."

"What?"

"A cop joke. Haul a suspect in and he accuses a mysterious bushy-haired stranger. They don't take those letters or the file folder seriously. Did they take a handwriting exemplar?"

"A what?"

"A writing sample. Did they ask for a sample of your handwriting?"

She nodded. "They asked me to print... They think I wrote that letter from Tim Service?"

"Or I did." He touched her chin with a finger and turned her to face him. "We can't solve this. The police will sort it out eventually. It's rough being a suspect." He snorted. "Found out today how rough it is. But we didn't do anything. We're clear. So we stick together, no more fighting. Deal?"

The next morning dawned partly cloudy and mild. A breeze blew lightly from the west. Melanie studied her neglected courtyard, eyeing the dusty wisteria leaves and begonias wilting in their gay Mexican pots, and felt guilty for neglecting to water or weed.

"Penny for your thoughts," Chris said.

She chuckled. "For once they're worth more than that. First normal thoughts I've had in days. The courtyard is a mess." She slid the glass door wide. The outdoor thermometer read seventy-two degrees. Clouds beyond the

Sandias hinted at possible rain in the next day or two. "May as well kill two birds with—" She winced at her choice of words. "I'm going to get Carmen. Let her enjoy a bath."

Chris folded the newspaper. "Want me to wash your car?"

Appreciating his understanding of her need for normalcy, she nodded. "Sure. Maybe that will make it rain." She took the keys to Victor's house and went out through the garage.

She fetched the macaw and carried her across the street. "Want a bath, pretty lady?" she asked as she settled Carmen on the outdoor perch. "Hmm, want to play in the water?"

"Bad bird," Carmen said. She rattled her feathers and extended her scarlet-yellow-and-blue wings to catch the sun.

"How about some company, bad bird? Want to play with my babies? Be nice to Heloise and she might talk to you." She reached for the door, and her words died in her throat.

A pink envelope lay on the doorstep. She blinked, certain it would disappear—a figment of her imagination and overwrought nerves. She blinked and blinked, but the envelope remained.

She backed away. "Chris?" She fumbled behind her and found the gate latch. "Chris!"

Holding the hose, he approached. "What's the matter?"

She pointed at the envelope.

Chris's jaw dropped. "What the hell—?" The hose nozzle clattered on the asphalt. He walked into the courtyard and reached for it, then stopped. He wiped his hands against his T-shirt, then picked the envelope up by the edges, as if handling a photograph, and carried it inside.

Melanie crowded his heels. Had Larry risen from the grave?

"I need tweezers," Chris said as he placed the envelope on the counter. Chris held the envelope with a pencil eraser while he slit it open with a knife. He used the tweezers to extract the note, then, with the tweezers and pencil, he unfolded the paper. He asked for a plastic bag. She gave him a quart-size zipper-lock bag, and he slid the envelope inside.

She leaned over his shoulder to read the note.

Cookie,
I am most upset with the castellan. He is my ears and eyes for when I, as a mortal must, lapse into thoughtless slumber. He allows the hordes to sully your sanctuary. Where was he when the dragon fouled your estate? Where was he when the loathsome knave smote your fragile flesh? I dismiss this vow-breaker, this tarnished knight! Henceforth, his charge is ended and I as your guardian, your protector and sworn knight, wield your banner alone and will destroy the fire-breathers and churls! Fear not those blackguards who dare persecute you. My lance is true, my arm unerring. You made your vow!!!! Break it not no matter what the temptation. You promised, you swore! You belong to me! If you cannot fulfill your chosen path then with great pain and woe in my heart you will force me into chastising you for breaking your oath! Most precious maid, fairest damsel, DON'T MAKE ME DO IT!

Dizzy, Melanie sat on a bar stool. "Who is this guy?"

Chris slid the opened note into the bag so that it was readable through the plastic. "It sure as hell isn't Larry." He called Whiteford.

Dazed, but needing something to do while waiting for the police, Melanie bathed the birds. Usually giving them a bath was a joy. They loved water, and it was a pleasure watching them preen and play on the perch. The eerie feeling that she was being watched made her skin itch.

When Whiteford and Grange arrived, Chris had the letter and the answering-machine tape with the threatening message ready for them.

The detectives read the letter and listened to the tape. Upon hearing the tape again, Melanie felt she knew the voice. Frustration burned that she could not pull a name from her brain.

Whiteford asked, "Do you have a typewriter, Melanie?"

Chris clamped his hands on his hips and glowered at the detective. "Can the attitude, man. If you had enough on us, you'd have a warrant. You want to search the premises? Try asking."

Melanie placed a hand on Chris's arm. "Did I tell you about Doug Harland, Detective Whiteford?" She stared at the note. "We dated in high school and for about two years afterward. He used to call me Cookie." That earned her a skeptical look from Whiteford. "He can't be writing these. He lives in Virginia. He's married."

Whiteford's skepticism remained. What had Chris said about bushy-haired strangers? Did Whiteford believe this was some elaborate plot to get away with murder?

Grange looked up from fussing over Winston. The Lab sat on his Frisbee, perfectly content to rest his massive head on the detective's knee. "This Doug Harland, you talked to him lately?"

"After I got that threatening message on the phone, I tried to call him. I spoke to his wife." She sighed. "I guess she never told him I called. I thought it was Larry sending the letters, trying to shake me up, make me crazy."

Whiteford watched the birds preening in the courtyard. "Tell me more about Doug Harland."

She stared at her fingernails. The crimson polish was chipped and sorely in need of repair, a perfect symbol of her tattered life. "We dated in high school. I went to college and he joined the navy, and we—"

Whiteford dropped his pencil. "A sailor?"

His demeanor shocked her and she moved closer to Chris. Then she noticed Chris giving her a strange look. "Yes, he was in the navy. On an aircraft carrier, the USS *America*."

The detectives exchanged glances.

"He lives in Virginia, he's married, with three kids. He doesn't have anything to do with this. He couldn't."

"Do you have his address?"

"I have his phone number."

"What kind of relationship did you have with him?"

What kind—? She slumped on a chair and dangled her hands between her knees. Nothing on God's green earth could make her believe Doug Harland had anything to do with killing anybody.

"We dated. Steady dating. When he joined the navy, we had been talking about marriage, possibly. I wrote him almost every day. He was out to sea for months at a time." She looked at Whiteford from the corner of her eye, trying to judge his reaction. "We grew up, grew apart."

"Who broke up with who?"

She shook her head. "Mutual, no hard feelings."

Whiteford stood. "I can check this out easy enough."

She met his gaze, and his animosity came through loud and clear. He wanted her to be guilty.

HER HANDS SHAKING, Melanie listened to the telephone ring. *Please, dear God, be there, Doug—and don't be a crazed killer.*

A man answered. "Hello."

"Doug? Is this Doug Harland?"

"Yes, it is. May I ask who's calling?"

"Melanie Rogers."

There was a pause, and a child screamed indignantly in the background. Doug snapped, "Brad, quit that! Sorry. Melanie?"

A pang of regret went through Melanie. No matter how badly her marriage had deteriorated, she had always longed for children. Years of trying had led nowhere. She was barren. She looked at Chris and knew he'd be a wonderful father. His kids would be smart and beautiful, tough little boys and saucy little girls. Not that it mattered. She passed off her broodiness as a symptom of depression.

"Do you remember me?"

"How could I forget? How are you doing? What's going on? Are you in town?"

He sounded so genuine, so innocent. She smiled at Chris to show him all was well. "I'm at home, in Albuquerque. I called before and left a message with your wife. I guess you never got it, huh?"

Another pause, then he chuckled. "I see. No, I never did." He lowered his voice. "Helen's been sort of insecure ever since Paul was born. Know what I mean? She looks great, but she thinks she's fat. You're married, right?"

"Divorced. That's why I need to talk to you. Have you got a few minutes? Can you talk?"

"Yes," he said slowly. "Is something wrong?"

"It's about all those letters we wrote. Do you still have the ones I wrote to you?"

He made a noise like a laugh, but sounded embarrassed. "No. I lost them."

"Lost? Moving or something?"

"Not exactly. Is this important?"

Her heart skipped. "What happened to the letters, Doug?"

"This is embarrassing. After we broke up, I...sort of carried a torch. I threw out most of the letters. I kept all your pictures and the...remember the Maid Marian letters? All the pledging of troths and calling me your knight in shining armor? You know, when you were taking that class in medieval history, and, well, those letters were really sweet. So I kept them."

Melanie swayed on the bar stool.

"Then somebody stole them," Doug said.

She nearly fell off the stool. "Who?"

He barked a short laugh. "Are you kidding? The *America* had forty-five hundred men aboard. If I knew who, I'd have gotten them back. What's going on? It's been, what, nine years? Almost ten?"

She envisioned the first letter. For years I sought you and now I've found you again... Pink paper...

"Doug, this is so very important. Do you even suspect anybody? Any ideas at all?"

Chris leaned closer.

Another long pause. Children laughed in the background. Helen called out that dinner was ready. "Sorry," he said. "I wish I could help, but it was so long ago. Melanie, this sounds serious."

Melanie had thought that knowing for sure Doug was innocent would make her feel better. It had the opposite effect. Somewhere out there was a demented stranger with a twisted sense of protectiveness. A murderer who killed in the name of love.

"Thanks, Doug. I have to warn you, the police will be contacting you. If you remember anything about those letters, no matter how insignificant it might seem, please tell them."

After she hung up, she told Chris what she'd learned.

"If this guy was in the navy, then his prints are on file somewhere. Maybe Whiteford can lift something off that letter."

"How did he find me?"

"Call your parents. That's where a stalker would start."

Calling them was more difficult than calling Doug. Did they know Larry was dead? Her mother answered. Without saying why, Melanie asked if in the past year anyone had asked about her.

"As a matter of fact, there was a gentleman asking about you," her mother said.

Melanie wiped sweat off her brow. "Who was he? What did he want?"

"Well, I don't know!" her mother said indignantly. "I told him you were very happily married and living in Albuquerque. You weren't interested in resuming old relationships."

Knowing her mother's snippiness when she thought she was right, Melanie drew a deep breath and prepared for the worst. "Mom, this is very important. Did he give you his name?"

A long silence was followed by a softening in her mother's tone. "Melanie? Are you in trouble?"

"Yes, Mom, I'm in a lot of trouble. I need your help. I don't need your lectures or your opinions, I just need your help. Please? Who was this man? What did he want?"

"I don't know." She sounded subdued. "I never saw him before."

"His name? What he looked like?"

"I don't...Charles, that's it. He said his name was Charles, and he was an old school friend of yours. College. I remember it was snowing, very hard. It must have been December, right before Christmas. Charles Lewis. Melanie, baby, what's the matter?"

"Can you remember what he looked like?" She tapped a piece of paper, then printed *Charles Lewis* for Chris. She underlined it twice.

"No—yes—not really. It was snowing, and he wore a cap and a heavy coat. Melanie, what is going on?"

Melanie bit back the urge to tell. Old hurts were too strong, and she felt too fragile to face her mother blaming her for Larry's death. Calling herself six kinds of coward, she gave her mother Henry Vandegraf's phone number and told her to call him as soon as possible. Then she hung up.

Supporting her face on one hand, Melanie said, "I don't know anybody named Charles Lewis. Why is he doing this to me?"

Chris let out a long, low whistle. "A lovesick loose cannon. Great, just great."

Chapter Thirteen

Melanie stared at the legal papers fanned out across the table. Maybe if she stared hard enough, something might make sense.

Chris lounged on the couch, watching the evening news. The sight of him soothed her eyes. He had one foot propped on the couch and was dangling a hand over his knee. Absently he raked back a wayward lock of sandy hair. She wondered if they could survive this turmoil to live a quiet, peaceful life.

It had been a normal day, yet normalcy now had a surreal quality, like an unfocused photograph—recognizable, but not quite right. Earlier they'd picked up Victor from the airport. On the way home, Victor had chatted about his problems in Chicago, and she and Chris had chatted back, even laughing. Victor was now preparing dinner for them, to say thanks for pet-sitting. Melanie suspected the dinner was also to offer condolences for her lost store and her myriad other problems.

The police had never shown up with a search warrant; Chris called it a good sign. Good? A crazy man was killing people because of her. Chris never said so, but she knew he had to think he might be next.

Shaking away the thoughts, she picked up a list of Larry's property holdings. Apartment buildings in New Mexico and Texas, condos in Aspen, a manufacturing plant, undeveloped land in California and a ranch in Wyoming. He owned—*she* owned—the mansion on Antonito and six residential rental properties in Albuquerque.

She wondered again, Why me? All she wanted was a bird shop, honest labor to fill her days, and Chris to love. "My Lord," she said, "what am I going to do with all this?"

Chris grinned, his eyes vivid across the living room. "Buy me a car? A red convertible?"

She scooped the papers into a pile. "This is so complicated. If for nothing else, I really hate Larry for doing this to me. What am I going to do with it?"

"Quit acting so guilty, for a start." Baseball scores held his attention for a moment, and then he aimed the remote and turned off the TV. He stood and stretched, catlike, then wandered to the table and tugged her hand. "I'm starving and there ain't no cooking like Vic's cooking."

Hand in hand, they left the house.

Victor and Winston were playing Frisbee in the street. Victor wore a pair of denims and an open-collared sport shirt. He looked relaxed and glad to be home from Chicago. He threw the Frisbee high and fast, and Winston shot after it like an eighty-pound bullet.

"Dinner in twenty minutes," Victor called cheerfully. "Winston insisted on a pickup game first."

Melanie caught Victor's quick appraisal. She knew Chris had talked to his brother about their problems. She smiled to show she felt okay.

Winston loped back with the Frisbee in his mouth. He stopped ten feet from them, looking confused about who to play with next. Victor snapped his fingers. As the dog approached, Chris bent to take the Frisbee.

What sounded like a car backfire echoed off the tall adobe walls. Melanie jumped, and her heart thudded. Winston shied violently, leaping to the side and landing in a crouch. Then he straightened and barked.

Victor grunted. He staggered sideways, then turned Chris a wide-eyed gaze full of puzzlement. A crimson flower blossomed below his left collarbone. He tugged his shoulders sideways as if trying to make his arm move. Then his knees crumpled and he collapsed to his hands and knees.

From the end of the compound, a woman screamed. Another terrible cracking echoed off the walls. A spray of gravel and dust exploded between Chris's feet, and a metallic *zing* buzzed like an angry wasp.

"Jesus!" Chris roared. He caught Melanie's arm, swinging her toward Victor's gate.

She stumbled, then ran. She caught the gate and shoved, almost falling into the courtyard. Heart pounding, she peered back into the street.

On her roof, outlined by the lowering sun, a man knelt. He held both arms extended, hands together. Melanie screamed, "Up there!" The man lowered his arms.

Breathing, "No, no, no," Melanie ran into the street. She waved both arms, wanting to shriek that this was a terrible mistake, but all she could do was gasp, "No, no, no." The man stood, and the sun outlined him in fire.

"Get inside!" Chris shouted. "Move, move!" Lugging Victor, he shuffled to the gate.

Another shot rang out. Pieces of adobe burst from the wall. Chris ducked, zagging to the side. Melanie screeched and raced after him.

"Door!" Chris barked.

Melanie shoved the front door. Victor's face was so white that the beard patterning on his face looked blue. Blood darkened his shirt and covered Chris's chest and arms. Chris laid his brother on the floor, then ripped off his T-shirt and crammed it against Victor's chest.

Melanie raced to the phone, shaking so hard she could barely punch in 911. She gulped several breaths before she told the operator that she needed an ambulance and the police.

She ran back to Chris. Blood crusted his arms and hands. The shirt he pressed against Victor was soaked. So much blood. The movies lied. They never showed this much blood. A long line of it led from the door, and it pooled on the bricks, tarry and glistening. It saturated Victor's shirt and covered Chris.

Chris's face was frightening in its intensity. "Come on, Vic, come on," he recited like a prayer.

"The ambulance is on the way. What can I do?"

Loud scratching and barking at the door made her jump. Chris's muscles looked ready to pop.

"Get Winston into the bedroom," Chris said. "No! Put your hands here, keep the pressure on."

She cringed; already the smell of blood made her sick. She pressed her hands against the slimy T-shirt. "Oh, Victor, oh, God. You'll be all right, Victor, it'll be okay." Victor's eyes were glassy, stunned, bewildered. His lips twitched. They were blue. His skin looked like paper, translucent.

She heard Chris open the door, heard Winston's claws clattering on the floor, heard Chris curse and Winston whine. The dog choked and gagged as Chris hauled him back to the bedroom and slammed the door.

Sirens wailed, growing loud.

CHRIS PASSED A HAND over his burning eyes. They felt as if they were filled with sand. He resisted scratching the bandage over his inner elbow. Both he and Melanie had given blood. Last he heard, Vic had taken three pints. He wished the doctors would hurry.

"Chris, you should sit down," Melanie said. She still held the limp, crumpled paper cup from the orange juice the blood technicians gave her hours ago. She unrolled and rolled the rim with trembling fingers. "Chris?"

To make her feel better, he sat. Her soft hand caressed his knee. Guilt darkened her eyes. He caught her hand, squeezing, feeling delicate bones and tendons working beneath her fragile skin. Remembered fear shuddered through him. Had she really run into the street, waving her arms, trying to stop bullets? He looked away.

Then he glowered and said harshly, "I can't believe you ran out in the street!"

She drew her head aside. "I don't know what you're talking about."

"Like hell. He'd have shot you."

"I didn't run into the street," she said stubbornly.

He opened his mouth to argue, but an orderly walked down the wide hallway and gave them a wary look before quickening his step and hurrying away.

To Chris's surprise, Melanie grinned. "You look bloody awful," she said. "And I mean that literally."

He glanced at his chest. A hospital robe barely reached around his torso. Caked blood covered his chest, and he could feel it crusting on his face. Melanie didn't look so good herself. Bloody splotches and streaks soiled her flame print blouse and green walking shorts.

"Don't change the subject," he muttered, wondering if she remembered running into the street—or if he could ever forget.

She squeezed his hand. "Victor's going to be okay."

Two figures walked toward them. Whiteford and Grange. Melanie tensed, her mouth curling in dislike. Chris stood. "Where the hell have you been? Did you catch him?" he demanded.

Whiteford beckoned with a flick of his hand.

Glowering, his jaw jutting forward, Chris stood his ground. Vic might die, because Whiteford wanted to believe Melanie was the criminal.

"Get over here, Glenn. I have to talk to you." Whiteford pushed open a door and peered inside. "Come here."

Chris stomped after the detective. "Is this how you guys run an investigation? Huh? Sit around cracking your knuckles and waiting to see who gets hit? It's been five hours. No, six. Is that—"

"Shut up, Glenn." Whiteford shut the door and leaned against it. "I got good news and bad news. First the bad news. Another body's been found. I've got a stalker slash serial killer on my hands, and I think Melanie's next.''

The strength drained out of Chris's legs, and he sat on the edge of a hospital bed. ''Who's the stiff?''

''John Doe.'' He jerked a thumb. ''Over on Central, in a rent-by-the-week motel. Tenants complained about the smell, and the manager opened the room. You ain't gonna believe— You ain't gonna like what we found.''

Chris finally noticed the weariness graying the detective's face, and his sagging shoulders. ''What happened to him?''

''The John Doe was trussed up like a pig for slaughter. Been dead a week, maybe, ten days.'' He hooked a finger over his shirt collar. ''Had an earring hooked on his shirt. The match to the one we found on Connalley's body.''

''Shot?''

''Neck broken.'' Although Whiteford gave the impression he was a man who'd seen it all, he shuddered. ''The killer's been living with the corpse. Manager said she saw him the day before yesterday, coming out of the room.''

Chris loosed a low whistle. ''What else?''

''Trophies.''

Working his jaw, Chris knew exactly what Whiteford meant. The killer kept his victim's belongings.

Whiteford raked his fingers through his hair. His eyes were bloodshot and bleak. ''Anne Marie Guererro's purse, paperwork I think came out of Service's office, Connalley's wedding band.''

''Wedding band?''

Whiteford nodded. ''His housekeeper said he always wore a wedding band, but he didn't have it when he was killed. We're pretty sure it's his. It's engraved. And there's more. The license plate off Melanie's car. Letters to Doug Harland from Melanie, dating back ten years. Hundreds of photographs, all of Melanie.''

Chris swallowed the unpleasant wetness in his mouth.

"Some are old, look like high school shots. But most of them are recent, taken in the area. He's been following her a long time."

"You checked out Doug Harland?" Chris asked.

Whiteford nodded. "Virginia Beach police questioned him and he's clean."

"What about the stolen letters?"

Whiteford shook his head. "We're running that down. We lifted a print off that last letter. We're hoping for more latents out of the motel." He pulled a face. "At the time the letters were stolen, the *America* was carrying a crew of four thousand six hundred and thirty men."

"Jesus. What about the motel manager?"

"The suspect rented the room under the name Rex Killeen. She gave us a description of his car. Late-model Ford, but the license plate was lifted off a yellow Ford that belongs to a little old lady who lives on the south side. She never realized her plate had been stolen. She never drives. I've got a hunch the Ford is stolen, too. We have the manager working on a sketch, but she claims every time she saw him he was wearing dark glasses."

"What about the shooting?" Chris asked. "There was a woman in the compound. Did she give you anything?"

"Eyewitness," the detective said with a snarl. "She says it's a man, but claims the sun was in her eyes. Can't even make up her mind what he was wearing." He sighed. "You know how that goes."

Chris did. "Tentative ID? Description?"

"Not yet. Melanie's in a lot of trouble, Glenn."

Chris shook his head. "He isn't trying to kill her." He met the detective's weary brown eyes. "He meant to kill me. You said there's good news?"

"Maybe. A fugitive bulletin came over the wire about Peter Osterman."

Chris straightened.

"He skipped bail. I made a call to your captain. He says Osterman beat it out of the country. Federal fugitive warrants and an APB are out. Captain Daws said an all-clear is on the way to you." Whiteford snorted. "I'm starting to think there's a target painted on your back. Get rid of one problem and pick up another."

Fearing Osterman had become almost second nature, and now all Chris could do was stare at Whiteford.

The detective opened the door. "You make it out of Albuquerque alive and who knows, you might get a promotion."

Two hours later, Chris and Melanie were allowed to see Victor. The bullet had passed through his brachial artery, sliced through his lung, then lodged in a rib. He'd lost a lot of blood and spent hours in surgery. He needed to stay in the hospital for a while, but he'd be all right.

Victor was awake, but groggy. He rolled his eyes.

Chris clasped Vic's hand. The quick burning in his eyes caught him off guard. He looked out the window, blinking rapidly until the burn faded and his throat loosened.

"Can I get you anything?"

Vic rasped, "Don't you dare call Mother.... She's upset enough about you." He closed his eyes.

Call Mother? His parents had lost track of Vic years ago. Chris decided Vic was still loopy from the anesthesia. "Get some sleep, Bro. Be back to see you tomorrow."

Chris and Melanie rode to her house in a patrol car. Chris considered the wisdom of finding a hotel room, but since they had no idea what Charles Lewis, aka Rex Killeen, looked like, a motel might be more dangerous than Melanie's house. After informing the police officers that he was armed, Chris guided Melanie inside.

It was nearly four in the morning. Exhaustion and nerves made him groggy. He headed for the shower.

He scrubbed blood off his face, arms and chest. He'd seen men die, and had killed one in the line of duty. Nasty business, but his perspective had always been impassive. Death was just a sorry fact of life. It surprised him how different it felt when the blood belonged to Vic. It surprised him how much it hurt.

A soft knock on the glass door startled him. Melanie asked, "Can I come in?" The door opened with a light pop of the magnetic catch.

She stood naked, arms dangling, looking weary and sore, and fragile as glass. He needed to touch her. He was thirty-four years old and had lived most of those years under the delusion that he didn't need anybody—but he needed to touch her.

He stepped back, and Melanie entered and closed the door. She glanced at the pinkish water swirling down the drain. Her lips tightened. He gathered her against his chest and closed his eyes against the pounding water. She was the one real, decent thing in the world, his proof that all wasn't ugly and hopeless.

For a long time they stood motionless while the hot water beat their skin and swirled down the drain. When she lifted her face to him, water dribbled down her cheeks and her hair hung in ropes over her shoulders. Her mouth was set in a solemn line. Steel darkened her amber eyes.

"We've got to stop him, Chris." Her voice was a whisper. "He can't get away with destroying our lives. We have to stop him."

He pressed a kiss between her eyebrows. "We will," he murmured.

MELANIE AND CHRIS walked into the police station for the second time. She held her head high, and her step was determined. Looking straight ahead, she went directly to Whiteford's and Grange's cubicle.

Grange offered her a seat. Chris remained standing and tugged the lapel of his linen jacket to better conceal the holstered Desert Eagle.

"Thanks for coming down," Whiteford said. The purple bags under his eyes and the downcast turn of his mouth spoke of long hours of overtime. Foam cups, stained with dark rings, littered his desk. He swept one aside and opened a manila folder. "We're dealing with one bad hombre. I want you two in protective custody."

"What do you mean?" Melanie asked.

"A safe house. Twenty-four-hour police protection."

One side of Melanie's mouth turned up, but her expression held no mirth. "I don't know who this man is, but he knows me. He'll find me."

Whiteford tapped the folder. "We ran the prints through the Department of Defense and got an ID. Charleton Lewis Richardson. Last known address Norfolk, Virginia."

Melanie shook her head. "Charles Lewis is the name he gave my mother. Do you have a photograph?"

Whiteford said, "Not yet. The navy is going through their files." He handed her a composite sketch. "This is what we got from the motel manager. He's five-ten or eleven, about a hundred and sixty-five pounds. Dark hair, clean-shaven."

While Melanie studied the sketch, Whiteford said, "Got an ID on the John Doe, Glenn. Thomas McRae. A gofer who worked for Connalley." He shuffled through the papers on his cluttered desk.

"Six-two, maybe two hundred and twenty pounds, with dark hair?" Chris asked. He accepted a photograph from Whiteford and studied the dead man's battered face. "Yeah, that's him."

Melanie grimaced. "That man who came into the store?"

He handed back the picture before Melanie saw it. "Uh-huh, Richardson must have seen him that day, too." He told the detectives about McRae carrying a message to Melanie, and about how he'd thrown the man out of the store.

Melanie handed back the sketch. "I'm sorry, I don't recognize this face. It's not a good picture."

"He must be the one Jim saw crawling all over the Beemer." Chris explained about the car salesman and the missing remote-control unit, and suggested the detectives might be able to get a better description from the salesman.

Whiteford promised to talk to Jim. Then he leaned forward and crossed his arms atop the desk. "Here's the scoop, you two. Richardson spent five years in the navy, three of them with the Seals—"

"What's that?" Chris asked. The acronym sounded vaguely familiar.

"Sea, Air, Land assault team. Some sort of supersquid. Kind of like the army Special Forces, but badder. He had an accident and got reassigned to the aircraft carrier *America*. But he had mental problems and got drummed out of the navy."

"What kind of mental problems?" Chris asked.

"Report doesn't say exactly, but my gut feeling is that it was pretty heavy-duty stuff. I'm running the computer now to see if he has any arrest record or a history in mental institutions. Considering the damage he's done around here, I'd say that info is pretty much moot. I need you in protective custody, Melanie."

She shook her head.

"Dr. Aniselle has gone over this case, and the evidence we pulled out of the motel. She's our resident expert on serial killers and stalkers."

Melanie twisted her skirt in her fingers and continued to shake her head.

"The doc says Richardson won't quit. She gave me a lot of psychobabble gobbledygook, but what it boils down to is this—Richardson thinks he's invincible, and he's got it in his head that you love him."

Melanie started. "Why?"

"Something called transference. He thinks that you wrote the love letters to him, and he's appointed himself your guardian. He's rescuing you, like you're some kind of damsel in distress. The doc says he might start killing cops."

"Now that you found his crash pad, won't he run?" Chris asked.

"Doc says no. Melanie is his reason for existing. He's addicted to her, and the killing is turning into a habit. We've got an APB out on him, got flyers out to all gun dealers and pawnshops in case he's looking for heavier hardware. We'll pick him up.''

Melanie peered around the doorway. She clenched her hands against her breast. ''He could be anybody. How can I hide if I don't know what he looks like? Is he going to kill me?''

Whiteford sighed. ''Doc says he's afraid of you.'' He shook his head. ''That's not the right word. He's in *awe* of you. It's everybody around you who has to worry.''

Chris thought hard, snatching at ideas, rejecting others. Vividly he saw her racing into the street, waving her arms at the gunman. Richardson had once had access to her house. He'd had plenty of opportunities to hurt her, but he hadn't. In awe of Melanie—addicted.

''We know he's following her,'' Chris said. ''Let's play tag.''

''No way, Glenn. He'll be expecting a trap. He's going to start killing cops. Dr. Aniselle says that shooting at you off the roof proves he isn't fixated on an MO. He'll use whatever method comes to mind. And he sure isn't stupid.''

''I've got an idea.''

''Forget it,'' Whiteford said.

''It'll work. Hear me out.''

Whiteford clamped his arms over his chest. ''Forget it.''

Chris dropped his hands on the desk and said, ''Listen . . .''

''THIS IS the screwiest plan I've ever heard,'' Melanie said.

Chris parked the Beretta. The garage door lumbered downward. ''Whiteford thinks it'll work.''

''Well, I don't like it. You're setting yourself up as a target, and I don't like it.'' She opened her car door.

Chris caught her arm. ''I'm a cop, honey. I know how to take care of myself. I'm wearing a vest.''

''Bulletproof vest,'' she muttered. ''What if he shoots at your head?''

He pulled her close and wrapped an arm around her neck. He kissed the tip of her nose. "The way I see it, we have two choices. Either go into protective custody for however long it takes to flush Richardson out, or do it this way. It'll work. As soon as he thinks you're leaving town, he'll panic."

"If they use a double for me, why can't they use one for you?"

He stroked her cheek with a knuckle. "They don't have anybody who can double for me. Besides, I'm a cop, not a civilian. I know what I'm doing."

"I'm scared. You sure this will work?"

He drew a deep breath. Then, patiently, he said, "The airport will be crawling with cops. The ticket clerk is a cop. Richardson will panic. He'll want to know what flight you're taking. And he'll have to ditch his weapon in order to get into the passenger loading area. No shoot-outs."

"What happens if you can't catch him at the airport?" Arguing was a delay tactic, and she knew it was futile, but she hated letting him go.

"I told you I talked to Daws."

"I know," she muttered.

"Officer Goldfield and I will get on the plane to Phoenix. We'll have a stakeout covering every arriving flight. If he doesn't show in twenty-four hours, we'll get you on a plane to Phoenix. It's covered, honey. I'm not going to let anything happen to you."

She twisted on the seat and grabbed his neck. "I'm so scared, I love you so much. I'd die if I lost you." She pressed her face against his neck and absorbed the sunshine scent of his skin.

He caressed the back of her neck, working his fingers under her hair. "I love you, honey, and nothing's going to happen to me. Now let's go inside and get this show on the road."

Two police officers waited inside her house. Officer Sandra Goldfield—"Call me Sandy"—shook Melanie's hand. Her eyes were shiny with excitement. She'd been in uniform when Melanie had met her at the police station. She looked feminine and fragile in civilian clothes.

Sandy Goldfield introduced the other officer as Detective John Burns. Then she said, "Ready?" and picked up a wig box from the table.

Melanie hesitated. "It'll work," Chris said, "trust me. Now where are your suitcases?"

"Guest room closet."

In her bedroom, Melanie undressed. Sandy said, "I wear a size six. I think I'm fatter than you."

"I wear a five. Close enough."

The policewoman winked. "Don't look so worried, Miss Rogers. We'll catch him."

Melanie handed over her yellow slacks and red-and-yellow print blouse. "I'm worried about Chris. Richardson wants to kill him." She pulled on shorts and a T-shirt.

While Sandy dressed, she said, "If my husband looked like that, I'd worry, too. About other women, though, not creeps like Richardson." She winked. "Glenn can take care of himself. He's a hero, you know."

Melanie decided she liked Sandy very much.

Sandy pinned up her fine blond hair and, with Melanie's help, fitted the curly dark brown wig in place. They stood side by side facing the mirror. They were the same height, the same slender build, and with the wig half obscuring Sandy's narrow face, the resemblance was uncanny.

"Amazing," Melanie said. "My long-lost sister."

Sandra ran a finger under the waistband of the slacks. "Hope I don't pop any buttons."

Melanie opened her jewelry box. "Pick what you like. I'll find a purse. Do you want big or small?"

"Make it big enough to hold my pistol and transmitter. Do these shoes look all—"

An angry squawk from the living room made both women jump. Melanie recognized the squawk as Abelard's and, with an inner groan, realized what it meant. She hurried into the living room.

Carmen paced the floor under the perch, while Abelard spread his wings and screeched. His normally curious expression was replaced by one of avian fury; raised feathers made him look twice his size. Heloise preened placidly, but she was watching Carmen.

"Oh, not now," Melanie whispered. Their cycle was off, probably caused by her stress and odd hours of the past few weeks. Melanie hadn't paid enough attention to the parrots to notice the signs. The Grays were preparing to breed.

Detective Burns sat rigid on the couch, eyeing Abelard as if the parrot might turn on him, too.

Chris snickered. "Carmen got a taste of her own medicine. Abelard got her a good one."

"It isn't funny, Chris. Abelard gets mean during breeding season." Melanie hoped their coming into season out of season didn't harm their health.

"Come on, Carmen." Melanie clenched a fist and let the macaw climb on. Gritting her teeth against the macaw's claws, she carried Carmen to the dining area and put her on the back of a chair.

"Everything okay?" Sandy asked as she came out. She sported big yellow earrings and carried Melanie's red-and-yellow straw purse. Abelard screeched and hissed, and Sandy jumped. "What's wrong with your birds?"

"Broody," Melanie said, trying to remember in which box she'd packed the disassembled nesting cage. She laughed wryly. "As if I don't have enough problems. No big deal."

Sandy turned a coquettish circle. "What do you guys think? Will I pass?"

Chris grinned, and his eyes sparkled with teasing light. "I like this seeing-double bit."

Melanie looked askance at him. "As long as you don't forget which is which." She wrapped her arms around his waist. Solemnly she said, "And don't forget I love you. Please be careful."

"Ready, Glenn?" Sandy asked. She slipped on a pair of Melanie's sunglasses to disguise her blue eyes.

Chris lowered his head and pressed a tender kiss to Melanie's lips. "I'll see you in a few hours, honey."

She hugged him tight, taking comfort from the stiff Kevlar vest and the outline of his holstered gun. After one last kiss, Chris and Sandy left the house. Melanie said, "Officer Goldfield is so brave."

Burns snorted. "She'll outgrow it. Can I trouble you for something to drink, ma'am?"

"Oh, sure." Melanie gave him a cup of coffee. She stared at Abelard and Heloise and called herself stupid for missing the signs of impending breeding. She racked her brain, trying to recall where she'd stored the brood cage.

Digging it out of the garage kept her busy enough not to worry about Chris—too much. After all, he was right. All those police officers knew what they were doing. This beat hiding out like a scared animal, too.

She lugged the disassembled cage into the house. A splat of white on the floor under Carmen made her sigh. Plus, Carmen was busily picking threads out of the chair's blue twill. In an hour the macaw would have the chair dismantled down to the frame.

"Detective Burns, I need to take Carmen home. Do you think it's safe? It's only across the street."

He frowned. "I guess so, but I need to go with you."

Melanie hoisted the macaw on the carrying bar. As she passed through the courtyard, Winston gave Melanie a mournful look. The Lab seemed to sense that something was terribly wrong with Victor. He ignored his Frisbee and refused to eat. Melanie wished she knew a way to assure the dog that Victor would soon be home.

Detective Burns entered the street first, his right hand inside his jacket. He stared at an open garage door from which emerged the whine of a saw. Melanie assured him it was a neighbor. They hurried to Victor's house.

Carmen began to fuss. She spread her wings, squawked and rocked violently on the bar. Speaking soothingly, Melanie studied the living-room floor. She and Chris had scrubbed the bricks, but did the macaw still smell blood? Feathers rattling and raised, the macaw lurched on the bar. "Okay, okay," Melanie said uneasily. "I'll take you back. You can sit outside. Hush, Carmen, hush, it's okay—"

Behind her, she heard a grunt, then a heavy thud. Carmen loosed a screech and launched herself into flight. Melanie gagged on the taste of feathers and sawdust.

Melanie spun around. Detective Burns was stretched out on the bricks, unmoving. Over him stood a man wearing a gray suit and an open-necked white shirt. Dark glasses concealed his eyes.

Carmen screamed and hit the perch so hard it rocked on its base. Melanie wanted to scream, too, but all she could do was gawk at the gun aimed at her head.

Chapter Fourteen

Sandy Goldfield laughed softly and sat on a molded plastic chair. Chris gave her a questioning look. "Sorry, Glenn. But I've never seen luggage that color before." She plucked at the leg of her slacks. "Miss Rogers really likes... bright stuff."

"Yeah, she really does," Chris murmured. Needing a clear head, he firmly clamped down thoughts of Melanie. A few hours, he thought, and this would all be over.

He studied the passenger lounge. One of the clerks behind the service counter was a real clerk, the other was a police officer. Half the people in the lounge, sitting on chairs, loitering near the windows overlooking airplanes on the tarmac and standing near a rest room door, were policemen.

Easy to pick out the cops, Chris mused. The alert ones, the men and women who looked at people's faces. He hoped Richardson was so fixated on Melanie that he wouldn't notice all the watchful passengers.

Detective Whiteford entered the lounge. He wore a big Western hat, cowboy boots and a casual jacket. He went to the service counter and stood in line to check his boarding pass.

Another man approached. The newcomer was a little under six feet tall and dark-haired. He wore dark glasses. Chris slid a stealthy hand inside his jacket. Sweat trickled down the middle of his back.

One by one the seated cops arose. Some stretched, some pretended to fuss over their hand luggage. Whiteford stepped away from the counter and pretended to inspect his boarding pass while he fumbled around inside his jacket.

A little girl raced across the floor, yelling, "Daddy!"

The dark-haired man glanced back, then extended a hand. The little girl grabbed his hand and babbled excitedly, pointing at a harassed looking woman who emerged from the ladies' rest room.

Chris could almost feel the collective sigh fluttering through the lounge.

"Damn it," Goldfield muttered. She pulled her hand out of her purse.

"Right," Chris murmured. "Wish we had a photo ID of the jerk."

Scratchy, distorted words came out of the public announcement system. If he heard, "Mr. Bird, pick up the white phone, please," it meant the officers at the main ticket counter downstairs had identified Richardson. He listened as the anonymous voice announced an arriving flight.

Whiteford scoped out a chair behind Chris and Goldfield and sat. He snapped open a newspaper. "Goldfield, take a stroll over to the ladies' room," he said. "See if anyone is interested."

"Right." She leaned close to Chris, pretending to kiss his cheek, and whispered, "These pants are too damned tight. If I busted out the butt, tell me."

Chris chuckled. When she had taken a few steps, he called, "Melanie?"

She looked over her shoulder.

"They aren't that tight."

"Thanks," she said dryly, and nudged her glasses higher on her nose.

"I don't think he's taking the bait," Whiteford said. "Maybe the doc was wrong. Maybe we did scare him off."

Watching for any male who might show more than a passing interest in Goldfield, Chris said, "No way. Richardson's like a damned shark. He's got blood in his nose. He won't quit. I didn't see any sign of a tail following us this morning, but he probably ditched the Ford."

Newspaper rustled. "Yeah, well, if he doesn't show by the time you and Goldfield board the plane, then I'm calling in the federal marshals."

Chris willed himself to not turn around. "What do you have in mind, Whiteford?"

"If he isn't at the airport, then that means he's back watching her house. Relax, Glenn, it's the same plan. But the feds are better equipped than our boys to handle this kind of situation. They'll take her into custody. She'll be safe, don't worry."

MELANIE WANTED to turn tail and run, scream or do anything except stare at the gun. Her limbs turned to lead and her blood froze. As the man advanced, the gun's bore seemed to swell to a monstrous size.

"Where's Glenn?" the man asked, his voice as icy as the rest of him.

She forced her eyes off the gun. Her face reflected in his glasses. Unable to think with Carmen screeching to wake the dead, she breathed, "Huh?"

"Glenn, Christopher Glenn, where is he?" He caught her wrist and squeezed, grinding bones, snapping her out of her stupor. She writhed in his grasp, and he raised the gun to her face. Stinking gun oil bit her nose.

She cut her eyes at Detective Burns. No blood, but she couldn't tell if the man was breathing. Cold, numbing panic stiffened her joints. I'm going to faint, and he'll kill me, she thought helplessly.

"Not here," she whispered.

"Where is he? Your place?"

Her mind raced in frantic circles. "I don't know where he is."

He forced her into the kitchen. With her arm locked in a merciless grip, she stumbled after him. His hand, strangely white and slick-feeling, made her flesh crawl. It took several seconds to realize he wore thin surgical gloves.

He punched in a number on the telephone. He said, "Got the woman. No sign of Glenn, just the brother... It's a bird making noise, sir.... Says she doesn't know... Yes, sir." He hung up, then picked up the gun. He pressed the barrel under her jaw, against the gland there, and shoved.

White-hot pain rocketed through Melanie's skull, leaving her eyes blurry with tears and her lungs choking for air. She clapped a hand over her jaw. Her teeth ached.

Impassively he said, "Believe me when I say I will hurt you." He jerked her arm, and she followed meekly, willing to do anything to keep him from hurting her like that again.

They were out the back door and the back gate before it hit Melanie what he had said. *Just the brother.* Did this man think Burns was Victor? He opened the rear door of a Cadillac and pushed her inside.

A man in the driver's seat hooked an arm over the seat and grinned at her. He had spiky white-blond hair and wore a loud print shirt. "Where's Glenn?"

"Drive, Jimmy. The man says we're gonna do it from his end."

Jimmy looked into the rearview mirror. "Hey, lady, this is a great town! Wow, nice air, clean streets. Is it true you can go skiing around here?"

Melanie's eyes widened. Was the man insane?

"Drive, Jimmy."

Jimmy made a fast U-turn on Candelaria, and Melanie lurched to the side. The gun hit her ribs. She caught the arm rest and jerked upright. She gaped at the big man, knowing he was staring back through the anonymous glasses. He showed all the emotion of a mannequin.

Whistling, Jimmy turned north on Rio Grande. The whistling stopped, and he glanced over his shoulder. "Hey,

Val, check out those houses, man. Hey, lady, doesn't that balloon guy live around here? Max, uh, what's his name?''

Stunned by his inanity, she said, "Maxie Anderson. He used to, but he died.''

"Ah, bummer. Man, I love hot-air balloons. Isn't the balloon festival here in Albuquerque like the biggest in the world?''

"Shut up and drive," Val said.

Melanie couldn't decide which was worse, the maniacal tourist in the driver's seat or this silent hulk with his steady gun. Jimmy gave a running commentary about the passing scenery, and when they passed a heavily fenced field containing bison he rubbernecked, nearly driving off the road.

Val said nothing at all. He held his right arm on his lap and kept the gun pointed at her belly.

Jimmy drove fast, whistling along with the radio, one hand draped casually over the steering wheel. He picked up I-25 north and drove faster. Melanie hoped a state highway patrolman saw the speeding Cadillac. Then considering Val's gun, she prayed one didn't. Jimmy took the Bernalillo exit and headed east toward Placitas. The road climbed toward the mountains. Melanie tried to ignore the nagging voice saying it was very bad that these men made no attempt to hide their identities or where they were taking her...very, very bad.

They turned south on a dirt road. Then at another dirt road, Jimmy slowed and swung wide into the curve. Melanie saw a mailbox marked 4210, but she had missed the street name.

Jimmy parked in a driveway next to a black Cadillac. At the end of the driveway was a small adobe house. It was whitewashed, the woodwork painted blue. Yuccas bloomed in circular garden plots. A sprawling wisteria was a purple blotch in the surrounding browns, golds, dusty greens and siennas.

Val ordered her out. Melanie's calves tingled with the urge to run. All she could see for miles was manzanita and yucca and wide-open spaces. She stared at two rows of black balls. They looked like cartoon bombs, with fuses sticking up. At intervals of about forty feet, they lined the dirt road.

Bombs?

Osterman liked high explosives. Was that what this was all about? Osterman? In sick horror, she stared at the black balls. Was that what high explosives looked like? Val urged her into the house.

The house smelled earthy, unused. Two men sat on folding chairs at a card table. Piles of red and blue chips indicated that they were playing poker. Melanie's flat heels clicked on the stone floor and echoed off the whitewashed walls. Except for the card table and a Spanish-style settee upholstered in blood-red velvet, the house was empty. Uncomfortable under the poker players' impassive stares, she hugged her elbows and wondered which one was Peter Osterman.

A man emerged from a doorway, wiping his hands on a paper towel. He was in his late fifties or early sixties, elegantly garbed in a three-piece suit, complete with a gold watch fob. The cut of his silver hair spoke of an expensive barber. He smiled at her as gently as anyone's kindly uncle or grandfather.

"Why, Mrs. Connalley, welcome. Please, my dear, be seated. May I call you Melanie?"

She cut her eyes at Val. He put the gun away and leaned his back against the front door. Jimmy joined the card players and ordered them to deal him in. Melanie sat on the settee.

This was Peter Osterman? She'd envisioned a corpulent gangster with piggy eyes and diamonds flashing on his pinkie fingers, not this distinguished-looking man. Clammy with sweat, she tugged at her shirt collar.

"You may call me Peter, my dear. Would you care for something to drink? It is terribly hot out there." He gazed up at the ceiling. "Lovely things, these adobes. Air-conditioning is quite unnecessary."

"Water, please." A sense of the bizarre made giggles lurch soundlessly in her throat—was she really exchanging pleasantries with a butcher? Be cool, she told herself harshly. Don't flip out. Don't!

"Jimmy, water for the lady." Peter sat beside her on the settee.

Determined to keep her mouth shut, Melanie clenched her hands on her lap. Since he called her Mrs. Connalley, and thought Detective Burns was Victor, then he knew far less than he'd like her to believe. It meant he was unaware of the police stakeout, or the fact that when Chris discovered her missing a hundred policemen would discover it, too.

If Chris discovered her missing before he boarded the plane to Phoenix.

She accepted a glass of iced mineral water from Jimmy.

Osterman rested his hands on his knees. His hands were white and soft-looking, with manicured fingernails. They reminded her of Larry's hands. She averted her gaze. He asked, "Where exactly is Detective Glenn?"

Forcing herself to meet his eyes, she said, "He sees no reason to keep me informed of every little move he makes."

"That's not what I've been told."

She took another sip. Every muscle tensed as she tried to keep from spilling water and keep her expression mild. "What is it you've been told?"

He laughed softly. "You're an intriguing woman, Melanie. It is very easy to see how Detective Glenn found himself entangled in such a mess." He cocked his head, and now his eyes were not grandfatherly in the least. "Did you kill your husband?"

A few drops of water splashed her walking shorts. "Is that how you found Chris? Because of me?"

His eyebrows twitched. "Actually, I learned a most interesting tidbit from his mother. I never knew Detective Glenn had a brother, or that he was such a shameful family secret."

She clenched the glass before it slipped through her fingers. "You hurt his mother?"

Running a hand over his lapels, he looked genuinely offended. "I merely offered her a friendly ear. Poor woman. Her sons are quite unworthy of her." He smiled distantly. "You've been causing quite a stir, though it puzzles me how such a lovely young woman could find herself in so much trouble." His gaze traveled slowly over her face and down to her bosom and then rested on her legs. "Did you kill your husband? Miss Rath believes so."

Melanie started. He'd talked to Phyllis? This was unreal. Chris claimed Osterman knew how to find and use people, but Phyllis?

Osterman chuckled. "I didn't think so. I doubt very much you could hurt anyone, despite the vehement words of that dear lady. Poor distraught woman. She was most helpful, almost too much so. Quite bitter. Very sad."

Melanie wanted to wrap her arms around herself and curl into a ball to escape his piercing perusal. "I don't know what you think you're doing, bringing me here. It won't do you any good." Muscles aching from the effort to present a relaxed demeanor, she added, "Chris left town. He should be on a plane to Phoenix right now."

Osterman started and shot a venomous glare at Val. Then he smiled. "The only place I appreciate lies, dear Melanie, is in bed." He checked his pocket watch. It was gold, inscribed with the initials PKO. He lifted a hand to Val.

Val picked up an old-fashioned rotary telephone. The other men stopped talking. Trailing the long cord, Val carried the phone to Peter and set it on the floor.

Peter handed her a card. "I will dial, and you will speak. Please read exactly what this says."

She glanced at the writing; it made no sense. She shook her head. "I'm telling you the truth! He left. He's gone. He talked to his friends and thought it was safe to go back to Phoenix." Her voice quavered, despite her effort to sound calm.

Again, Osterman gave her an offended grimace. "My dear, this is strictly a business matter. Detective Glenn has cost me a great deal of time and money. Circumstances have forced me to take an extended vacation, and I should like to make arrangements for a repayment plan before I leave."

Repayment? He meant to blow Chris up again. "If all you're interested in is the money, then we should talk."

He picked up the handset.

"I inherited over six million dollars from my husband. That's why Phyllis is so bitter. I got it and she didn't."

Peter froze with a finger in the rotary dial.

"Call Henry Vandegraf. He's the executor of the estate. He'll tell you, call him. You can have all of it. Just leave Chris alone."

"Now this is very interesting." He slowly hung up the phone, then sat back and stroked his chin. "Remarkable. Why, it does my heart good to know such loyalty exists in this harsh old world. You would actually give up six million dollars? For love?"

Sensing he was toying with her, but not knowing what else to do, she nodded.

"Does Detective Glenn return your feelings?" He touched her cheek, and it took everything she could muster to keep from bursting off the settee and running screaming around the room.

He continued, "Have you ever been to Argentina? I own a charming little villa there. We'll talk again of your six million dollars once we get there." He dialed the telephone, then handed it to her.

She held it on her lap, telling him with her eyes to go straight to hell. She heard the ring, from far away heard Victor's voice on the answering machine and then the beep. Peter looked up at Val.

Val shot out a beefy hand and caught her throat, finding the tender glands under her jaw, and squeezed. White pain exploded in her head.

"Enough," Peter said, and Val released her.

She slumped forward, clawing at her throat, twisting her head against the fiery pain. She gagged, choking down the urge to vomit.

"Now speak."

She could barely see through her tears, but she read hoarsely, "The meadow is large enough for only one fox. To learn your options, call 555-1212." Peter took the handset from her and hung up. Val returned the telephone to the table. Melanie rubbed her wounded throat and muttered, "You son of a bitch."

Peter made a delicate face. "*Tsk.* Such language from a lady." He leaned back on the settee.

"Chris will kill you."

Smiling, he opened a briefcase, brought out a well-thumbed copy of *War and Peace* and settled back to read.

CHRIS CHECKED HIS WATCH. Twenty minutes to boarding, and not a peep out of Richardson.

"Relax, Glenn," Goldfield said quietly. "He's a cool customer. He's around here, I'm certain of it. He'll follow us onto the—"

The officer disguised as an airline clerk spoke into a microphone on the service counter, "Mr. Wren? Mr. Wren? You have a message at the service counter. Mr. Wren?"

Chris's heart thumped hard against his chest. "Mr. Wren" was the emergency signal. He stared straight ahead, aware of the other cops listening and watching.

Whiteford went to the counter and said in a husky drawl, "I'm Wren." He took the telephone.

Bolting upright, so hard his hat tipped, Whiteford lost his slouch and his cool. He gestured wildly, beckoning. Books thumped against stools, luggage rustled. Real passengers looked startled as half the people in the lounge converged on the service counter.

"Damn it," Whiteford said.

Chris shouldered his way through the crowd. Whiteford's slack mouth scared him.

"We've got problems, people," the detective said. "Burns is down. Richardson snatched Melanie."

MELANIE SHIFTED on the settee. The longer she sat, the harder it felt. Osterman gave her a magazine. Its glossy pages lay open and unread on her lap.

She watched patches of sunshine creep across the floor, growing more golden but dimmer as the sun set. She wondered where Chris was now. Was Detective Burns dead, alive? Had Chris heard the message?

Leave a message for Chris? She wanted to laugh—and laugh and laugh and laugh. Creeping edges of rising hysteria made her lurch and clutch the settee. If she told Osterman that Chris never answered telephones, would he believe it? She prayed Chris didn't answer the phone.

The house grew gloomy, and Val turned on a small lamp next to Osterman. He continued to read.

Chris? she called with her mind. Don't answer the phone, don't pay any attention to that message. I didn't mean to do it, I didn't, but he hurt me. . . .

The phone rang. Val answered with a grunt, then brought the phone to Osterman. He listened, smiling, then said, "Good. Very good." Nestling the handset under his chin, he looked at his watch. "We can keep to a tight schedule now. Remember, when you pick him up, I want him alive." He hung up. He turned a smile on Melanie.

"He's smarter than you think," she said. "You aren't going to get away with this."

"This is a very private affair between Detective Glenn and myself," Osterman replied. "Jimmy?"

The pale-haired man leaped to his feet, grinning loopily. He clapped his hands once, then rubbed the palms together. "In or out, Mr. O.?"

Osterman looked around the room. "In, I do believe." He leaned closer to Melanie and said in an aside, "Do excuse Jimmy's enthusiasm. He does so love bright lights and noise. Ah, but I cannot complain about a man who loves his work.''

CHRIS SHUT DOWN the Beretta, then listened to the engine tick. He stared at the Cadillac parked under the sodium arc light in the parking lot of the Winrock shopping mall. When Whiteford had gotten the call that Burns was down, everyone had thought Richardson had snatched Melanie. But when they'd received the message from Melanie, all the players had changed.

Chris checked the Desert Eagle's load, slamming the clip home with a satisfying click. Osterman had made two deadly errors. He thought Chris was stupid and he was smart. He leaned forward and shoved the Eagle into the waistband of his jeans at the small of his back.

He glanced at the Kevlar vest on the passenger seat. If he wore it, he'd have to put on a jacket to conceal it, and a jacket would make him look like more of a threat. He had never liked the things anyway. They were too damned hot.

He glanced at the parking lot entrances, able to see the waiting police cars only because he knew they were there. A shadowy movement behind a van marked an officer with a riot gun taking position. Whiteford didn't like this, but to hell with him. Chris knew Osterman. For years he'd been studying the man, marking his habits, learning his methods.

Chris had made the first phone call from Vic's house—after Whiteford had traced the number, learned it was a public phone on the university campus and had four plain-clothes in place to pick up whoever answered. An anonymous voice had told Chris to go to a pay phone downtown and call another number. Chris had known then Osterman meant to pick him up.

Osterman was in Albuquerque because he wanted to oversee Chris's death personally. He wouldn't do it in a parking lot in the middle of town. That was definitely not Osterman's style.

He left the car and stood, his arms away from his sides. Night air bit his bare arms, raising gooseflesh. *Chris Cool, nice and easy.*

The doors opened on both sides of the Cadillac, and two men stepped out. Chris recognized the driver.

"Hey, Evander," he called. "When did they let you out of San Quentin?"

Evander narrowed his eyes and raised a .45 over the top of the car door. "Throw down your piece, Glenn."

Chris held his hands high, palms open. "Nothing. Where's Osterman?"

"Stop right there."

Thigh muscles tensed to keep his limp to a minimum, he kept walking. The Eagle dragged at his jeans.

"I said stop!"

"Hey, Evander, be cool, we're old buddies. How's the food at Quentin, anyway? Looks like they fed you pretty good." He kept walking.

Chris reached the Cadillac and plunked both hands on the hood. He cut his eyes between both men, wondering if either of them intended to get stupid.

Evander was a loser, short on brains but long on ambition. He'd been popped in Barstow, California three years ago on a hijack charge. How Osterman had managed to spring him out of prison, Chris didn't know. At the moment he didn't care. All that mattered was that Osterman wanted him alive. That gave him all the edge he needed.

The lights came on—headlights from parked cars; flashers on patrol cars; heavy-duty spots guaranteed to blind a person for twenty minutes. Like a string of firecrackers, shotguns were pumped and shells loaded with oily snaps.

Chris dropped to a squat in front of the Cadillac and pulled out his gun, flicking off the safety with his thumb. He called, "Hard or easy, Evander?"

"Screw it," Evander replied, dropping the .45. Hands high, he stepped away from the car, blinking stupidly as police officers spilled from behind and inside parked cars,

surrounding the Cadillac. To the sound of sirens screaming, the parking lot filled with marked cars.

Chris rose and casually aimed at Evander, watching until
he and the other punk were handcuffed and Mirandized.
Then he looked to Whiteford and said, "Mind?"

Whiteford shook his head, "Only a crazy man walks up
on a perp like that. Got ice water in your veins, Glenn. But
I can't argue with a crazy man. Go for it."

Police officers stepped back and looked away. Evander
rolled his eyes and began to sweat.

"Well, well," Chris said, and caught Evander's shirt-
front. He slammed the man against the Cadillac's hood,
then hooked the fleshy part of Evander's ear with the Eagle's barrel. "All these cops and not a civilian or lawyer in
sight. *Hmm . . .* That could be bad, Evander. Very bad."

Evander's breath stank of onions and rank fear.

"Got ten rounds, man," Chris said quietly. "By my calculations, I'll use all ten before anybody starts worrying
about police brutality. By then you'll be missing ten essen-
tial body parts. I suggest you tell me where Osterman is."

PETER OPENED his pocket watch, then closed his book and
slipped it inside a briefcase. "Jimmy," he said mildly, "how
are you doing? By my calculations, Detective Glenn should
be arriving within twenty minutes. Nolan, go light the
smudge pots."

Whistling, Jimmy stepped back from the table. He
clasped his hands against his chest and cocked his head,
looking like a farm wife admiring a freshly baked cherry pie.

Half a dozen pale, shiny balls sat atop the table, along
with spools of wire and a pair of walkie-talkies. Jimmy said,
"Okay now, Mr. O., do we go for depth, or do you want me
to bring the whole place in?" He formed a mound in the air.
"I kind of see a tomb thing, sort of, you know, a monu-
ment. What you think?"

Nolan, a slouch-shouldered man, picked up a small propane torch. He turned a valve, then lit it with a disposable lighter and adjusted the flame.

Melanie shot Osterman an astonished look. "What is he talking about? Peter, please, if you want money, I'll give it to you. But don't hurt Chris. Please."

Melanie watched the man named Enrico open a suitcase and bring out rolls of surgical tape and a cassette recorder.

Jimmy cradled the shiny balls, going around the room. He whistled as he flattened the balls along the walls at intervals. He ran wires to the balls, then connected all the wires to one walkie-talkie.

A bomb. That was what he was going to do to Chris. Osterman planned to turn this house into a bomb and blow him up.

Hoisting a walkie-talkie, Jimmy said, "Okay, this is your unit, Mr. O. Hit the button and bye-bye. Simple." He set the walkie-talkie next to its twin, then pulled a folding chair to the center of the room. He turned the chair this way and that, adjusting its position by millimeters. Finally he stepped back and grinned broadly. "Right here! Ground zero. Perfect." He placed the wired walkie-talkie on the chair seat.

Jimmy said, "But I need more, Mr. O. Got enough wire to do the outside, too. This is gonna be great, my best ever." Flashing a wide smile at Melanie, he ambled to the door. He paused. "Hey, when is the balloon festival? Did I miss it already for this year?"

All Melanie could do was stare at him.

Osterman said, "Jimmy, work first, play later." After Jimmy shrugged and left the house, Osterman clucked his tongue. "He's quite brilliant, actually, but he does have his quirks."

Val turned away from a window and frowned at Peter. "Sir? Nolan isn't lighting the pots."

"Do you see him?"

Val shook his head, then looked out the window again. "I don't see Jimmy, either. That goof must've found a rabbit or something." Val went to the door and opened it. He called, "Nolan? Jimmy, what the hell are—"

Orange light filled the windows. An explosive roar slapped Melanie's head, and her eardrums felt as if they had burst. Glass shattered. The blast threw Melanie against Osterman, and both of them hit the floor.

She heard a wet snap, like green wood breaking. She gasped, trying to breathe, but the air was gone, vanished, replaced by heat. She choked, struggling for breath and a strangled croak emerged from her throat. Crackling, like television snow, filled her head. Something clattered overhead, like hail hitting the roof. Roaring and thunderous booming made the floor vibrate.

Osterman roughly shoved her aside. Pain flared through her shoulder and chest and her cheek cracked against stone. Flashes of sickening color made a light show in her head. Whimpering, she tried to rise, attempting to escape the heat and the nauseating stink of burning paint. Her left arm hung useless, throbbing.

Orange light dimmed and turned yellow and flickering, casting crazy shadows inside the house. The sweet metallic smell of burning gasoline made the air hot and vile.

On hands and knees, with blood trickling from his ears, Val crawled blindly on the floor. Tears streamed from his eyes. His face was blackened and twisted in a grimace. The lamp had tipped over, and it shone like a spotlight through the top of the stiff pleated shade. Val crawled in and out of the light like a demented clown seeking his props.

"That idiot blew himself up," Enrico said. He shot Osterman a startled look, then pulled and jerked at the cracked, askew door until he got it open wide enough to slip through.

Through a fog of pain, Melanie heard, "My dear? Are you hurt? Yes, I can see that you are." Osterman eased her back against the settee and touched her face gently. "Val? Val, can you hear me?"

The big man grunted and found his gun. He scooted back to the door.

"Can you hear me?" Osterman demanded.

"What? I can't hear you, sir."

Melanie focused on the telephone. She glanced at a doorway leading to a bathroom—the phone cord was long enough to reach. Eyes locked on the men, she scooted on her buttocks toward the phone. Pain weighted her chest, and every breath burned. She bit her inner cheek to stop her cries, and tasted blood. The explosion had broken the door and cracked the walls. Melanie suspected it had also broken her arm.

Osterman turned his head, and Melanie froze. "Melanie," he said patiently, "both cars are burning. There is enough light to draw the curious from Santa Fe. I am not in a mood to tolerate any foolishness. Sit perfectly still." He turned back to Val and said loudly, "Get out there and help Enrico!"

Val swayed, studying Osterman's lips intently. He hitched his shoulders, then eased through the opening and went outside.

Osterman paced and kept glancing out the window.

Melanie focused again on the phone. Her left arm hung, numb, tingling with an unpleasant sensation of being encased in cement. Icy sweat slicked her face. She clutched the telephone in her right hand; it felt as though it weighed a hundred pounds. Dull panic shook her. She had no strength.

Osterman said, "Melanie, please." He moved the telephone out of her reach.

"I'm going to vomit," she whispered. She stared at her throbbing left arm and wondered if it made any difference if she got sick or not. She couldn't feel worse. She tried to lift her wounded arm. Knives cut through the muscle, and she gasped and bit her lower lip.

Osterman looked out the window, then back at her. "Something appears quite amiss. I sent men out and they haven't returned. Do you think I underestimated Detective

Glenn's resiliency?'' His tone was mild, but strained. He pulled out a gun.

A heavy thud made the front door vibrate. Wood cracked with a sharp report, and the top hinge ripped loose with a screech.

Osterman dropped to a crouch and swung his gun at the door.

Val burst into the room.

The big man seemed to fly—a swan dive in a graceful arc, head down, legs together, arms tucked at his sides. He hit the floor in a slide, and Melanie blinked, dully puzzled by the way his head folded under his body.

Peter jerked her upright. The Fourth of July exploded in her brain, and then the world grayed, turned fuzzy. Something cold and hard pressed her throat. *Don't hurt me,* she tried to tell Peter. She couldn't take any more pain. She'd faint.

A man, outlined in fire, filled the doorway. In a deadly calm voice tinged by the soft slurring of a southern accent, he said, ''Cookie.''

Chapter Fifteen

Events happened too fast for Melanie's shock-numbed mind. One second Osterman held her, his gun at her throat. After that, the room was a blur of fiery orange light and flying feet and thumps and cries of pain. Then she found herself sitting on the floor, legs splayed and head reeling, while a man loomed over Osterman, clutching Osterman's tie and cramming a gun barrel into his mouth.

Befuddled, she stared at the two men. Her mind groaned. She tried to convince herself that this was a strange dream and if she closed her eyes it would all disappear. But when she looked away, her gaze fell on Val. Bile rose in her throat, mingling with blood. No, she protested silently, I'm not in a house with a dead man.

The roar of flames receded to a dull background crackle. Melanie heard a pitiful sound and realized it was Osterman. His eyes were very round, pleading.

She looked, transfixed, at the other man, and again her mind rebelled. *No, he's too shy, a mumbler, a bumbler, that can't be...*

"Roddy?" she mouthed, clumsily regaining her feet. It *was* him. He even wore one of his nice jackets, although it was streaked and smudged. The lamp spotlit Roddy's hand... and the gun. She saw his finger twitch. "Roddy!" she yelled.

His shoulders jerked. He was going to murder Osterman before her eyes, and he'd lie limp and motionless like Val, with his blood pooling on the floor.

She searched frantically for what Whiteford had said. Addicted—killing was a habit. *Awe.* That was the word, that was what Roddy felt for her, awe.

Roddy stood frozen, as if undecided, with his shoulders rounded and his head pulled into his neck. Self-doubt filled Melanie. Awe, awesome, awe-inspiring—words to describe another, not her, never her.

Then she remembered the letters to Doug, the ones she had written when she took a course in medieval history. The letters Roddy had stolen and believed she'd written to him. *Dear Sir Rodney, my beloved white knight from your beloved Maid Cookie...* The name Sir Rodney had been a whimsical form of address for Doug. Was that how Roddy had come by his current alias?

With all the strength she could muster, with all the command she could force into her voice, she said, "Sir Rodney! Stop it! Put it down!"

Roddy looked over his shoulder. Black hummingbird eyes darted, sliding past her. His mouth set in an anguished line.

Maybe she remembered wrong. Oh, God, wasn't it Sir Rodney? What was it—?

"He hurt you," Roddy said, as if that explained everything.

"My beloved Sir Rodney isn't a murderer. Let him go!"

"He'll hurt you. I can't let him go." His words lifted at the end on a hesitant note.

Melanie swallowed the thickness in her throat. The idea of sitting back down tantalized her. She wanted to rest, to close her eyes, ears and mind. She hurt so much. Sensibility cried out indignantly that Peter Osterman was a murderer, he had tried to kill Chris, he'd tried to kill her. She stared into Osterman's terrified eyes, saw his lips pulled back, recoiling from the gun barrel. *Close your eyes and let him die.*

''No! Stop it, stop it now. If you kill him, I'll never forgive you. Ever.''

''You love me.'' He sounded as petulant as a little boy.

Love him? He was Charles Lewis, Charleton Richardson, the author of the Cookie letters, a murderer... She forced a step, forced her right arm up, and turned her hand in a gesture of command. *One of these days you'll try that on a truly vicious animal and earn yourself some nasty bites... low dog in the pack... bad, bad dog!*

She squinted until Roddy came into focus. Crackling white noise filled her ears. ''I don't like blood. It... it offends me.''

Roddy flinched.

''If you don't turn him loose, I'll go away, far away, and I'll find somebody who doesn't offend me. Do you hear me? I'll find another protector. A true knight. Somebody who cares about me!''

A buzzing drone grew loud. She shook her head, but the noise grew louder and she realized it was the roar of an engine. She caught the way Osterman's eyes darted at the doorway. An airplane. Those black balls made sense now. Smudge pots. Lights to guide the airplane. Could she let him escape? Dull panic clawed at her chest.

Roddy cringed like a dog brought up short on a choke chain. For a moment his darting eyes stilled. Melanie stared deep into those dark eyes, and her belly turned to ice. Dead eyes, soulless eyes. Eyes that saw everything and felt nothing.

The plane's buzzing grew louder, closer, flying over the house and drowning out the sound of the flames. Then, fainter, came the sound of sirens.

Roddy's eyes narrowed. He pulled back the gun, then jerked Osterman, who snapped to his feet as if yanked by a rope. Melanie watched, disbelieving. Roddy wasn't that big, he wasn't that strong—yet he had broken Tim Service's neck, tied up Larry and tortured him.... He slammed Osterman against the wall so hard the man clung to it for a second before slowly sliding downward.

"I don't mean to offend you." He ducked his head and rounded his shoulders, inching toward Melanie. His lips pulled back in an ingratiating grin. "You long for a strong arm, for a shield against the wicked world. I am your arm, your shield. I've always been there for you."

Not knowing what else to do, she nodded. "You read my letters?"

He took a step away. "I saved them all, memorized them. Poetry." He sighed. "Songs in my heart."

On hands and knees, Osterman crawled toward the gaping door. Melanie had to stop him, to warn Roddy—but Roddy would kill him, and Osterman's blood would stain her hands forever. Frozen by indecision, she met Osterman's eyes.

Sirens grew louder. She didn't know if the plane landed or flew away. Peter Osterman slipped out the door.

Roddy said, "He's a worm. He won't be back, the coward." He frowned and huffed a soft sigh. His head bobbed, and his free hand waggled aimlessly. The hand holding the gun was rock-steady. "You don't have to suffer cowards. That man, he is a knave, isn't he? At first I thought he had good intentions." His face metamorphosed into a dark and furious mask. "I trusted him!"

She inched a step backward. "Who? I don't know what you're talking about."

"*Him!* I trusted him, and he abused my trust. He tried to seduce you, didn't he?" He panted, as if the very thought pained him. "I can't believe I cheered him. I laughed when he tossed that oaf out of your store. But then he let him burn it down!" He snapped up his head and shook the gun at her. "I told you to get rid of him!"

He meant Chris. She licked her lips. "I did. I sent him away, exactly like you said, and now look at this mess. It's your fault. Look what you've done."

"I do everything for you."

The sirens were screams now, overpowering the crackle of flames, coming closer. Desperately she said, "Did you really do all this for me, Roddy? Because you love me?"

He nodded. "I won't let anyone hurt you. Ever." He tugged at his ear and shuffled his feet. "That's why I have to take you away. It wasn't supposed to be this way. Our love is different, it's...pure. Maid Marian and Robin Hood, Ivanhoe and Rowena."

His shuffling drew him closer, and she recoiled. "I want you to take me home now. I'm hurt and I'm tired. I want to go home."

He raised the gun; she froze. "You are going home. Our home. I can't protect you out there. It's for your own good. You're delicate, like the white flowers. You're hurt?"

She nodded. "I think my arm is broken. Please, if you love me, let me go home."

He frowned, as if he were considering it. "You threw away my flowers. You shouldn't have thrown them away. I got them especially for you."

"I'm sorry. I didn't know you sent them."

"Yes, you did. I made that bastard confess to hurting you, and then you threw my flowers away! You treated them like garbage!"

He strode forward and grasped her arm in a grip of steel. Too shocked to protest, she stumbled bonelessly into the bathroom.

"Forgive me," he said, and then turned on the water in the sink. It emerged in a chunky spray, knocking in the pipes, rusty. Melanie cut her eyes right and left, seeking escape, but Roddy stood between her and the door, and the bathroom had no window. A sickening refrain echoed in her mind. *He killed Annie and Service and Larry, and who knows who else, and now he'll kill me.*

He ordered her to sit; she sat on the commode. He dabbed water on her face. At each touch, he flinched and apologized.

"Helicopters. Police cars. They're coming," he said, sounding regretful. "They don't understand. They can't understand you and me. We belong together. Remember what you said? 'We are creatures of a higher order.' That's true."

"Listen to me," she whispered. "You listen to me now. If you love me, truly love me, you have to prove it now. You have to—" A choppy *wup-wup-wup* caught her attention. Blue and red lights strobed through the narrow opening of the bathroom door. "You have to give yourself up."

He slipped out the door. Melanie leaped to her feet, but he was back, pushing her back down on the toilet. He caught her shoulder, and the throbbing pain turned to fire. She screamed.

Clapping a hand to his mouth, Roddy stumbled backward. Like a chameleon, he changed and was once again the stumble-tongued bumbler, unable to meet her eyes.

Blinking back tears, she cried, "You hurt me! What kind of protection is that, huh?"

"I'm sorry...sorry, forgive...I'm sorry." He waved a hand downward. "I'm sorry."

She panted, blinking away sweat, licking her lips and tasting rank salt. Her arm throbbed and burned. She gazed at the discolored flesh puffing around the hem of her T-shirt sleeve and felt sick.

"I'll fix it, okay? I can fix it, I can fix anything." He stared at the gun, then slowly turned the barrel so that it pointed at his face.

"They won't let us go. They won't let me protect you. The world is full of bad people. Everywhere! That nasty girl, speaking ill of you, telling lies about you. She said you had a lover. What kind of pervert would tell lies like that about you? And that bastard burning our store! It was going to be a wonderful store. We were going to put birds in it. I like birds, lots of birds. It would have been perfect for us, but he burned it down."

The beaten-dog look rounded his shoulders and he sighed and sighed again, staring intently into the barrel of the gun.

"Roddy, don't," she whispered. "Please, let them help you. Don't."

"Then he hit you. I almost killed him right there. But that was too good for him. He had to suffer, the way he made you suffer." He lowered the gun. "I don't want to lose you, Cookie." He looked at the ceiling, and his Adam's apple bobbed convulsively. "It took so long to find you again. I can't live without you. They'll take you away from me. They don't understand. They're bad!"

"I'll help you," she whispered.

His face changed again. The pain was gone, and his eyes darted, flicking left to right, alive in movement but dead in their depths. Noises outside seemed to pulsate through the thick adobe walls—a cacophony of sirens, shouting men, and the thunderous *wup-wup* of a helicopter. "I don't believe in death," he said simply.

He fitted a red rubber stopper in the drain hole of the claw-footed bathtub. "Some things possess true immortality. You taught me that. Souls, love. Love like ours." He turned on the faucet knob and held his hand under the brownish, spurting water. "No hot water," he said in a musing tone, then shrugged.

Fixated by the running water, she said, "What are you doing?"

He looked at the gun, turning it this way and that. He held the barrel to his ear. "I can't shoot you." He smiled. "I'll never cause you pain. I'm *not* one of the bad guys."

He swung the gun on her. "But you are not very grateful sometimes. That upsets me. Cavorting with that—that bastard! I saw you laughing at me that day in the restaurant. You shouldn't laugh at people who do you favors, Cookie. That's bad. It's unseemly for a lady of your high station."

"So you smashed my car? Trashed my house? Is that how you show me you love me?" She felt more than heard the booming bullhorns and sirens outside the house.

"I could've done worse." His eyes widened. "Don't be afraid. We'll be together forever, our souls one, joined." He glanced at the tub. "Drowning isn't painful."

Something sly and knowing filled his face, curled his mouth, reminding Melanie of a little boy with a nasty secret. Blood pounded in her ears.

"I drowned once," he said. "In the sea. The light called me. But those bastards forced me back."

She stared at the slowly filling tub. Drowning? Her mouth filled with fear, and she choked on it, envisioning water smothering her.

"It's fate, Cookie. You can't deny fate."

CHRIS JUMPED out of the helicopter. Head down, he ran past the blades. County fire engines were parked a hundred yards beyond the house. Firemen, warned of possible gunmen, milled on the safe sides of the big pumpers, watching the hulks of two cars burning. One car had its rear end blown away. Paramedics stood around a corpse, or rather what was left of one. Two others bodies lay under sheets some distance away.

Threatening Evander had proved unnecessary. The idiot had had a map in the Cadillac, with the route to this house marked in thick black pencil. Then, before the helicopter had arrived at the mall, word had come in that a trucker had reported a huge fire on Placitas Ridge.

"Mother Mary, look at this mess," Whiteford said behind Chris. "The trucker reported a fire, not World War III." He spoke into his radio, ordering the helicopter back up to pursue the airplane they'd seen circling the house.

Chris stared at the house. Shattered windows, an askew door, black streaks and uprooted yuccas spoke of the explosion's power. Had Osterman's expert set off an accidental explosion? He half listened to Whiteford's superior officer confer with the county sheriff about a ground search for Osterman and paid a lot more attention to the paramedics, who were searching for body parts, knowing that if they reported finding anything female...

The plane probably belonged to Osterman. Judging by the smudge pots lining the road, he meant to use the road as a runway. Chris watched state troopers and more sheriffs' vehicles arriving.

"You're the expert, Glenn," Whiteford said, and peeked under a sheet. He shone a flashlight over the dead man's face. "What have we got here?"

"Don't know." He looked at both corpses. He recognized Maurice Nolan and Rico Enrico, hoods he'd long suspected of being Osterman's henchmen.

Why was the damned house so quiet?

"They didn't die in the explosion," he told Whiteford.

"Brilliant, detective. So who killed them, and why?" He exhaled deeply. "This was a nice quiet town before you showed up."

"I'm going in for a look-see."

"Like hell you are."

"Osterman isn't in there." Sweating under the Kevlar vest that he had put on in the chopper, he cut to the left, seeking a window on the dark side of the house.

Whiteford caught his arm. "Can the iceman act, Glenn! This ain't your territory. Back off."

Chris twisted away.

"I understand your concern, but if you go charging in there, you'll get yourself killed."

"Quick lesson in Osterman psychology, man. Rule number one, he doesn't get his hands dirty. He's not in that house, but Melanie probably is. I'm taking a look."

Alert for any movement from the house, he zigzagged through the sagebrush and manzanita. He kept to the shadows past the circle of fire and emergency lights.

"Damn you, Glenn!" Whiteford muttered, following. Gravel clattered, and he panted heavily. "I'm too old for this crap."

Chris crouched behind a bush, staring at the door, willing himself to see beyond it. He pointed at a window. "Cover me." He took a step, then looked back. "You got a radio?"

Whiteford worked a radio off his belt and spoke into it, warning his men not to shoot him or Chris.

Hunched over, Chris ran to the side of the house and flattened himself against the wall. The rough adobe caught at his vest and hair. A voice bellowed through a bullhorn for Osterman to throw down his weapons and come out with his hands up. Chris rolled against the wall until he could see through the window. Emergency lights and firelight through the open door and windows made the interior look like a discotheque. A body lay on the floor.

Staying low, weapon at the ready, Whiteford scuttled to the house and took up position on the other side of the window.

"A body. Male," Chris whispered. "No sign of Melanie."

He looked again. He said, "There's a door, partially open. Light behind it, and I can see shadows. I think there's someone moving in there."

"Maybe she's tied up, can't get out," Whiteford whispered.

Chris inched his head higher. A lamp had fallen over, half its light illuminating a table. Chris stared at the items on the table, unsure of what he was seeing. Then he shifted his perusal to a chair sitting in the middle of the room. Slowly, as he grew used to the flickering light and shifting shadows, he followed lines. Those were wires, and they led to a walkie-talkie on the chair, and the wires traced back to...

He slammed his back against the wall and dropped to a crouch. Sweat burst out on his forehead, and he clutched his gun with both hands.

"Glenn?"

Paralysis gripped him, and images filled his head, crowding out reality. Billy Scopes's confused face... heat, the stink of burning metal . . . Billy Scopes and running and yelling . . .

"Jesus," he whispered. "The whole damned house is wired. It's a bomb."

RODDY CROUCHED by the tub and swirled his hand in the rising water. "I'm sorry it's cold," he said.

"I am not drowning!" Melanie screamed and lurched against the toilet tank, jerked both feet off the floor and pistoned them straight out.

She slammed both feet into the small of Roddy's back. His thighs caught on the high tub rim, his arms pinwheeled, and he shot forward. His head cracked against the tiles. Blood splattered, and he fell face first into the water. A comma mark of red marred the tile.

Gasping, blinded by tears and terror, Melanie scrambled to the door. Water splashed her legs and back.

"Cookie!" Roddy screamed.

She ran, her hard-soled sandals slipping on the floor. She hit the table, and it toppled, spilling the walkie-talkie and the wire spools. She tripped, and her chin cracked against the floor, but the flashes of bright light and shards of pain piercing her face spurred her. She churned her legs, unable to make her arms work, unable to find her footing. Too charged to feel pain, she huffed and grunted, trying to reach her feet.

"Cookie!"

Roddy grabbed her ankle, and she screeched, kicking at him.

"Let her go!" Chris yelled.

Chris crouched in the doorway, holding his gun in both hands. Melanie flung out her hand, straining for him, reaching for him. Another set of arms shot through the doorway, and firelight sparked off the blue steel barrel of a revolver.

"Let her go!" Chris shouted, and his eyes glittered like silver in the shifting light.

Melanie lunged at Chris, jerking her foot. "Chris," she breathed. "Oh, Chris..."

Roddy snarled, getting slowly to his feet. He raised his hands. He held a walkie-talkie.

Chris straightened, raising the gun level with Roddy's chest. "Melanie, honey, can you get up?"

Shaking, she struggled to her knees. Her broken arm had surpassed pain. With grunts of effort, she made it to her feet.

"Get out of the way, Melanie."

She stared at Chris's face. Sweat poured off his brow, and his eyes were wide and blank. He trembled.

She looked back. Roddy had his hands in the air, but he held the walkie-talkie. Melanie stared at the overturned table, following wires with her disbelieving gaze. The other walkie-talkie was connected to wires—wires connected to shiny blobs of plastic explosive.

Roddy said, "I won't let them take you away from me, Cookie. We belong together. Forever."

"You twitch and I blow your goddamned head off," Chris whispered huskily. The tremble turned into a shake. His nostrils flared. "Melanie, honey, come to me, slowly, get out of the way."

Melanie looked from man to man. Chris looked paralyzed; Roddy had his thumb on the button.

Hit the button and bye-bye.

"Sir Rodney," she said softly, "is this what you meant by forever? Blown to bits? Bloody? Offensive? Is this what you mean by true love? Hurt me, frighten me, and now you want to blow me up? Some knight in shining armor you turned out to be."

"Come here," Chris whispered.

Melanie shook her head. "No, you go, Chris. Out the door. He won't hurt me. Will you, Sir Rodney? You're my protector."

"I love you," he moaned.

"I'll help you," she said. She heard her weakness and knew she couldn't remain upright much longer.

Roddy's face changed again, becoming a mask of despair. "I did it for you," he whispered. "I did everything for you." He dived and hit the bathroom door with a crash.

Stunned by how quickly he moved, Melanie stared.

"Oh, damn it to hell," Chris muttered. He snatched her around the waist and ran.

Melanie screeched.

Deaf to her agony, Chris raced out the door. His feet pounded the dirt, flinging gravel. The damned trucks looked a million miles away.

Arms pumping, Whiteford ran like an Olympic track star. "Get down!" Whiteford yelled. "It's going to blow!"

Chris tightened his grip on Melanie's limp body. He dived into a shallow ditch. All around him men hit the dirt.

Melanie screeched again, and he rolled atop her, shouting, "It's going to blow!"

She groaned, then choked. He stroked her face. She was dripping with icy sweat. She squeaked, "Chris...arm."

"It's okay, baby, help's here, *shh,* I love you." He covered her with his body, his exposed back itching. Seconds ticked past.

Nearby, Whiteford lifted his head and peered at the house. "What happened?"

Chris lifted his head. Realization hit him, and he laughed. It sounded dry and strained. His worst nightmare had been only that, a nightmare. "No juice, man." He laughed again. "The walkie-talkies must not have been turned on. No power. Oh, Jesus."

Whiteford muttered an obscenity. "You mean we have to talk that nut out of—"

The house blew up.

CHRIS LIT THE CANDLES. He studied the effect of the white tapers and the bright flowers. Red roses, purple hyacinths, orange lilies, pink asters—colors for Melanie. Had a woman ever lived who loved color as much as Melanie?

The telephone rang, and he answered.

"How are you doing, Lucky?"

Chris pulled a face. "What do you want, Whiteford?"

"I've got a lady reporter cooling her heels down the hall. Get this, she wants to write a book about that mess out on Placitas Ridge. She says it'll be a best-seller."

Chris laughed. "Civilians. So tell her the story."

Whiteford grunted irritably. Chris doubted if the man would ever fully forgive him for almost getting him blown up.

"Believe it or not, she wants to talk to you and Melanie," Whiteford said. "She says you're the real story. Can I give her your number?"

Chris heard the rumbling of the garage door. "Later," he said. "Much later. I have things to do." Chris smiled as Melanie and Victor walked into the house. "Gotta go." He hung up.

She gave him a funny smile, one he'd never seen before. It was a little strained, a little...embarrassed? She looked at the colorful table, and the line between her eyebrows deepened.

Chris jutted his chin at the cast on her left arm. "What did the doc say?"

"I'll live." She stroked the cast. It was bright with flowers, geometric designs and ridiculous animals. Chris and she had spent a giggly evening covering the white plaster with designs in acrylic paint. A bright red scarf served as a sling and matched her tropical print camp shirt. "It smells good. Uh, give me a minute. I'll be right out."

She brushed his cheek with an absent kiss, then walked past him into the bedroom and closed the door. He turned his puzzlement to Victor. Melanie had been in a chipper mood when Victor drove her to the hospital so that they could make their respective checkups.

Chris whispered, "What happened at the hospital?"

Victor shrugged. "She's been in this mood since we left the doctor. I asked, but she doesn't wish to talk about it."

"Her arm's going to be all right, isn't it?" Actually, Chris worried more about her mental health. He had spent many nights in the past few weeks sitting up in bed and rocking her, soothing away her nightmares.

Victor said, "As far as I know, the doctor gave her a clean bill of health." He turned a smile to the steaming pots on the stove. "She'll tell you, I'm certain. I'll leave the pair of you alone. I sense an air of something special cooking—"

Chris patted a stool. "Cop a squat for a minute, Vic. I called Mom this afternoon. She's ticked at both of us."

Victor sat. "Oh, dear."

"Oh, dear is right, Bro. After she finished crying, she chewed me out royally." He clamped a hand over Vic's bony wrist and squeezed. "I told her as soon as I get back to Phoenix I'll come see her. And you'll be with me."

Victor started, his dark blue eyes wide and wary. Chris had the disjointed feeling of being the older brother, the brother in charge. Vic said, "Father..."

"Come on, Vic, he turns eighty next month. Do we let him go to his grave insisting he only has one son? Hiding out is stupid. Come with me. Do it for Mom. The worst Dad can do is disown both of us." He grinned and hung his head. "You're my brother, Vic... and I love you and I'm proud of you. And if Dad can't accept it, that's his problem."

"Why, Chris, that's the nicest thing you've ever said to me."

Melanie paused in the doorway. She flicked her gaze between the brothers and puzzled over Victor's shiny eyes. From down the hall she heard Heloise's irritable squawk. No doubt Abelard was looking too closely at the newly hatched chick again. She started down the hall, then stopped. The birds didn't need her; she needed to talk to Chris.

"The table looks beautiful, Chris." It was set for two, with her good china and crystal, and pink napkins fan-folded on the plates. "Victor, are you joining us?" In cowardly desperation, she hoped so. She and Chris had been through so much, and now another problem?

He rose from the stool. "I'm afraid not. I promised Ernesto my undivided attention this afternoon. He's swamped in invoices and tax forms. The poor man will certainly earn his Christmas bonus this year." He patted Chris's shoulder. "I'll see myself out."

"Think about what I said, Vic," Chris said.

"I will." He nodded graciously and left.

Chris swung around on the bar stool and held out a hand. "Everything okay, honey? You didn't run into Phyllis again, did you?"

She winced. With the case closed on Larry's murder, Phyllis Rath had turned her energy to winning some of Larry's estate. She claimed Larry had meant to name her as his heir in light of their engagement. Melanie preferred to leave the woman to her delusions and all the problems to Henry Vandegraf.

She forced a smile. "What are you cooking? It smells wonderful." She took his hand.

"Beef Stroganoff. Let's hope it tastes okay." He drew her close and wrapped his arm about her waist. "Melanie, what's wrong?"

"Uh, Chris..." she began, appalled by her cowardice. After everything that had happened, it surprised her that anything could scare her. She noticed a brown-paper-wrapped package on the counter. "What's that?"

He looked, then shrugged. "For you. It came in the mail."

Thankful for the distraction, she stepped away from Chris's arm and pulled the package near. She flashed him a smile. "I feel fine. The doctor said the cast can come off in two weeks. No infection." She lifted her chin. "He said plastic surgery will get rid of the scar. Do you think it's that bad?"

"I can barely see it. Want some help?"

"This one-handed stuff is driving me crazy." She watched him unwrap the package and wondered how to tell him what she'd learned today. Wondered how he'd take it.

For the past few weeks he'd been so solicitous, so gentle. He took care of her, drove her where she needed to go, helped her dress and did the cooking and housecleaning. Making love with him was awful, funny and wonderful. He was so afraid of hurting her, and she invariably hit him at least once a night with the cast. They usually ended up more giggly than passionate, and he was so wonderfully patient with her. Now this?

"What were you and Victor looking so serious about?"

Chris lifted the top off a white cardboard box and revealed white foam peanuts. He said, "I have to go back to Phoenix. I think Vic ought to go with me. He needs—*we* need—to see my parents."

The casual words held the power of a blow to the solar plexus. Back to Phoenix? She jerked a wide-eyed gaze to the beautiful table. This couldn't be goodbye.

"I've used up my convalescent leave, and all my vacation time." He let out a long breath, then caught her right hand in both of his. "I need to take care of some details. I'm resigning from the force, Melanie."

It took a moment for that to sink in. She blinked slowly. "You're quitting the police force?"

He nodded, grinning. His blue eyes glowed. "Hey, I'm not going to leech off you, honey. I've got enough in savings so I can finish up my degree. I ought to be able to find something to do in Albuquerque. Maybe something with Vic. I'm pretty good with my hands, and if nothing else, I've got a strong back. Or maybe help you out with your new store. That is, if you don't mind me hanging around?"

She sagged with relief, then, without thinking, blurted, "I'm pregnant, Chris."

His grin faded, and his eyebrows drew into a deep V. He tightened his fingers.

"Oh, God, I'm sorry. I didn't know, I mean, I thought I couldn't... I wasn't using any birth control, I never have... Oh, Chris, I didn't know I could have a baby."

Amusement and surprise flickered across his face, and then he loosed a wry laugh. He lifted her hand to his mouth and gave it a quick kiss, then went to the table and lifted the artfully folded napkin off her plate. She gaped at him, unable to judge if he was happy, or upset, or what.

"This is one time you can't accuse me of crappy timing," he said. "In fact, I couldn't have planned this better."

A small velvet-covered box sat on her plate.

Quietly he said, "Will you marry me, Melanie?" He nestled the box in both hands, presenting it to her. "We can make it a real short engagement." He opened the box and revealed a perfect solitaire diamond, flashing fire under the skylight.

She looked at it helplessly, knowing she'd never get the ring onto her swollen left hand. "You aren't upset?"

"Surprised." He lifted his shoulders. "Maybe embarrassed. I'm kind of old for whoopsies." He touched a knuckle to her cheek. "I love you, honey. I'm not upset about a baby. Not at all, not as long as you're okay." His grin turned lopsided and supremely pleased. "Hey, we're going to make a beautiful kid—as long as it looks like you."

To her dismay, she began to cry. Making soothing noises, Chris gathered her into his arms and pressed soft kisses to her hair. He asked, "You aren't unhappy, are you?"

She shook her head against his chest.

"Then you'll marry me?"

She nodded.

He gently eased her back. Through tear blurs, she watched him lift her right hand and slip the diamond ring on her ring finger. The diamond winked at her; so did Chris. "That'll do until the cast comes off."

Then he cupped her face in both hands and kissed her on the lips, long and deep and slow, the way he did it best. He used his thumbs to ease away her tears.

"I love you, Chris," she whispered.

"Yeah, and you better quit looking at me like that, or dinner is going to burn." He urged her to sit on a bar stool. "Are you feeling okay?"

The anxious note in his voice touched her, and she smiled. "I'm fine—now." She held her hand to the light and admired the ring. The future looked glorious, bright and shiny, irresistible.

Grinning at her, Chris fished around in the box and brought out a long, slim, velvet-covered box . . . and an envelope. Melanie frowned at it. "Who's that from?"

He checked the brown wrapping, then pulled a face.

Her belly chilled and rolled with a thud. "Oh, God, not another secret admirer . . ."

Chris opened the box, revealing a gold necklace. The pendant was a golden fox, with a ruby for an eye. Color drained from Chris's face, and he slowly placed the box on the counter. Chris and Melanie recoiled.

Peter Osterman—now a fugitive, hiding out in Argentina. Guilty remorse rocketed through Melanie, leaving her shaking. She'd let Osterman get away; she had allowed his escape. Was the nightmare beginning again?

Chris opened the envelope. It contained a card with a laughing fox wearing a deerstalker cap and holding an oversize pipe. The caption read, "I've deduced . . ."

Throat working, Chris opened the card. Inside, it read, "You'll get well soon!" Then, below it, in flowing script, was a note:

My dear Melanie, I regret you and I did not meet under kinder circumstances. You are a genuinely lovely lady. I hope you can find it in your heart to forgive me. Please, let it never be said I am a man who ever forgets a debt. In your honor, I have forgiven Detective

Glenn's debt to me. I hope he is man enough to appreciate what you've done. Affectionately, Peter.

Melanie breathed outward in a sound that was halfway between a laugh and a sigh.

"Jesus," Chris said, blinking. Then he laughed and perched the card on the countertop so that the fox stared owlishly back at them.

"Is that for real, Chris?"

"I never heard of Osterman going back on his word." He laughed again.

In his throaty laughter, Melanie heard freedom. Freedom from fear, freedom from the past, freedom to begin a new life. The cage door stood open, and she could finally fly.

Fifty red-blooded, white-hot, true-blue hunks from every State in the Union!

Beginning in May, look for MEN: MADE IN AMERICA! Written by some of our most popular authors, these stories feature fifty of the strongest, sexiest men, each from a different state in the union! Favorite stories by such bestsellers as Debbie Macomber, Jayne Ann Krentz, Mary Lynn Baxter, Barbara Delinsky and many, many more!

Plus, you can receive a FREE gift, just for enjoying these special stories!

You won't be able to resist MEN: MADE IN AMERICA!

Two titles available every other month at your favorite retail outlet.

OFFICIAL RULES • MILLION DOLLAR BIG BUCKS SWEEPSTAKES
NO PURCHASE OR OBLIGATION NECESSARY TO ENTER

To enter, follow the directions published. **ALTERNATE MEANS OF ENTRY:** Hand print your name and address on a 3″ ×5″ card and mail to either: Harlequin "Big Bucks," 3010 Walden Ave., P.O. Box 1867, Buffalo, NY 14269-1867, or Harlequin "Big Bucks," P.O. Box 609, Fort Erie, Ontario L2A 5X3, and we will assign your Sweepstakes numbers. (Limit: one entry per envelope.) For eligibility, entries must be received no later than March 31, 1994. No responsibility is assumed for lost, late or misdirected entries.

Upon receipt of entry, Sweepstakes numbers will be assigned. To determine winners, Sweepstakes numbers will be compared against a list of randomly preselected prizewinning numbers. In the event all prizes are not claimed via the return of prizewinning numbers, random drawings will be held from among all other entries received to award unclaimed prizes.

Prizewinners will be determined no later than May 30, 1994. Selection of winning numbers and random drawings are under the supervision of D.L. Blair, Inc., an independent judging organization, whose decisions are final. One prize to a family or organization. No substitution will be made for any prize, except as offered. Taxes and duties on all prizes are the sole responsibility of winners. Winners will be notified by mail. Chances of winning are determined by the number of entries distributed and received.

Sweepstakes open to persons 18 years of age or older, except employees and immediate family members of Torstar Corporation, D.L. Blair, Inc., their affiliates, subsidiaries and all other agencies, entities and persons connected with the use, marketing or conduct of this Sweepstakes. All applicable laws and regulations apply. Sweepstakes offer void wherever prohibited by law. Any litigation within the province of Quebec respecting the conduct and awarding of a prize in this Sweepstakes must be submitted to the Régies des Loteries et Courses du Quebec. In order to win a prize, residents of Canada will be required to correctly answer a time-limited arithmetical skill-testing question. Values of all prizes are in U.S. currency.

Winners of major prizes will be obligated to sign and return an affidavit of eligibility and release of liability within 30 days of notification. In the event of non-compliance within this time period, prize may be awarded to an alternate winner. Any prize or prize notification returned as undeliverable will result in the awarding of that prize to an alternate winner. By acceptance of their prize, winners consent to use of their names, photographs or other likenesses for purposes of advertising, trade and promotion on behalf of Torstar Corporation without further compensation, unless prohibited by law.

This Sweepstakes is presented by Torstar Corporation, its subsidiaries and affiliates in conjunction with book, merchandise and/or product offerings. Prizes are as follows: Grand Prize—$1,000,000 (payable at $33,333.33 a year for 30 years). First through Sixth Prizes may be presented in different creative executions, each with the following approximate values: First Prize—$35,000; Second Prize—$10,000; 2 Third Prizes—$5,000 each; 5 Fourth Prizes—$1,000 each; 10 Fifth Prizes—$250 each; 1,000 Sixth Prizes—$100 each. Prizewinners will have the opportunity of selecting any prize offered for that level. A travel-prize option, if offered and selected by winner, must be completed within 12 months of selection and is subject to hotel and flight accommodations availability. Torstar Corporation may present this Sweepstakes utilizing names other than Million Dollar Sweepstakes. For a current list of all prize options offered within prize levels and all names the Sweepstakes may utilize, send a self-addressed, stamped envelope (WA residents need not affix return postage) to: Million Dollar Sweepstakes Prize Options/Names, P.O. Box 4710, Blair, NE 68009.

The Extra Bonus Prize will be awarded in a random drawing to be conducted no later than May 30, 1994 from among all entries received. To qualify, entries must be received by March 31, 1994 and comply with published directions. No purchase necessary. For complete rules, send a self-addressed, stamped envelope (WA residents need not affix return postage) to: Extra Bonus Prize Rules, P.O. Box 4600, Blair, NE 68009.

For a list of prizewinners (available after July 31, 1994) send a separate, stamped, self-addressed envelope to: Million Dollar Sweepstakes Winners, P.O. Box 4728, Blair, NE 68009.   SWP-H393